# TORTILLA FLAT

# OF MICE AND MEN

# TORTILLA FLAT

# OF MICE AND MEN

# JOHN STEINBECK

BOOK-OF-THE-MONTH CLUB
NEW YORK

# TORTILLA
# FLAT

ILLUSTRATED BY RUTH GANNETT

# CHAPTER HEADINGS

# TORTILLA FLAT

# PREFACE

THIS is the story of Danny and of Danny's friends and of Danny's house. It is a story of how these three became one thing, so that in Tortilla Flat if you speak of Danny's house you do not mean a structure of wood flaked with old whitewash, overgrown with an ancient untrimmed rose of Castile. No, when you speak of Danny's house you are understood to mean a unit of which the parts are men, from which came sweetness and joy, philanthropy and, in the end, a mystic sorrow. For Danny's house was not unlike the Round Table, and Danny's friends were not unlike the knights of it. And this is the story of how that group came into being, of how it flourished and grew to be an organization beautiful and wise. This story deals with the adventuring of Danny's friends, with the good they did, with their thoughts and their endeavors. In the end, this story tells how the talisman was lost and how the group disintegrated.

In Monterey, that old city on the coast of California, these things are well known, and they are repeated and sometimes elaborated. It is well that this cycle be put down on paper so that in a future time scholars, hearing the legends, may not say as they say of Arthur and of Roland and of Robin Hood—"There was no Danny nor any group of Danny's friends, nor any house. Danny is a nature god and his friends primitive symbols of the wind, the sky, the sun." This history is designed now and ever to keep the sneers from the lips of sour scholars.

Monterey sits on the slope of a hill, with a blue bay below it and with a forest of tall dark pine trees at its back. The lower parts of the town are inhabited by Americans, Italians, catchers and canners of fish. But on the hill where the forest and the town intermingle, where the streets are innocent of asphalt and the corners free of street lights, the old inhabitants of Monterey are embattled as the Ancient Britons are embattled in Wales. These are the paisanos.

They live in old wooden houses set in weedy yards, and the pine trees from the forest are about the houses. The paisanos are clean of commercialism, free of the complicated systems of American business, and, having nothing that can be stolen, exploited or mortgaged, that system has not attacked them very vigorously.

What is a paisano? He is a mixture of Spanish, Indian, Mexican and assorted Caucasian bloods. His ancestors have lived in California for a hundred or two years. He speaks English with a paisano accent and Spanish with a paisano accent. When questioned concerning his race, he indignantly claims pure Spanish blood and rolls up his sleeve to show that the soft inside of his arm is nearly white. His color, like that of a well-browned meerschaum pipe, he ascribes to sunburn. He is a paisano, and he lives in that uphill district above the town of Monterey called Tortilla Flat, although it isn't a flat at all.

Danny was a paisano, and he grew up in Tortilla Flat and every one liked him, but he did not stand out particularly from the screeching children of Tortilla Flat.

He was related to nearly every one in the Flat by blood or romance. His grandfather was an important man who owned two small houses in Tortilla Flat and was respected for his wealth. If the growing Danny preferred to sleep in the forest, to work on ranches and to wrest his food and wine from an unwilling world, it was not because he did not have influential relatives. Danny was small and dark and intent. At twenty-five his legs were bent to the exact curves of a horse's sides.

Now when Danny was twenty-five years old, the war with Germany was declared. Danny and his friend Pilon (Pilon, by the way, is something thrown in when a trade is concluded—a boot) had two gallons of wine when they heard about the war. Big Joe Portagee saw the glitter of the bottles among the pines and he joined Danny and Pilon.

As the wine went down in the bottles, patriotism arose in the three men. And when the wine was gone they went down the hill arm in arm for comradeship and safety, and they walked into Monterey. In front of an enlistment station they cheered loudly for America and dared Germany to do her worst. They howled menaces at the German Empire until the enlistment sergeant

awakened and put on his uniform and came into the street to silence them. He remained to enlist them.

The sergeant lined them up in front of his desk. They passed everything but the sobriety test and then the sergeant began his questions with Pilon.

"What branch do you want to go in?"

"I don' give a god-dam," said Pilon jauntily.

"I guess we need men like you in the infantry." And Pilon was written so.

He turned then to Big Joe, and the Portagee was getting sober. "Where do you want to go?"

"I want to go home," Big Joe said miserably.

The sergeant put him in the infantry too. Finally he confronted Danny, who was sleeping on his feet. "Where do you want to go?"

"Huh?"

"I say, what branch?"

"What you mean, 'branch'?"

"What can you do?"

"Me? I can do anything."

"What did you do before?"

"Me? I'm a mule skinner."

"Oh, you are? How many mules can you drive?"

Danny leaned forward, vaguely and professionally. "How many you got?"

"About thirty thousand," said the sergeant.

Danny waved his hand. "String 'em up!" he said.

And so Danny went to Texas and broke mules for the duration of the war. And Pilon marched about Oregon with the infantry, and Big Joe, as shall be later made clear, went to jail.

# I

*How Danny, home from the wars, found himself*
*an heir, and how he swore to protect the helpless.*

Wₕₑₙ Danny came home
from the army he learned that he was an heir and an
owner of property. The viejo, that is the grandfather,
had died leaving Danny the two small houses on Tortilla Flat.

When Danny heard about it he was a little weighed
down with the responsibility of ownership. Before he
ever went to look at his property he bought a gallon of
red wine and drank most of it himself. The weight of
responsibility left him then, and his very worst nature
came to the surface. He shouted, he broke a few chairs
in a poolroom on Alvarado Street; he had two short but
glorious fights. No one paid much attention to Danny.
At last his wavering bow-legs took him toward the

wharf where, at this early hour in the morning, the Italian fishermen were walking down in rubber boots to go out to sea.

Race antipathy overcame Danny's good sense. He menaced the fishermen. "Sicilian bastards," he called them, and "Scum from the prison island," and "Dogs of dogs of dogs." He cried, *"Chinga tu madre, Piojo."* He thumbed his nose and made obscene gestures below his waist. The fishermen only grinned and shifted their oars and said, "Hello, Danny. When'd you get home? Come around to-night. We got new wine."

Danny was outraged. He screamed, *"Pon un condo a la cabeza."*

They called, "Good-by, Danny. See you to-night." And they climbed into their little boats and rowed out to the lampara launches and started their engines and chugged away.

Danny was insulted. He walked back up Alvarado Street, breaking windows as he went, and in the second block a policeman took him in hand. Danny's great respect for the law caused him to go quietly. If he had not just been discharged from the army after the victory over Germany, he would have been sentenced to six

18

months. As it was, the judge gave him only thirty days.

And so for one month Danny sat on his cot in the Monterey city jail. Sometimes he drew obscene pictures on the walls, and sometimes he thought over his army career. Time hung heavy on Danny's hands there in his cell in the city jail. Now and then a drunk was put in for the night, but for the most part crime in Monterey was stagnant, and Danny was lonely. The bedbugs bothered him a little at first, but as they got used to the taste of him and he grew accustomed to their bites, they got along peacefully.

He started playing a satiric game. He caught a bedbug, squashed it against the wall, drew a circle around it with a pencil and named it "Mayor Clough." Then he caught others and named them after the City Council. In a little while he had one wall decorated with squashed bedbugs, each named for a local dignitary. He drew ears and tails on them, gave them big noses and mustaches. Tito Ralph, the jailer, was scandalized; but he made no complaint because Danny had not included either the justice of the peace who had sentenced him, nor any of the police force. He had a vast respect for the law.

One night when the jail was lonely, Tito Ralph came into Danny's cell bearing two bottles of wine. An hour later he went out for more wine, and Danny went with him. It was cheerless in the jail. They stayed at Torrelli's, where they bought the wine, until Torrelli threw them out. After that Danny went up among the pines and fell asleep, while Tito Ralph staggered back and reported his escape.

When the brilliant sun awakened Danny about noon, he determined to hide all day to escape pursuit. He ran and dodged behind bushes. He peered out of the undergrowth like a hunted fox. And, at evening, the rules having been satisfied, he came out and went about his business.

Danny's business was fairly direct. He went to the back door of a restaurant. "Got any old bread I can give my dog?" he asked the cook. And while that gullible man was wrapping up the food, Danny stole two slices of ham, four eggs, a lamb chop and a fly swatter.

"I will pay you sometime," he said.

"No need to pay for scraps. I throw them away if you don't take them."

Danny felt better about the theft then. If that was the

way they felt, on the surface he was guiltless. He went back to Torrelli's, traded the four eggs, the lamb chop and the fly swatter for a water glass of grappa and retired toward the woods to cook his supper.

The night was dark and damp. The fog hung like limp gauze among the black pines that guard the landward limits of Monterey. Danny put his head down and hurried for the shelter of the woods. Ahead of him he made out another hurrying figure; and as he narrowed the distance, he recognized the scuttling walk of his old friend Pilon. Danny was a generous man, but he recalled that he had sold all his food except the two slices of ham and the bag of stale bread.

"I will pass Pilon by," he decided. "He walks like a man who is full of roast turkey and things like that."

Then suddenly Danny noticed that Pilon clutched his coat lovingly across his bosom.

"Ai, Pilon, *amigo!*" Danny cried.

Pilon scuttled on faster. Danny broke into a trot. "Pilon, my little friend! Where goest thou so fast?"

Pilon resigned himself to the inevitable and waited. Danny approached warily, but his tone was enthusiastic. "I looked for thee, dearest of little angelic friends, for see, I have here two great steaks from God's own pig, and a sack of sweet white bread. Share my bounty, Pilon, little dumpling."

Pilon shrugged his shoulders. "As you say," he muttered savagely. They walked on together into the woods.

Pilon was puzzled. At length he stopped and faced his friend. "Danny," he asked sadly, "how knewest thou I had a bottle of brandy under my coat?"

"Brandy?" Danny cried. "Thou hast brandy? Perhaps it is for some sick old mother," he said naïvely. "Perhaps thou keepest it for Our Lord Jesus when He comes again. Who am I, thy friend, to judge the destination of this brandy? I am not even sure thou hast it. Besides I am not thirsty. I would not touch this brandy. Thou art welcome to this big roast of pork I have, but as for thy brandy, that is thine own."

Pilon answered him sternly. "Danny, I do not mind sharing my brandy with you, half and half. It is my duty to see you do not drink it all."

Danny dropped the subject then. "Here in the clearing I will cook this pig, and you will toast the sugar cakes in this bag here. Put thy brandy here, Pilon. It is better here, where we can see it, and each other."

They built a fire and broiled the ham and ate the stale bread. The brandy receded quickly down the bottle. After they had eaten, they huddled near the fire and sipped delicately at the bottle like effete bees. And the fog came down upon them and grayed their coats with moisture. The wind sighed sadly in the pines about them.

And after a time, a loneliness fell upon Danny and Pilon. Danny thought of his lost friends.

"Where is Arthur Morales?" Danny asked, turning his palms up and thrusting his arms forward. "Dead in France," he answered himself, turning the palms down and dropping his arms in despair. "Dead for his country. Dead in a foreign land. Strangers walk near his grave and they do not know Arthur Morales lies there." He raised his hands palms upward again. "Where is Pablo, that good man?"

"In jail," said Pilon. "Pablo stole a goose and hid in the brush; and that goose bit Pablo and Pablo cried out and so was caught. Now he lies in jail for six months."

Danny sighed and changed the subject, for he realized that he had prodigally used up the only acquaintance in any way fit for oratory. But the loneliness was still on him and demanded an outlet. "Here we sit," he began at last.

"—broken hearted," Pilon added rhythmically.

"No, this is not a poem," Danny said. "Here we sit, homeless. We gave our lives for our country, and now we have no roof over our head."

"We never did have," Pilon added helpfully.

Danny drank dreamily until Pilon touched his elbow and took the bottle. "That reminds me," Danny said, "of a story of a man who owned two whore houses——" His mouth dropped open. "Pilon!" he cried. "Pilon! my little fat duck of a baby friend. I had forgotten! I am an heir! I own two houses."

"Whore houses?" Pilon asked hopefully. "Thou art a drunken liar," he continued.

"No, Pilon. I tell the truth. The viejo died. I am the heir. I, the favorite grandson."

"Thou art the only grandson," said the realist, Pilon. "Where are these houses?"

"You know the viejo's house on Tortilla Flat, Pilon?"

"Here in Monterey?"

"Yes, here in Tortilla Flat."

"Are they any good, these houses?"

Danny sank back, exhausted with emotion. "I do not know. I forgot I owned them."

Pilon sat silent and absorbed. His face grew mournful. He threw a handful of pine needles on the fire, watched the flames climb frantically among them and die. For a long time he looked into Danny's face with deep anxiety, and then Pilon sighed noisily, and again he sighed. "Now it is over," he said sadly. "Now the great times are done. Thy friends will mourn, but nothing will come of their mourning."

Danny put down the bottle, and Pilon picked it up and set it in his own lap.

"Now what is over?" Danny demanded. "What do you mean?"

"It is not the first time," Pilon went on. "When one is poor, one thinks, 'If I had money I would share it with my good friends.' But let that money come and charity flies away. So it is with thee, my once-friend. Thou art lifted above thy friends. Thou art a man of property. Thou wilt forget thy friends who shared everything with thee, even their brandy."

His words upset Danny. "Not I," he cried. "I will never forget thee, Pilon."

"So you think now," said Pilon coldly. "But when you have two houses to sleep in, then you will see. Pilon will be a poor paisano, while you eat with the mayor."

Danny arose unsteadily and held himself upright against a tree. "Pilon, I swear, what I have is thine. While I have a house, thou hast a house. Give me a drink."

"I must see this to believe it," Pilon said in a discouraged voice. "It would be a world wonder if it were so. Men would come a thousand miles to look upon it. And besides, the bottle is empty."

# II

*How Pilon was lured by greed of position to for-sake Danny's hospitality.*

THE lawyer left them at the gate of the second house and climbed into his Ford and stuttered down the hill into Monterey.

Danny and Pilon stood in front of the paintless picket fence and looked with admiration at the property, a low house streaked with old whitewash, uncurtained windows blank and blind. But a great pink rose of Castile was on the porch, and grandfather geraniums grew among the weeds in the front yard.

"This is the best of the two," said Pilon. "It is bigger than the other."

Danny held a new skeleton key in his hand. He tiptoed over the rickety porch and unlocked the front door. The main room was just as it had been when the viejo had lived there. The red rose calendar for 1906, the silk banner on the wall, with Fighting Bob Evans looking between the super-structures of a battleship, the bunch of red paper roses tacked up, the strings of dusty red peppers and garlic, the air-tight stove, the battered rocking chairs.

Pilon looked in the door. "Three rooms," he said breathlessly, "and a bed and a stove. We will be happy here, Danny."

Danny moved cautiously into the house. He had bitter memories of the viejo. Pilon darted ahead of him, and into the kitchen. "A sink with a faucet," he cried. He turned the handle. "No water. Danny, you must have the company turn on the water."

They stood and smiled at each other. Pilon noticed that the worry of property was settling on Danny's face. No more in life would that face be free of care. No more would Danny break windows now that he had windows of his own to break. Pilon had been right—he had been raised among his fellows. His shoulders had straightened to withstand the complexity of life. But one cry of pain escaped him before he left for all time his old and simple existence.

"Pilon," he said sadly, "I wish you owned it and I could come to live with you."

While Danny went to Monterey to have the water turned on, Pilon wandered into the weed-tangled back yard. Fruit trees were there, bony and black with age, and gnarled and broken from neglect. A few tent-like chicken coops lay among the weeds, A pile of rusty barrel hoops, a heap of ashes and a sodden mattress. Pilon looked over the fence into Mrs. Morales' chicken yard, and after a moment of consideration he opened a few small holes in the fence for the hens. "They will like to make nests in the tall weeds," he thought kindly. He considered how he could make a figure-four trap in case the roosters came in too and bothered the hens and kept them from the nests. "We will live happily," he thought again.

Danny came back indignant from Monterey. "That company wants a deposit," he said.

"Deposit?"

"Yes. They want three dollars before they will turn on the water."

"Three dollars," Pilon said severely, "is three gallons

of wine. And when that is gone, we will borrow a bucket of water from Mrs. Morales, next door."

"But we haven't three dollars for wine."

"I know," Pilon said. "Maybe we can borrow a little wine from Mrs. Morales."

The afternoon passed. "To-morrow we will settle down," Danny announced. "To-morrow we will clean and scrub. And you, Pilon, will cut the weeds and throw the trash in the gulch."

"The weeds?" Pilon cried in horror. "Not *those* weeds." He explained his theory of Mrs. Morales' chickens.

Danny agreed immediately. "My friend," he said, "I am glad you have come to live with me. Now, while I collect a little wood, you must get something for dinner."

Pilon, remembering his brandy, thought this unfair. "I am getting in debt to him," he thought bitterly. "My freedom will be cut off. Soon I shall be a slave because of this Jew's house." But he did go out to look for some dinner.

Two blocks away, near the edge of the pine wood, he came upon a half-grown Plymouth Rock rooster scratching in the road. It had come to that adolescent age when its voice cracked, when its legs and neck and breast were naked. Perhaps because he had been thinking of Mrs. Morales' hens in a charitable vein, this little rooster engaged Pilon's sympathy. He walked slowly on toward the dark pine woods, and the chicken ran ahead of him.

Pilon mused, "Poor little bare fowl. How cold it must be for you in the early morning, when the dew falls and the air grows cold with the dawn. The good God is not always so good to little beasts." And he thought, "Here you play in the street, little chicken. Some day an automobile will run over you; and if it kills you, that will be the best that can happen. It may only break your leg or your wing. Then all of your life you will drag along in misery. Life is too hard for you, little bird."

He moved slowly and cautiously. Now and then the chicken tried to double back, but always there was Pilon in the place it chose to go. At last it disappeared into the pine forest, and Pilon sauntered after it.

To the glory of his soul be it said that no cry of pain came from that thicket. That chicken, which Pilon had prophesied might live painfully, died peacefully, or at least quietly. And this is no little tribute to Pilon's technique.

Ten minutes later he emerged from the woods and walked back toward Danny's house. The little rooster, picked and dismembered, was distributed in his pockets. If there was one rule of conduct more strong than any other to Pilon, it was this: Never under any circumstances bring feathers, head or feet home, for without these a chicken cannot be identified.

In the evening they had a fire of cones in the air-tight stove. The flames growled in the chimney. Danny and Pilon, well-fed, warm and happy, sat in the rocking chairs and gently teetered back and forth. At dinner they had used a piece of candle, but now only the light from the stove cracks dispelled the darkness of the room. To make it perfect, rain began to patter on the roof. Only a little leaked through, and that in places where no one wanted to sit anyway.

"It is good, this," Pilon said. "Think of the nights when we slept in the cold. This is the way to live."

"Yes, and it is strange," Danny said. "For years I

had no house. Now I have two. I cannot sleep in two houses."

Pilon hated waste. "This very thing has been bothering me. Why don't you rent the other house?" he suggested.

Danny's feet crashed down on the floor. "Pilon," he cried. "Why didn't I think of it!" The idea grew more familiar. "But who will rent it, Pilon?"

"I will rent it," said Pilon. "I will pay ten dollars a month in rent."

"Fifteen," Danny insisted. "It's a good house. It is worth fifteen."

Pilon agreed grumbling. But he would have agreed to much more, for he saw the elevation that came to a man who lived in his own house; and Pilon longed to feel that elevation.

"It is agreed, then," Danny concluded. "You will rent my house. Oh, I will be a good landlord, Pilon. I will not bother you."

Pilon, except for his year in the army, had never possessed fifteen dollars in his life. But, he thought, it would be a month before the rent was due, and who could tell what might happen in a month.

They teetered contentedly by the fire. After a while Danny went out for a few moments and returned with some apples. "The rain would have spoiled them anyway," he apologized.

Pilon, not to be outdone, got up and lighted the candle; he went into the bedroom and in a moment returned with a wash bowl and pitcher, two red glass vases and a bouquet of ostrich plumes. "It is not good to have so many breakable things around," he said. "When they are broken you become sad. It is much better never to have had them." He picked the paper roses from the wall. "A compliment for Señora Torrelli," he explained as he went out the door.

Shortly afterward he returned, wet through from the rain, but triumphant in manner, for he had a gallon jug of red wine in his hand.

They argued bitterly later, but neither cared who won, for they were tired with the excitements of the day. The wine made them drowsy, and they went to sleep on the floor. The fire died down; the stove cricked as it cooled. The candle tipped over and expired in its own grease, with little blue, protesting flares. The house was dark and quiet and peaceful.

# III

*How the poison of possessions wrought with Pilon*
*and how evil temporarily triumphed in him.*

THE next day Pilon went to live in the other house. It was exactly like Danny's house, only smaller. It had its pink rose of Castile over the porch, its weed-grown yard, its ancient, barren fruit trees, its red geraniums—and Mrs. Soto's chicken yard was next door.

Danny became a great man, having a house to rent, and Pilon went up the social scale by renting a house.

It is impossible to say whether Danny expected any rent, or whether Pilon expected to pay any. If they did, both were disappointed. Danny never asked for it, and Pilon never offered it.

The two friends were often together. Let Pilon come by a jug of wine or a piece of meat and Danny was sure to drop in to visit. And, if Danny were lucky or astute in the same way, Pilon spent a riotous night with him. Poor Pilon would have paid the money if he ever had any, but he never did have—not long enough to locate Danny. Pilon was an honest man. It worried him sometimes to think of Danny's goodness and his own poverty.

One night he had a dollar, acquired in a manner so astounding that he tried to forget it immediately for fear the memory might make him mad. A man in front of the San Carlos hotel had put the dollar in his hand, saying, "Run down and get four bottles of ginger-ale. The hotel is out." Such things were almost miracles, Pilon thought. One should take them on faith, not worry and question them. He took the dollar up the road to give to Danny, but on the way he bought a gallon of wine, and with the wine he lured two plump girls into his house.

Danny, walking by, heard the noise and joyfully went in. Pilon fell into his arms and placed everything at Danny's disposal. And later, after Danny had helped to dispose of one of the girls and half of the wine, there was a really fine fight. Danny lost a tooth, and Pilon had his shirt torn off. The girls stood shrieking by, and kicked whichever man happened to be down. At last Danny got up off the floor and butted one of the girls in the stomach, and she went out the door croaking like a frog. The other girl stole two cooking pots and followed her.

For a little while, Danny and Pilon wept over the perfidy of women.

"Thou knowest not what bitches women are," Danny said wisely.

"I do know," said Pilon.

"Thou knowest not."

"I do know."

"Liar."

There was another fight, but not a very good one.

After that, Pilon felt better about the unpaid rent. Had he not been host to his landlord?

A number of months passed. Pilon began again to worry about the rent. And as time went by, the worry grew intolerable. At last in desperation he worked a whole day cleaning squids for Chin Kee and made two dollars. In the evening he tied his red handkerchief around his neck, put on his father's revered hat and started up the hill to pay Danny the two dollars on account.

But on the way he bought two gallons of wine. "It is better so," he thought. "If I give him hard money, it does not express how warmly I feel toward my friend. But a present, now. And I will tell him the two gallons cost five dollars." This was silly, and Pilon knew it, but he indulged himself. No one in Monterey better knew the price of wine than Danny.

Pilon was proceeding happily. His mind was made up; his nose pointed straight toward Danny's house. His feet moved, not quickly, but steadily, in the proper direction. Under each arm he carried a paper bag, and a gallon of wine was in each bag.

It was purple dusk, that sweet time when the day's sleeping is over, and the evening of pleasure and conversation has not begun. The pine trees were very black against the sky, and all objects on the ground were obscured with dark; but the sky was as mournfully bright as memory. The gulls flew lazily home to the sea rocks after a day's visit to the fish canneries of Monterey.

Pilon was a lover of beauty and a mystic. He raised his face into the sky and his soul arose out of him into the sun's afterglow. That not too perfect Pilon, who plotted and fought, who drank and cursed, trudged slowly on; but a wistful and shining Pilon went up to the sea gulls where they bathed on sensitive wings in the evening. That Pilon was beautiful, and his thoughts were unstained with selfishness and lust. And his thoughts are good to know.

"Our Father is in the evening," he thought. "These birds are flying across the forehead of the Father. Dear birds, dear sea gulls, how I love you all. Your slow wings stroke my heart as the hand of a gentle master strokes the full stomach of a sleeping dog, as the hand of Christ stroked the heads of little children. Dear birds," he thought, "fly to our Lady of Sweet Sorrows with my open heart." And then he said the loveliest words he knew, "Ave Maria, gratia plena——"

The feet of the bad Pilon had stopped moving. In truth the bad Pilon for the moment had ceased to exist. (Hear this, recording angel!) There was, nor is, nor ever has been a purer soul than Pilon's at that moment. Galvez' bad bulldog came to Pilon's deserted legs standing alone in the dark. And Galvez' bulldog sniffed and went away without biting the legs.

A soul washed and saved is a soul doubly in danger, for everything in the world conspires against such a soul. "Even the straws under my knees," says Saint Augustine, "shout to distract me from prayer."

Pilon's soul was not even proof against his own memories; for, as he watched the birds, he remembered that Mrs. Pastano used sea gulls sometimes in her tamales, and that memory made him hungry, and hunger tumbled his soul out of the sky. Pilon moved on, once more a cunning mixture of good and evil. Galvez' bad bulldog turned snarling and stalked back, sorry now that he had let go such a perfect chance at Pilon's legs.

Pilon hunched his arms to ease the weight of the bottles.

It is a fact verified and recorded in many histories that the soul capable of the greatest good is also capable of the greatest evil. Who is there more impious than a backsliding priest? Who more carnal than a recent virgin? This, however, may be a matter of appearance.

Pilon, just back from Heaven, was, although he did not know it, singularly receptive of every bitter wind, toward every evil influence that crowded the night

about him. True, his feet still moved toward Danny's house, but there was neither intention nor conviction in them. They awaited the littlest signal to turn about. Already Pilon was thinking how stupendously drunk he could get on two gallons of wine, and more, how long he could stay drunk.

It was almost dark now. The dirt road was no longer visible, nor the ditches on either side. No moral conclusion is drawn from the fact that at this moment, when Pilon's impulses were balanced as precariously as a feather, between generosity and selfishness, at this very moment Pablo Sanchez happened to be sitting in the ditch at the side of the road wishing he had a cigarette and a glass of wine.

Ah, the prayers of the millions, how they must fight and destroy each other on their way to the throne of God.

Pablo first heard footsteps, then saw a blurred figure, and then recognized Pilon. "Ai, *amigo*," he called enthusiastically. "What great burden is it thou carriest?"

Pilon stopped dead and faced the ditch. "I thought you were in jail," he said severely. "I heard about a goose."

"So I was, Pilon," Pablo said jocularly. "But I was not well received. The judge said the sentence did me no good, and the police said I ate more than the allowance for three men. And so," he finished proudly, "I am on parole."

Pilon was saved from selfishness. True, he did not take the wine to Danny's house, but instantly he invited Pablo to share it at the rented house. If two generous paths branch from the highroad of life and only one can be followed, who is to judge which is best?

Pilon and Pablo entered the little house joyfully. Pilon lighted a candle and produced two fruit jars for glasses.

"Health!" said Pablo.

"*Salud!*" said Pilon.

And in a few moments, "*Salud!*" said Pablo.

"Mud in your eye!" said Pilon.

They rested a little while. "*Su servidor,*" said Pilon.

"Down the rat-hole," said Pablo.

Two gallons is a great deal of wine, even for two paisanos. Spiritually the jugs may be graduated thus: Just below the shoulder of the first bottle, serious and concentrated conversation. Two inches farther down, sweetly sad memory. Three inches more, thoughts of old and satisfactory loves. An inch, thoughts of old and bitter loves. Bottom of the first jug, general and undirected sadness. Shoulder of the second jug, black, unholy despondency. Two fingers down, a song of death or longing. A thumb, every other song each one knows. The graduations stop here, for the trail splits and there is no certainty. From this point on anything can happen.

But let us go back to the first mark, which says serious and concentrated conversation, for it was at that place that Pilon made his coup.

"Pablo," he said, "dost thou never get tired of sleeping in ditches, wet and homeless, friendless and alone?"

"No," said Pablo.

Pilon mellowed his voice persuasively. "So *I* thought, my friend, when I was a dirty gutter-dog, I too, was content, for I did not know how sweet a little house is, and a roof, and a garden. Ah, Pablo, this is indeed living."

"It's pretty nice," Pablo agreed.

Pilon pounced. "See, Pablo, how would you like to rent part of my house? There would never be the cold

44

ground for you any more. Never the hard sand under the wharf with crabs getting in your shoes. How would you like to live here with me?"

"Sure," said Pablo.

"Look, you will pay only fifteen dollars a month! And you may use all the house except my bed, and all the garden. Think of it, Pablo! And if some one should write you a letter, he will have some place to send it to."

"Sure," said Pablo. "That's swell."

Pilon sighed with relief. He had not realized how the debt to Danny rode on his shoulders. The fact that he was fairly sure Pablo would never pay any rent did not mitigate his triumph. If Danny should ever ask for money, Pilon could say, "I will pay when Pablo pays."

They moved on to the next graduation, and Pilon remembered how happy he had been when he was a little boy. "No care then, Pablo. I knew not sin. I was very happy."

"We have never been happy since," Pablo agreed sadly.

# IV

*How Jesus Maria Corcoran, a good man, became an unwilling vehicle of evil.*

LIFE passed smoothly on for Pilon and Pablo. In the morning when the sun was up clear of the pine trees, when the blue bay rippled and sparkled below them, they arose slowly and thoughtfully from their beds.

It is a time of quiet joy, the sunny morning. When the glittery dew is on the mallow weeds, each leaf holds a jewel which is beautiful if not valuable. This is no time for hurry or for bustle. Thoughts are slow and deep and golden in the morning.

Pablo and Pilon in their blue jeans and blue shirts walked in comradeship into the gulch behind the house, and after a little time they returned to sit in the sun on the front porch, to listen to the fish horns on the streets

47

of Monterey, to discuss in wandering, sleepy tones the doings of Tortilla Flat; for there are a thousand climaxes on Tortilla Flat for every day the world wheels through.

They were at peace there on the porch. Only their toes wriggled on the warm boards when the flies landed on them.

"If all the dew were diamonds," Pablo said, "we would be very rich. We would be drunk all our lives."

But Pilon, on whom the curse of realism lay uneasily, added. "Everybody would have too many diamonds. There would be no price for them, but wine always costs money. If only it would rain wine for a day, now, and we had a tank to catch it in."

"But good wine," interjected Pablo. "Not rotgut swill like the last you got."

"I didn't pay for it," said Pilon. "Some one hid it in the grass by the dance hall. What can you expect of wine you find?"

They sat and waved their hands listlessly at the flies. "Cornelia Ruiz cut up the black Mexican yesterday," Pilon observed.

Pablo raised his eyes in mild interest. "Fight?" he asked.

"Oh no, the black one did not know Cornelia got a new man yesterday, and he tried to come in. So Cornelia cut him."

"He should have known," Pablo said virtuously.

"Well, he was down in the town when Cornelia got her new man. The black one just tried to go in through the window when she locked the door."

"The black one is a fool," said Pablo. "Is he dead?"

"Oh, no. She just cut him up a little bit on the arms. Cornelia was not angry. She just didn't want the black one to come in."

"Cornelia is not a very steady woman," said Pablo. "But still she has masses sung for her father, ten years dead."

"He will need them," Pilon observed. "He was a bad man and never went to jail for it, and he never went to confession. When old Ruiz was dying, the priest came to give him solace, and Ruiz confessed. Cornelia says that priest was white as buckskin when he came out of the sickroom. But afterwards that priest said he didn't believe half what Ruiz confessed."

Pablo, with a cat-like stroke, killed a fly that landed on his knee. "Ruiz was always a liar," he said. "That soul will need plenty of masses. But do you think a mass has virtue when the money for that mass comes out of men's pockets while they sleep in wine at Cornelia's house?"

"A mass is a mass," said Pilon. "Where you get two-bits is no interest to the man who sells you a glass of wine. And where a mass comes from is of no interest to God. He just likes them, the same as you like wine. Father Murphy used to go fishing all the time, and for months the Holy Sacrament tasted like mackerel, but that did not make it less holy. These things are for priests to explain. They are nothing for us to worry about. I wonder where we could get some eggs to eat. It would be good to eat an egg now."

Pablo tilted his hat down over his eyes to keep the sun from bothering him. "Charlie Meeler told me that Danny is with Rosa Martin, that Portagee girl."

Pilon sat upright in alarm. "Maybe that girl will want to marry Danny. Those Portagees always want to marry, and they love money. Maybe when they are married Danny will bother us about the rent. That Rosa will want new dresses. All women do. I know them."

Pablo, too, looked annoyed. "Maybe if we went and talked to Danny——" he suggested.

"Maybe Danny has some eggs," said Pilon. "Those chickens of Mrs. Morales are good layers."

They put on their shoes and walked slowly toward Danny's house.

Pilon stooped and picked up a beer bottle cap and cursed and threw it down. "Some evil man has left it there to deceive people," he said.

"I tried it last night," said Pablo. He looked into a yard where the green corn was ripe, and made a mental note of its ripeness.

They found Danny sitting on his front porch, behind the rose bush, wriggling his toes to keep the flies off.

"Ai, *amigos*," he greeted them listlessly.

They sat down beside him and took off their hats and their shoes. Danny took out a sack of tobacco and some papers and passed them to Pilon. Pilon looked mildly shocked, but made no comment.

"Cornelia Ruiz cut up the black Mexican," he said.

"I heard about it," said Danny.

Pablo spoke acidly. "These women, there is no virtue in them any more."

"It is dangerous to lie with them," said Pilon. "I have heard that there is one young Portagee girl here on the Flat who can give a man something to remember her by, if he goes to the trouble to get it."

Pablo made disapproving clucking noises with his tongue. He spread his hands in front of him. "What is a man to do?" he asked. "Is there no one to trust?"

They watched Danny's face, and saw no alarm appear there.

"This girl's name is Rosa," said Pilon. "I would not say her last name."

"Oh, you mean Rosa Martin," Danny observed with very little interest. "Well, what can you expect of a Portagee?"

Pablo and Pilon sighed with relief.

"How are Mrs. Morales' chickens getting along?" Pilon asked casually.

Danny shook his head sadly. "Every one of those chickens is dead. Mrs. Morales put up some string-beans in jars, and the jars blew up, and she fed the beans to the chickens, and those chickens all died, every one."

"Where are those chickens now?" Pablo demanded.

Danny waved two fingers back and forth in negation. "Some one told Mrs. Morales not to eat those chickens or she would be sick, but we scraped the insides good and sold them to the butcher."

"Has anybody died?" Pablo asked.

"No. I guess those chickens would have been all right."

"Perhaps you bought a little wine with the money from those chickens?" Pilon suggested.

Danny smiled cynically at him. "Mrs. Morales did, and I went to her house last night. That is a pretty woman in some lights, and not so old, either."

The alarm came back to Pablo and Pilon.

"My cousin Weelie says she is fifty years old," Pilon said excitedly.

Danny spread his hands. "What is it how old in years she is?" he observed philosophically. "She is lively, that one. She owns her house and has two hundred dollars in the bank." Then Danny became a little embarrassed. "I would like to make a present to Mrs. Morales."

Pilon and Pablo regarded their feet, and tried by

strenuous mental effort to ward off what was coming. But their effort had no value.

"If I had a little money," said Danny, "I would buy her a box of big candy." He looked meaningly at his tenants, but neither one answered him. "I would need only a dollar or two," he suggested.

"Chin Kee is drying squids," Pilon observed. "Perhaps you could cut squids for half a day."

Danny spoke pointedly. "It would not look well for a man who owns two houses to cut squids. But perhaps if a little rent were ever paid——"

Pilon arose angrily. "Always the rent," he cried. "You would force us into the streets—into the gutters, while you sleep in your soft bed. Come, Pablo," Pilon said angrily, "we will get money for this miser, this Jew."

The two of them stalked off.

"Where will we get money?" Pablo asked.

"I don't know," said Pilon. "Maybe he won't ask again." But the inhuman demand had cut deep into their mental peace. "We will call him 'Old Jew' when we see him," said Pilon. "We have been his friends for years. When he was in need, we fed him. When he was cold, we clothed him."

"When was that?" Pablo asked.

"Well, we would have, if he needed anything and we had it. That is the kind of friends we were to him. And now he crushes our friendship into the ground for a box of big candy to give to an old fat woman."

"Candy is not good for people," said Pablo.

So much emotion had exhausted Pilon. He sat down in the ditch beside the road and put his chin in his hands and was disconsolate.

Pablo sat down too, but he only did it to rest, for his friendship with Danny was not as old and beautiful as Pilon's was.

The bottom of the ditch was choked with dry grass and bushes. Pilon, staring downward in his sorrow and resentment, saw a human arm sticking out from under a bush. And then, beside the arm, a half-full gallon bottle of wine. He clutched Pablo's arm and pointed.

Pablo stared. "Maybe he is dead, Pilon."

Pilon had got his breath and his fine clear vision again. "If he is dead, the wine will do him no good. He can't be buried with it."

The arm stirred, swept back the bushes, and disclosed the frowsy face and red stubble beard of Jesus Maria

Corcoran. "Ai, Pilon. Ai, Pablo," he said hazily. *"Que tomas?"*

Pilon leaped down the bank on him. *"Amigo,* Jesus Maria! you are not well!"

Jesus Maria smiled sweetly. "Just drunk," he murmured. He rose to his knees. "Come have a drink, my friends. Drink deep. There is plenty more."

Pilon tilted the bottle over his elbow. He swallowed four times and over a pint left the jug. Then Pablo took the bottle from him, and Pablo played with it as a cat plays with a feather. He polished the mouth with his sleeve. He smelled the wine. He took three or four preliminary sips and let a few drops run all around his mouth, to tantalize himself. At last, "Madre de Dios, *que vino!*" he said. He raised the jug and the red wine gurgled happily down his throat.

Pilon's hand was out long before Pablo had to breathe again. Pilon turned a soft and admiring countenance to his friend Jesus Maria. "Hast thou discovered a treasure in the woods?" he asked. "Has some great man died and named thee in his will, my little friend?"

Jesus Maria was a humanitarian, and kindness was always in him. He cleared his throat and spat. "Give me a drink," he said. "My throat is dry. I will tell you how it was." He drank dreamily, like a man who has so much wine that he can take his time in drinking it, can even spill a little without remorse. "I was sleeping on the beach two nights ago," he said. "Out on the beach near Seaside. In the night the little waves washed a rowboat to the shore. Oh, a nice little rowboat, and the oars were there. I got in and rowed it down to Monterey. It was easily worth twenty dollars, but trade was slow, and I only got seven."

"Thou hast money left?" Pilon put in excitedly.

"I am telling you how it was," Jesus Maria said with some dignity. "I bought two gallons of wine and brought them up here to the woods, and then I went to walk with Arabella Gross. For her I bought one pair of silk drawers in Monterey. She liked them—so soft they were, and so pink. And then I bought a pint of whisky for Arabella, and then after a while we met some soldiers and she went away with them."

"Oh, the thief of a good man's money!" Pilon cried in horror.

"No," said Jesus Maria dreamily. "It was time she went anyway. And then I came here and went to sleep."

"Then thou hast no more money?"

"I don't know," said Jesus Maria. "I will see." He fished in his pocket and brought out three crumpled dollar bills and a dime. "To-night," he said, "I will buy for Arabella Gross one of those little things that goes around higher up."

"You mean the little silk pockets on a string?"

"Yes," said Jesus Maria, "and not so little as you might think, either." He coughed to clear his throat.

Instantly Pilon was filled with solicitude. "It is the night air," he said. "It is not good to sleep out in the open. Come, Pablo, we will take him to our house and cure this cold of his. The malady of the lungs has a good start, but we will cure it."

"What are you talking about?" said Jesus Maria. "I'm all right."

"So you think," said Pilon. "So Rudolfo Kelling thought. And you yourself went to his funeral a month ago. So Angelina Vasquez thought. She died last week."

Jesus Maria was frightened. "What do you think is the matter?"

"It is sleeping in this night air," Pilon said sagely. "Your lungs will not stand it."

Pablo wrapped the wine jug in a big weed, so disguising it that any one passing would have been consumed with curiosity until he knew what that weed contained.

Pilon walked beside Jesus Maria, touching him now and then under the elbow to remind him that he was not a well man. They took him to their house and laid him on a cot, and although the day was warm, they covered him with an old comforter. Pablo spoke movingly of those poor ones who writhed and suffered with tuberculosis. And then Pilon pitched his voice to sweetness. He spoke with reverence of the joy of living in a little house. When the night was far gone, and all the talk and wine were gone, and outside the deadly mists clung to the ground like the ghosts of giant leeches, then one did not go out to lie in the sickly damp of a gulch. No, one got into a deep, soft, warm bed and slept like a little child.

Jesus Maria went to sleep at this point. Pilon and Pablo had to wake him up and give him a drink. Then Pilon spoke movingly of the mornings when one lay in one's warm nest until the sun was high enough to be of some use. One did not go shivering about in the dawn, beating one's hands to keep them from freezing.

At last Pilon and Pablo moved in on Jesus Maria as two silent hunting Airedales converge on their prey. They rented the use of their house to Jesus for fifteen dollars a month. He accepted happily. They shook hands all around. The jug came out of its weed. Pilon drank deeply, for he knew his hardest task was before him. He said it very gently and casually, while Jesus Maria was drinking out of the bottle.

"And you will pay only three dollars on account now."

Jesus Maria put down the bottle and looked at him in horror. "No," he exploded. "I made a promise to Arabella Gross to buy one of those little things. I will pay the rent when it is time."

Pilon knew he had blundered. "When you lay on that beach at Seaside, God floated the little rowboat to you. Do you think the good God did it so you could buy silk drawers for a cannery slut? No! God did it so you would not die from sleeping on the ground in the cold. Do you think God is interested in Arabella's breasts? And besides, we will take a two dollar deposit," he went on. "For one dollar you can get one of those things big enough to hold the udders of a cow."

Still Jesus Maria protested.

"I will tell you," Pilon went on, "unless we pay Danny two dollars we shall all be turned into the street, and it will be your fault. You will have it on your soul that we sleep in ditches."

Under so many shots, coming from so many directions, Jesus Maria Corcoran succumbed. He passed two of the crumpled bills to Pilon.

And now the tense feeling went out of the room, and peace and quiet and a warm deep comradeship took its place. Pilon relaxed. Pablo took the comforter back to his own bed, and conversation sprang up.

"We must take this money to Danny."

Their first appetite over, they were sipping the wine out of fruit jars now.

"What is this great need Danny has for two dollars?" Jesus Maria asked.

Pilon grew confidential. His hands came into play like twin moths, restrained only by his wrists and arms from flying out the door. "Danny, our friend, is taking up with Mrs. Morales. Oh, don't think Danny is a fool.

61

Mrs. Morales has two hundred dollars in the bank. Danny wants to buy a box of big candy for Mrs. Morales."

"Candy is not good for people," Pablo observed. "It makes their teeth ache."

"That is up to Danny," said Jesus Maria. "If he wants to ache Mrs. Morales' teeth, that is his business. What do we care for Mrs. Morales' teeth?"

A cloud of anxiety had settled on Pilon's face. "But," he interposed sternly, "if our friend Danny takes big candy to Mrs. Morales, he will eat some too. So it is the teeth of our friend that will ache."

Pablo shook his head anxiously. "It would be a bad thing if Danny's friends, on whom he depends, should bring about the aching of his teeth."

"What shall we do, then?" asked Jesus Maria, although he and every one else knew exactly what they would do. They waited politely, each one for another, to make the inevitable suggestion. The silence ran on. Pilon and Pablo felt that the suggestion should not come from them, since, by some lines of reasoning, they might be considered interested parties. Jesus Maria kept silence in duty to his hosts, but when their silence made him aware of what was required of him, he came in-stantly into the breach.

"A gallon of wine makes a nice present for a lady," he suggested in a musing tone.

Pilon and Pablo were astonished at his brilliance. "We can tell Danny it would be better for his teeth to get wine."

"But maybe Danny will pay no heed to our warning. If you give money to that Danny, you can't tell what he will do with it. He might buy candy anyway, and then all our time and worry are wasted."

They had made of Jesus Maria their feeder of lines, their opener of uneasy situations. "Maybe if we buy the wine ourselves and then give it to Danny there is no danger," he suggested.

"That is the thing," cried Pilon. "Now you have it."

Jesus Maria smiled modestly at being given credit for this. He felt that sooner or later this principle would have been promulgated by some one in the room.

Pablo poured the last little bit of wine into the fruit jars and they drank tiredly after their effort. It was a matter of pride to them that the idea had been arrived at so logically, and in such a philanthropic cause.

"Now I am hungry," said Pablo.

Pilon got up and went to the door and looked at the sun. "It is after noon," he said. "Pablo and I will go to Torrelli's to get the wine, while you, Jesus Maria, go into Monterey for something to eat. Maybe Mrs. Bruno, on the wharf, will give you a fish. Maybe you can get a little bread some place."

"I would rather go with you," said Jesus Maria, for he suspected that another sequence, just as logical, and just as inevitable, was beginning to grow in the heads of his friends.

"No, Jesus Maria," they said firmly. "It is now two o'clock, or about that. In an hour it will be three o'clock. Then we will meet you here and have something to eat. And maybe a little glass of wine to go with it."

Jesus Maria started for Monterey very reluctantly, but Pablo and Pilon walked happily down the hill toward Torrelli's house.

# V

*How St. Francis turned the tide and put a gentle punishment on Pilon and Pablo and Jesus Maria.*

T HE afternoon came down as imperceptibly as age comes to a happy man. A little gold entered into the sunlight. The bay became bluer and dimpled with shore-wind ripples. Those lonely fishermen who believe that the fish bite at high tide left their rocks, and their places were taken by others, who were convinced that the fish bite at low tide.

At three o'clock the wind veered around and blew softly in from the bay, bringing all manner of fine kelp odors. The menders of nets in the vacant lots of Monterey put down their spindles and rolled cigarettes. Through the streets of the town, fat ladies, in whose eyes lay the weariness and the wisdom one sees so often in the eyes of pigs, were trundled in overpowered motor cars toward tea and gin fizzes at the Hotel Del Monte. On Alvarado Street, Hugo Machado, the tailor, put a sign in his shop door, "Back in Five Minutes," and went home for the day. The pines waved slowly and voluptuously. The hens in a hundred hen yards complained in placid voices of their evil lot.

Pilon and Pablo sat under a pink rose of Castile in Torrelli's yard, and quietly drank wine and let the afternoon grow on them as gradually as hair grows.

"It is just as well that we do not take two gallons of wine to Danny," said Pilon. "He is a man who knows little restraint in drinking."

Pablo agreed. "Danny looks healthy," he said, "but it is just such people that you hear of dying every day. Look at Rudolfo Kelling. Look at Angelina Vasquez."

Pilon's realism arose mildly to the surface. "Rudolfo fell into the quarry above Pacific Grove," he observed in mild reproof. "Angelina ate a bad can of fish. But," he continued kindly, "I know what you mean. And there are plenty of people who die through abuse of wine."

All Monterey began to make gradual instinctive preparations against the night. Mrs. Guttierez cut little chiles into her enchilada sauce. Rupert Hogan, the seller of spirits, added water to his gin and put it away to be served after midnight. And he shook a little pepper into his early evening whisky. At El Paseo dancing pavilion, Bullet Rosendale opened a carton of pretzels and arranged them like coarse brown lace on the big courtesy plates. The Palace Drug Company wound up its awnings. A little group of men who had spent the afternoon in front of the post office, greeting their friends, moved toward the station to see the Del Monte Express from San Francisco come in. The sea gulls arose glutted from the fish cannery beaches and flew toward the sea rocks. Lines of pelicans pounded doggedly over the water wherever they go to spend the night. On the purse-seine fishing boats the Italian men folded their nets over the big rollers. Little Miss Alma Alvarez, who was ninety years old, took her daily bouquet of pink geraniums to the Virgin on the outer wall of the church of San Carlos. In the neighboring and Methodist village of Pacific Grove the W.C.T.U. met for tea and discussion, listened while a little lady described the vice and prostitution of Monterey with energy and color. She thought a committee should visit these resorts to see exactly how terrible conditions really were. They had gone over the situation so often, and they needed new facts.

The sun went westering and took on an orange blush. Under the rose bush in Torrelli's yard Pablo and Pilon

finished the first gallon of wine. Torrelli came out of his house and passed out of the yard without seeing his erstwhile customers. They waited until he was out of sight on the way to Monterey; whereupon Pablo and Pilon went into the house, and with a conscious knowledge of their art, cozened their supper out of Mrs. Torrelli. They slapped her on the buttocks and called her a "Butter Duck" and took little courteous liberties with her person, and finally left her, flattered and slightly tousled.

Now it was evening in Monterey, and the lights went on. The windows glowed softly. The Monterey Theater began to spell "Children of Hell—Children of Hell" over and over with its lights. A small but fanatic group of men who believe that the fish bite in the evening took their places on the cold sea rocks. A little fog drifted through the streets and hung about the chimneys, and a fine smell of burning pine wood filled the air.

Pablo and Pilon went back to their rose bush and sat on the ground, but they were not as contented as they had been. "It is cool here," said Pilon, and he took a drink of wine to warm himself.

"We should go to our own house where it is warm," said Pablo.

"But there is no wood for the stove."

"Well," said Pablo, "if you will take the wine, I will meet you at the corner of the street." And he did, in about half an hour.

Pilon waited patiently, for he knew there are some

things even one's friends cannot help with. While he waited, Pilon kept a watchful eye aimed down the street in the direction Torrelli had taken, for Torrelli was a forceful man to whom explanations, no matter how carefully considered nor how beautifully phrased, were as chaff. Moreover, Torrelli had, Pilon knew, the Italians' exaggerated and wholly quixotic ideal of marital relations. But Pilon watched in vain. No Torrelli came brutally home. In a little while Pablo joined him, and Pilon noticed with admiration and satisfaction that he carried an armful of pine sticks from Torrelli's wood pile.

Pablo made no comment on his recent adventure until they arrived at their house. Then he echoed Danny's words, "A lively one, that Butter Duck."

Pilon nodded his head in the dark and spoke with a quiet philosophy. "It is seldom that one finds all things at one market—wine, food, love and fire wood. We must remember Torrelli, Pablo, my friend. There is a man to know. We must take him a little present sometime."

Pilon built a roaring fire in the cast-iron stove. The two friends drew their chairs close and held their fruit jars to the heat to warm the wine a little. This night the light was holy, for Pablo had bought a candle to burn for San Francisco. Something had distracted his attention before that sacred plan had consummated. Now the little wax taper burned beautifully in an abalone shell, and it threw the shadows of Pablo and Pilon on the wall and made them dance.

"I wonder where that Jesus Maria has gone," Pilon observed.

"He promised he would come back long ago," said Pablo. "I do not know whether that is a man to trust or not."

"Perhaps some little thing happened to detain him, Pablo. Jesus Maria, with that red beard and that kind heart is nearly always in some kind of trouble with ladies."

"His is a grasshopper brain," said Pablo. "He sings and plays and jumps. There is no seriousness in him."

They had no great time to wait. They had barely started their second fruit jar of wine when Jesus Maria staggered in. He held each side of the door to steady himself. His shirt was torn and his face was bloody. One eye showed dark and ominous in the dancing candle-light.

Pablo and Pilon rushed to him. "Our friend! He is hurt. He has fallen from a cliff. He has been run over by a train!" There was not the slightest tone of satire, but Jesus Maria knew it for the most deadly kind of satire. He glared at them out of the eye which still had some volition in such matters.

"Both thy mothers were udderless cows," he remarked.

They fell back from him in horror at the vulgarity of the curse. "Our friend is wandering in his mind."

"The bone of his head has been broken."

"Pour him a little wine, Pablo."

Jesus Maria sat morosely by the fire and caressed his fruit jar, while his friends waited patiently for an explanation of the tragedy. But Jesus Maria seemed content to leave his friends in ignorance of the mishap. Although Pilon cleared his throat several times, and although Pablo looked at Jesus Maria with eyes which offered sympathy and understanding, Jesus Maria sat sullenly and glared at the stove and at the wine and at the blessed candle, until at length his discourteous reticence drove Pilon to an equal discourtesy. Afterwards he did not see how he could have done it.

"Those soldiers again?" he asked.

"Yes," Jesus Maria growled. "This time they came too soon."

"There must have been twenty of them to have used thee so," Pablo observed, for the good of his friend's spirit. "Every one knows thou art a bad man in a fight."

And Jesus Maria did look a little happier then.

"They were four," he said. "Arabella Gross helped, too. She hit me on the head with a rock."

Pilon felt a wave of moral resentment rising within him. "I would not remind thee," he said severely, "how thy friends warned thee against this cannery slob." He wondered whether he had warned Jesus Maria, and seemed to remember that he had.

"These cheap white girls are vicious, my friend," Pablo broke in. "But did you give her that little thing that goes around?"

Jesus Maria reached into his pocket and brought out a crumpled pink rayon brassiere. "The time had not come," he said. "I was just getting to that point; and besides, we had not come into the woods yet."

Pilon sniffed the air and shook his head, but not without a certain sad tolerance. "Thou hast been drinking whisky."

Jesus Maria nodded.

"Where did this whisky come from?"

"From those soldiers," said Jesus Maria. "They had it under a culvert. Arabella knew it was there, and she told me. But those soldiers saw us with the bottle."

The story was gradually taking shape. Pilon liked it this way. It ruined a story to have it all come out quickly. The good story lay in half-told things which must be filled in out of the hearer's own experience. He took the pink brassiere from Jesus Maria's lap and ran his fingers over it, and his eyes went to musing. But in a moment they shone with a joyous light.

"I know," he cried. "We'll give this thing to Danny as a gift to Mrs. Morales."

Every one except Jesus Maria applauded the idea, and he felt himself hopelessly outnumbered. Pablo, with a delicate understanding of the defeat, filled up Jesus Maria's fruit jar.

When a little time had passed, all three men began to smile. Pilon told a very funny story of a thing that had happened to his father. Good spirits returned to the company. They sang. Jesus Maria did a shuffling dance to prove he was not badly hurt. The wine went down and down in the jug, but before it was gone the three friends grew sleepy. Pilon and Pablo staggered off to bed, and Jesus Maria lay comfortably on the floor, beside the stove.

The fire died down. The house was filled with the deep sounds of slumber. In the front room only one thing moved. The blessed candle darted its little spear-pointed flame up and down with incredible rapidity.

Later, this little candle gave Pilon and Pablo and Jesus Maria some ethical things to think about. Simple small rod of wax with a string through it: Such a thing, you would say, is answerable to certain physical laws, and to none other. Its conduct, you would think, was guaranteed by certain principles of heat and combustion. You light the wick; the wax is caught and drawn up the wick; the candle burns a number of hours, goes out, and that is all. The incident is finished. In a little while the candle is forgotten, and then, of course, it has never existed.

Have you forgotten that this candle was blessed? That

in a moment of conscience or perhaps pure religious exaltation, it was designed by Pablo for San Francisco? Here is the principle which takes the waxen rod outside the jurisdiction of physics.

The candle aimed its spear of light at heaven, like an artist who consumes himself to become divine. The candle grew shorter and shorter. A wind sprang up

outside and sifted through the cracks in the wall. The candle sagged sideways. A silken calendar, bearing the face of a lovely girl looking out of the heart of an American Beauty rose, floated out a little distance from the wall. It came into the spear of flame. The fire licked up the silk and raced toward the ceiling. A loose piece of wallpaper caught fire and fell flaming into a bundle of newspapers.

In the sky, saints and martyrs looked on with set and unforgiving faces. The candle was blessed. It belonged to Saint Francis. Saint Francis will have a big candle in its place to-night.

If it were possible to judge depth of sleep, it could be said with justice that Pablo, whose culpable action was responsible for the fire, slept even more soundly than his two friends. But since there is no gauge, it can only be said that he slept very very soundly.

The flames ran up the walls and found little holes in the roof, and leaked through into the night. The house filled with the roar of fire. Jesus Maria turned over uneasily and began, in his sleep, to take off his coat. Then a flaming shingle dropped in his face. He leaped up with a cry, and stood shocked at the fire that raged about him.

"Pilon!" he shrieked. "Pablo!" He ran into the other room, pulled his friends out of bed and pushed them out of the house. Pilon still grasped the pink brassiere in his fingers.

They stood outside the burning house, and looked in the open fire-curtained door. They could see the jug standing on the table with a good two inches of wine in it.

Pilon sensed the savage incipient heroism of Jesus Maria. "Do not do it," he shouted. "It must be lost in the fire as a punishment on us for leaving it."

The cry of sirens came to them, and the roar of trucks climbing the hill in second gear from the fire house in Monterey. The big red fire vehicles drew near and their searchlights played among the pine trunks.

Pilon turned hastily to Jesus Maria. "Run and tell Danny his house is burning. Run quickly, Jesus Maria."

"Why don't you go?"

"Listen," said Pilon. "Danny does not know you are one who rents his house. He may be a little bit angry with Pablo and me."

Jesus Maria grasped this logic and raced toward Danny's house. The house was dark. "Danny," Jesus Maria cried. "Danny, your house is on fire!" There was no answer. "Danny!" he cried again.

A window went up in Mrs. Morales' house next door. Danny sounded irritable. "What the hell do you want?"

"Your other house is on fire, the one Pablo and Pilon live in."

For a moment Danny did not answer. Then he demanded, "Is the fire department there?"

"Yes," cried Jesus Maria.

The whole sky was lighted up by now. The crackling of burning timbers could be heard. "Well," said Danny, "if the fire department can't do anything about it, what does Pilon expect me to do?"

Jesus Maria heard the window bang shut, and he turned and trotted back toward the fire. It was a bad time to call Danny, he knew, but then how could one tell? If Danny had missed the fire, he might have been angry. Jesus Maria was glad he had told him about it anyway. Now the responsibility lay on Mrs. Morales.

It was a little house, there was plenty of draft, the walls were perfectly dry. Perhaps not since old Chinatown had burned had there been such a quick and thorough fire. The men of the fire department took a look at the blazing walls and then began wetting the brush and the trees and the neighboring houses. In less than an hour the house was completely gone. Only then did the hoses play on the heap of ashes to put out the coals and the sparks.

Pilon and Pablo and Jesus Maria stood shoulder to

shoulder and watched the whole thing. Half the population of Monterey and all the population of Tortilla Flat except Danny and Mrs. Morales stood happily about and watched the fire. At last, when it was all over, when only a cloud of steam arose from the black heap, Pilon turned silently away.

"Where goest thou?" Pablo called.

"I go," said Pilon, "to the woods to have out my sleep. I counsel you to come too. It will be well if Danny does not see us for a little while." They nodded gravely and followed him into the pine forest. "It is a lesson to us," said Pilon. "By this we learn never to leave wine in a house overnight."

"Next time," Pablo said hopelessly, "you will take it outside and some one will steal it."

# VI

*How three sinful men, through contrition, attained peace. How Danny's Friends swore comradeship.*

WHEN the sun was clear of the pines, and the ground was warm, and the night's dew was drying on the geranium leaves, Danny came out on his porch to sit in the sunshine and to muse warmly of certain happenings. He slipped off his shoes and wriggled his toes on the sun-warmed boards of the porch. He had walked down earlier in the morning and viewed the square black ashes and twisted plumbing which had been his other house. He had indulged in a little conventional anger against careless friends, had mourned for a moment over that transitory quality of earthly property which made spiritual property so much more valuable. He had thought over the ruin of his status as a man with a house to rent; and, all this clutter of necessary and decent emotion having been satisfied and swept away, he had finally slipped into his true emotion, one of relief that at least one of his burdens was removed.

"If it were still there, I would be covetous of the rent," he thought. "My friends have been cool toward me because they owed me money. Now we can be free and happy again."

But Danny knew he must discipline his friends a little, or they would consider him soft. Therefore, as he sat on his porch, warding off flies with a moving hand which conveyed more warning than threat to the flies, he went over the things he must say to his friends before he allowed them back into the corral of his affection. He must show them that he was not a man to be imposed upon. But he yearned to get it over and to be once more that Danny whom every one loved, that Danny whom people sought out when they had a gallon of wine or a piece of meat. As the owner of two houses he had been considered rich, and he had missed a great many tidbits.

Pilon and Pablo and Jesus Maria Corcoran slept a long time on the pine needles in the forest. It had been a night of terrible excitement, and they were tired. But at length the sun shone into their faces with noonday ardor and the ants walked on them, and two blue jays stood on the ground nearby, calling them all manner of sharp names.

What finished their sleep, though, was a picnic party which settled just on the other side of the bush from them and opened a big lunch basket from which moving smells drifted to Pilon and Pablo and Jesus Maria. They awakened; they sat up; and then the enormity of their situation burst upon them.

"How did the fire start?" asked Pablo plaintively, and no one knew.

"Perhaps," said Jesus Maria, "we had better go to another town for a while—to Watsonville or to Salinas; those are nice towns."

Pilon pulled the brassiere from his pocket and ran his fingers over its pink smoothness. And he held it to the sunlight and looked through it.

"That would only delay matters," he decided. "I think it would be better to go to Danny and confess our fault, like little children to a father. Then he can't say anything without being sorry. And besides, have we not this present for Mrs. Morales?"

His friends nodded agreement. Pilon's eyes strayed through the thick brush to the picnic party, and particularly to that huge lunch basket from which came the penetrating odors of deviled eggs. Pilon's nose wrinkled a little, like a rabbit's. He smiled in a quiet reverie. "I am going to walk, my friends. In a little while I will meet you at the quarry. Do not bring the basket if you can help it."

They watched sadly as Pilon got up and walked away, through the trees, in a direction at right angles to the picnic and the basket. Pablo and Jesus Maria were not surprised a few moments later, to hear a dog bark, a rooster crow, high shrill laughter, the snarl of a wild cat, a little short scream and a cry for help; but the picnic party was surprised and fascinated. The two men and two women left their basket and trotted away toward these versatile sounds.

Pablo and Jesus Maria obeyed Pilon. They did not take the basket, but always afterwards their hats and their shirts were stained with deviled eggs.

At about three o'clock in the afternoon the three

penitents walked slowly toward Danny's house. Their arms were loaded with offerings of reconciliation: oranges and apples and bananas, bottles of olives and pickles, sandwiches of pressed ham, egg sandwiches, bottles of soda pop, a paper carton of potato salad and a copy of the Saturday Evening Post.

Danny saw them coming, and he stood up and tried to remember the things he had to say. They lined up in front of him and hung their heads.

"Dogs of dogs," Danny called them, and "thieves of decent folks' other house," and "spawn of cuttlefish." He named their mothers cows and their fathers ancient sheep.

Pilon opened the bag he held and exposed the ham sandwiches. And Danny said he had no more trust in friends, that his faith had been frostbitten and his friendship trampled upon. And then he began to have a little trouble remembering, for Pablo had taken two deviled eggs out of his bosom. But Danny went back to the grand generation and criticized the virtue of its women and the potency of its men.

Pilon pulled the pink brassiere from his pocket and let it dangle listlessly from his fingers.

Danny forgot everything, then. He sat down on the porch and his friends sat down, and the packages came open. They ate to a point of discomfort. It was an hour later, when they reclined at ease on the porch, giving attention to little besides digestion, when Danny asked casually, as about some far-off object, "How did the fire start?"

"We don't know," Pilon explained. "We went to sleep, and then it started. Perhaps we have enemies."

"Perhaps," said Pablo devoutly, "perhaps God had a finger in it."

"Who can say what makes the good God act the way He does?" added Jesus Maria.

When Pilon handed over the brassiere and explained how it was a present for Mrs. Morales, Danny was reticent. He eyed the brassiere with some skepticism. His friends, he felt, were flattering Mrs. Morales. "That is not a woman to give presents to," he said finally. "Too often we are tied to women by the silk stockings we give them." He could not explain to his friends the coolness that had come to his relationship with Mrs. Morales since he was the owner of only one house; nor could he, in courtesy to Mrs. Morales, describe his own pleasure at that coolness. "I will put this little thing away," he said. "Some day it may be of use to some one."

When the evening came, and it was dark, they went into the house and built a fire of cones in the air-tight stove. Danny, in proof of his forgiveness, brought out a quart of grappa and shared its fire with his friends.

They settled easily into the new life. "It is too bad Mrs. Morales' chickens are all dead," Pilon observed.

But even here was no bar to happiness. "She is going to buy two dozen new ones on Monday," said Danny.

Pilon smiled contentedly. "Those hens of Mrs. Soto's were no good," he said. "I told Mrs. Soto they needed oyster shells, but she paid no attention to me."

They drank the quart of grappa, and there was just enough to promote the sweetness of comradeship.

"It is good to have friends," said Danny. "How lonely it is in the world if there are no friends to sit with one and to share one's grappa."

"Or one's sandwiches," Pilon added quickly.

Pablo was not quite over his remorse, for he suspected the true state of celestial politics which had caused the

burning of the house. "In all the world there are few
friends like thee, Danny. It is not given to many to
have such solace."

Before Danny sank completely under the waves of his
friends, he sounded one warning. "I want all of you to

keep out of my bed," he ordered. "That is one thing I
must have to myself."

Although no one had mentioned it, each of the four
knew they were all going to live in Danny's house.

Pilon sighed with pleasure. Gone was the worry of the
rent; gone the responsibility of owing money. No longer

was he a tenant, but a guest. In his mind he gave thanks for the burning of the other house.

"We will all be happy here, Danny," he said. "In the evenings we will sit by the fire and our friends will come in to visit. And sometimes maybe we will have a glass of wine to drink for friendship's sake."

Then Jesus Maria, in a frenzy of gratefulness, made a rash promise. It was the grappa that did it, and the night of the fire, and all the deviled eggs. He felt that he had received great gifts, and he wanted to distribute a gift. "It shall be our burden and our duty to see that there is always food in the house for Danny," he declaimed. "Never shall our friend go hungry."

Pilon and Pablo looked up in alarm, but the thing was said; a beautiful and generous thing. No man could with impunity destroy it. Even Jesus Maria understood, after it was said, the magnitude of his statement. They could only hope that Danny would forget it.

"For," Pilon mused to himself, "if this promise were enforced, it would be worse than rent. It would be slavery."

"We swear it, Danny!" he said.

They sat about the stove with tears in their eyes, and

their love for one another was almost unbearable.

Pablo wiped his wet eyes with the back of his hand, and he echoed Pilon's remark. "We shall be very happy living here," he said.

# VII

*How Danny's Friends became a force for Good. How they succored the poor Pirate.*

A GREAT many people saw the Pirate every day, and some laughed at him, and some pitied him; but no one knew him very well, and no one interfered with him. He was a huge, broad man, with a tremendous black and bushy beard. He wore jeans and a blue shirt, and he had no hat. In town he wore shoes. There was a shrinking in the Pirate's eyes when he confronted any grown person, the secret look of an animal that would like to run away if it dared turn its back long enough. Because of this expression, the paisanos of Monterey knew that his head had not grown up with the rest of his body. They called him The Pirate because of his beard. Every day people saw him wheeling his barrow of pitchwood about the streets until he sold the load. And always in a cluster at his heels walked his five dogs.

Enrique was rather houndish in appearance, although his tail was bushy. Pajarito was brown and curly, and these were the only two things you could see about him. Rudolph was a dog of whom passers-by said, "He is an American dog." Fluff was a Pug and Señor Alec Thompson seemed to be a kind of an Airedale. They walked in a squad behind the Pirate, very respectful toward him, and very solicitous for his happiness. When he sat down to rest from wheeling his barrow, they all tried to sit in his lap and have their ears scratched.

Some people had seen the Pirate early in the morning on Alvarado Street; some had seen him cutting pitchwood; some knew he sold kindling; but no one except Pilon knew everything the Pirate did. Pilon knew everybody and everything about everybody.

The Pirate lived in a deserted chicken house in the yard of a deserted house on Tortilla Flat. He would have thought it presumptuous to live in the house itself. The dogs lived around and on top of him, and the Pirate liked this, for his dogs kept him warm on the coldest nights. If his feet were cold, he had only to put them against the warm belly of Señor Alec Thompson. The chicken house was so low that the Pirate had to crawl in on his hands and knees.

Early every morning, well before daylight, the Pirate crawled out of his chicken house, and the dogs followed him, roughing their coats and sneezing in the cold air. Then the party went down to Monterey and worked along an alley. Four or five restaurants had their back doors on this alley. The Pirate entered each one, into a restaurant kitchen, warm and smelling of food. Grumbling cooks put packages of scraps in his hands at each place. They didn't know why they did it.

When the Pirate had visited each back door and had his arms full of parcels, he walked back up the hill to Munroe Street and entered a vacant lot, and the dogs excitedly swarmed about him. Then he opened the parcels and fed the dogs. For himself he took bread or a piece of meat out of each package, but he did not pick the best for himself. The dogs sat down about him, licking their lips nervously, and shifting their feet while they waited for food. They never fought over it, and that was a surprising thing. The Pirate's dogs never fought each other, but they fought everything else that wandered the streets of Monterey on four legs. It was a fine thing to see the pack of five, hunting fox-terriers and Pomeranians like rabbits.

Daylight had come by the time the meal was over. The Pirate sat on the ground and watched the sky turn blue with the morning. Below him he saw the schooners put out to sea with deckloads of lumber. He heard the bell buoy ringing sweetly off China Point. The dogs sat about him and gnawed at the bones. The Pirate seemed to be listening to the day rather than seeing it, for while his eyes did not move about, there was an air of attentiveness in him. His big hands strayed to the dogs and his fingers worked soothingly in the coarse hair. After about half an hour, the Pirate went to the corner of the vacant lot, threw the covering of sacks from his wheelbarrow and dug up his ax out of the ground where he buried it every evening. Then up the hill he pushed the barrow, and into the woods, until he found a dead tree, full of pitch. By noon he had a load of fine kindling; and then, still followed by his dogs, he walked the streets until he had sold the load for twenty-five cents.

It was possible to observe all this, but what he did

with the quarter, no one could tell. He never spent it. In the night, guarded from danger by his dogs, he went into the woods and hid the day's quarter with hundreds of others. Somewhere he had a great hoard of money.

Pilon, that acute man, from whom no details of the life of his fellows escaped, and who was doubly delighted to come upon those secrets that nestled deep in the brains of his acquaintances, discovered the Pirate's hoard by a logical process. Pilon reasoned thus: "Every day that Pirate has a quarter. If it is two dimes and a nickel, he takes it to a store and gets a twenty-five cent piece. He never spends any money at all. Therefore, he must be hiding it."

Pilon tried to compute the amount of the treasure. For years the Pirate had been living in this way. Six days a week he cut pitchwood, and on Sundays he went to church. His clothes he got from the back doors of houses, his food at the back doors of restaurants. Pilon puzzled with the great numbers for a while, and then gave it up. "The Pirate must have at least a hundred dollars," he thought.

For a long time Pilon had considered these things. But it was only after the foolish and enthusiastic promise to feed Danny that the thought of the Pirate's hoard gained any personal significance to Pilon.

Before he approached the subject at all, Pilon put his mind through a long and stunning preparation. He felt very sorry for the Pirate. "Poor little half-formed one," he said to himself. "God did not give him all the brain he should have. That poor little Pirate cannot look after himself. For see, he lives in filth in an old chicken house. He feeds upon scraps fit only for his dogs. His clothes are thin and ragged. And because his brain is not a good one, he hides his money."

Now, with his groundwork of pity laid, Pilon moved on to his solution. "Would it not be a thing of merit," he thought, "to do those things for him which he cannot do for himself? To buy him warm clothes, to feed him food fit for a human? But," he reminded himself, "I have no money to do these things, although they lie squirming in my heart. How can these charitable things be accomplished?"

Now he was getting somewhere. Like the cat, which during a long hour closes in on a sparrow, Pilon was ready for his pounce. "I have it!" his brain cried. "It is like this: The Pirate has money, but he has not the brain to use it. I have the brain! I will offer my brain to his use. I will give freely of my mind. That shall be my charity toward this poor little half-made man."

It was one of the finest structures Pilon had ever built. The urge of the artist to show his work to an audience came upon him. "I will tell it to Pablo," he thought. But he wondered whether he would dare do such a thing. Was Pablo strictly honest? Would he not want to divert some of this money to his own ends? Pilon decided not to take the chance, right then, anyway.

It is astounding to find that the belly of every black and evil thing is as white as snow. And·it is saddening to discover how the concealed parts of angels are leprous. Honor and peace to Pilon, for he had discovered how to uncover and to disclose to the world the good that lay in every evil thing. Nor was he blind, as so many saints are, to the evil of good things. It must be admitted with sadness that Pilon had neither the stupidity, the self-righteousness nor the greediness for reward ever to become a saint. Enough for Pilon to do good and to be rewarded by the glow of human brotherhood accomplished.

That very night he paid a visit to the chicken house where the Pirate lived with his dogs. Danny, Pablo and Jesus Maria, sitting by the stove, saw him go and said nothing. For, they thought delicately, either a vapor of love had been wafted to Pilon or else he knew where he could get a little wine. In either case it was none of their business until he told them about it.

It was well after dark, but Pilon had a candle in his pocket, for it might be a good thing to watch the expression on the Pirate's face while he talked. And Pilon had a big round sugar cookie in a bag, that Susie Francisco, who worked in a bakery, had given him in return for a formula for getting the love of Charlie Guzman. Charlie was a Postal Telegraph messenger and rode a motorcycle; and Susie had a man's cap to put on backward in case Charlie should ever ask her to ride with him. Pilon thought the Pirate might like the sugar cookie.

The night was very dark. Pilon picked his way along a narrow street bordered with vacant lots and with weed-grown, neglected gardens.

Galvez' bad bulldog came snarling out of Galvez' yard, and Pilon spoke soothing compliments to him.

"Nice dog," he said gently, and "Pretty dog," both of them palpable lies. They impressed the bulldog, however, for he retired into Galvez' yard.

Pilon came at last to the vacant property where the Pirate lived. And now he knew he must be careful, for the Pirate's dogs, if they suspected ill of any one toward their master, were known to become defending furies. As Pilon stepped into the yard, he heard deep and threatening growls from the chicken house.

"Pirate," he called. "It is thy good friend Pilon, come to talk with thee."

There was silence. The dogs stopped growling.

"Pirate, it is only Pilon."

A deep surly voice answered him, "Go away. I am sleeping now. The dogs are sleeping. It is dark, Pilon. Go to bed."

"I have a candle in my pocket," Pilon called. "It will make a light as bright as day in thy dark house. I have a big sugar cookie for thee, too."

A faint scuffling sounded in the chicken house. "Come then," the Pirate said. "I will tell the dogs it is all right."

As he advanced through the weeds, Pilon could hear

101

the Pirate talking softly to his dogs, explaining to them that it was only Pilon, who would do no harm. Pilon bent over in front of the dark doorway and scratched a match and lighted his candle.

The Pirate was seated on the dirt floor, and his dogs were all about him. Enrique growled, and had to be reassured again. "That one is not so wise as the others," the Pirate said pleasantly. His eyes were the pleased eyes of an amused child. When he smiled his big white teeth glistened in the candlelight.

Pilon held out the bag. "It is a fine cake for you," he said.

The Pirate took the bag and looked into it; then he smiled delightedly, and brought out the cookie. The dogs all grinned and faced him, and moved their feet and licked their lips. The Pirate broke his cookie into seven pieces. The first he gave to Pilon, who was his guest. "Now, Enrique," he said. "Now Fluff. Now Señor Alec Thompson." Each dog received his piece and gulped it and looked for more. Last, the Pirate ate his and held up his hands to the dogs. "No more, you see," he told them. Immediately the dogs lay down about him.

Pilon sat on the floor and stood the candle on the ground in front of him. The Pirate questioned him self-consciously with his eyes. Pilon sat silently, to let many questions pass through the Pirate's head. At length he said, "Thou art a worry to thy friends."

The Pirate's eyes filled with astonishment. "I? To my friends? What friends?"

Pilon softened his voice. "Thou hast many friends who think of thee. They do not come to see thee because thou art proud. They think it might hurt thy pride to have them see thee living in this chicken house, clothed in rags, eating garbage with thy dogs. But these friends of thine worry for fear the bad life may make thee ill."

The Pirate was following his words with breathless astonishment, and his brain tried to realize these new things he was hearing. It did not occur to him to doubt them, since Pilon was saying them. "I have all these friends?" he said in wonder. "And I did not know it. And I am a worry to those friends. I did not know, Pilon. I would not have worried them if I had known." He swallowed to clear his throat of emotion. "You see, Pilon, the dogs like it here. And I like it because of

them. I did not think I was a worry to my friends."
Tears came into the Pirate's eyes.

"Nevertheless," Pilon said, "thy mode of living keeps
all thy friends uneasy."

The Pirate looked down at the ground and tried to
think clearly, but as always, when he attempted to cope
with a problem, his brain grew gray and no help came
from it, but only a feeling of helplessness. He looked to
his dogs for protection, but they had gone back to sleep,
for it was none of their business. And then he looked
earnestly into Pilon's eyes. "You must tell me what to
do, Pilon. I did not know these things."

It was too easy. Pilon was a little ashamed that it
should be so easy. He hesitated; nearly gave it up; but
then he knew he would be angry with himself if he
did. "Thy friends are poor," he said. "They would like
to help thee, but they have no money. If thou hast
money hidden, bring it out into the open. Buy thyself
some clothes. Eat food that is not cast out by other
people. Bring thy money out of its hiding place, Pirate."

Pilon had been looking closely at the Pirate's face
while he spoke. He saw the eyes droop with suspicion
and then with sullenness. In a moment Pilon knew two

things certainly; first, that the Pirate had money hidden; and second, that it was not going to be easy to get at it. He was pleased at the latter fact. The Pirate had become a problem in tactics such as Pilon enjoyed.

Now the Pirate was looking at him again, and in his eyes was cunning, and on top of that, a studied ingenuousness. "I have no money anywhere," he said.

"But every day, my friend, I have seen thee get a quarter for thy wood, and never have I seen thee spend it."

This time the Pirate's brain came to his rescue. "I give it to a poor old woman," he said. "I have no money anywhere." And with his tone he closed a door tightly on the subject.

"So it must be guile," Pilon thought. So those gifts, that in him were so sharpened, must be called into play. He stood up and lifted his candle. "I only thought to tell thee how thy friends worry," he said critically. "If thou wilt not try to help, I can do nothing for thee."

The sweetness came back into the Pirate's eyes. "Tell them I am healthy," he begged. "Tell my friends to come and see me. I will not be too proud. I will be glad to see them any time. Wilt thou tell them for me, Pilon?"

"I will tell them," Pilon said ungraciously. "But thy friends will not be pleased when they see thou dost nothing to relieve their minds." Pilon blew out his candle and went away into the darkness. He knew that the Pirate would never tell where his hoard was. It must be found by stealth, taken by force and then all the good things given to the Pirate. It was the only way.

And so Pilon set himself to watch the Pirate. He followed him into the forest when he went to cut kindlings. He lay in wait outside the chicken house at night. He talked to him long and earnestly, and nothing came of it. The treasure was as far from discovery as ever. Either it lay buried in the chicken house or it was hidden deep in the forest, and was only visited at night.

The long and fruitless vigils wore out the patience of Pilon. He knew he must have help and advice. And who could better give it than those comrades, Danny, Pablo and Jesus Maria? Who could be so stealthy, so guileful? Who could melt to kindness with more ease?

Pilon took them into his confidence; but first he prepared them, as he had prepared himself: The Pirate's poverty, his helplessness, and finally—the solution. When he came to the solution, his friends were in a philanthropic frenzy. They applauded him. Their faces shone with kindness. Pablo thought there might be well over a hundred dollars in the hoard.

When their joy had settled to a working enthusiasm, they came to plans.

"We must watch him," Pablo said.

"But I have watched him," Pilon argued. "It must be that he creeps off in the night, and then one cannot follow too close, for his dogs guard him like devils. It is not going to be so easy."

"You've used every argument?" Danny asked.

"Yes. Every one."

In the end it was Jesus Maria, that humane man, who found the way out. "It is difficult while he lives in that chicken house," he said. "But suppose he lived here, with us? Either his silence would break under our kindness, or else it would be easier to know when he goes out at night."

The friends gave a good deal of thought to this suggestion. "Sometimes the things he gets out of restaurants are nearly new," mused Pablo. "I have seen him with a steak out of which only a little was missing."

"It might be as much as two hundred dollars," said Pilon.

Danny offered an objection. "But those dogs—he would bring his dogs with him."

"They are good dogs," said Pilon. "They obey him exactly. You may draw a line around a corner and say, 'Keep thy dogs within this line.' He will tell them, and those dogs will stay."

"I saw the Pirate one morning, and he had nearly half a cake, just a little bit damp with coffee," said Pablo.

The question settled itself. The house resolved itself into a committee, and the committee visited the Pirate.

It was a crowded place, that chicken house, when they all got inside. The Pirate tried to disguise his happiness with a gruff tone.

"The weather has been bad," he said socially. And, "You wouldn't believe, maybe, that I found a tick as big as a pigeon's egg on Rudolph's neck." And he spoke disparagingly of his home, as a host should. "It is too small," he said. "It is not a fit place for one's friends to come. But it is warm and snug, especially for the dogs."

Then Pilon spoke. He told the Pirate that worry was killing his friends; but if he would go to live with them, then they could sleep again, with their minds at ease.

It was a very great shock to the Pirate. He looked at his hands. And he looked to his dogs for comfort, but they would not meet his glance. At last he wiped the happiness from his eyes with the back of his hand, and he wiped his hand on his big black beard.

"And the dogs?" he asked softly. "You want the dogs, too? Are you friends of the dogs?"

Pilon nodded. "Yes, the dogs, too. There will be a whole corner set aside for the dogs."

The Pirate had a great deal of pride. He was afraid he might not conduct himself well. "Go away now," he said pleadingly. "Go home now. To-morrow I will come."

His friends knew how he felt. They crawled out of the door and left him alone.

"He will be happy with us, that one," said Jesus Maria.

"Poor little lonely man," Danny added. "If I had

known, I would have asked him long ago, even if he had no treasure."

A flame of joy burned in all of them.

They settled soon into the new relationship. Danny, with a piece of blue chalk, drew a segment of a circle, enclosing a corner of the living room, and that was where the dogs must stay when they were in the house. The Pirate slept in that corner too, with the dogs.

The house was beginning to be a little crowded, with five men and five dogs; but from the first, Danny and his friends realized that their invitation to the Pirate had been inspired by that weary and anxious angel who guarded their destinies and protected them from evil.

Every morning, long before his friends were awake, the Pirate arose from his corner and, followed by his dogs, he made the rounds of the restaurants and the wharves. He was one of those for whom every one feels a kindliness. His packages grew larger. The paisanos received his bounty and made use of it; fresh fish, half pies, untouched loaves of stale bread, meat that required only a little soda to take the green out. They began really to live.

And their acceptance of his gifts touched the Pirate

111

more deeply than anything they could have done for him. There was a light of worship in his eyes as he watched them eat the food he brought.

In the evening, when they sat about the stove and discussed the doings of Tortilla Flat with the lazy voices of fed gods, the Pirate's eyes darted from mouth to mouth, and his own lips moved, whispering again the words his friends said. The dogs pressed in about him jealously.

These were his friends, he told himself in the night, when the house was dark, when the dogs snuggled close to him so that all might be warm. These men loved him so much that it worried them to have him live alone. The Pirate had often to repeat this to himself, for it was an astounding thing, an unbelievable thing. His wheelbarrow stood in Danny's yard now, and every day he cut his pitchwood and sold it. But so afraid was the Pirate that he might miss some word his friends said in the evening, might not be there to absorb some stream of the warm companionship, that he had not visited his hoard for several days to put the new coins there.

His friends were kind to him. They treated him with a sweet courtesy; but always there was some eye open and upon him. When he wheeled his barrow into the woods, one of the friends walked with him, and sat on a log while he worked. When he went into the gulch, the last thing at night, Danny or Pablo or Pilon or Jesus Maria kept him company. And in the night he must have been very quiet to have crept out without a shadow behind him.

For a week, the friends merely watched the Pirate. But at last the inactivity tired them. Direct action was out of the question, they knew. And so one evening the subject of the desirability of hiding one's money came up for discussion.

Pilon began it. "I had an uncle, a regular miser, and he hid his gold in the woods. And one time he went to look at it, and it was gone. Some one had found it and stolen it. He was an old man, then, and all his money was gone, and he hanged himself." Pilon noticed with some satisfaction, the look of apprehension that came upon the Pirate's face.

Danny noticed it, too; and he continued, "The viejo, my grandfather, who owned this house, also buried money. I do not know how much, but he was reputed a rich man, so there must have been three or four hundred dollars. The viejo dug a deep hole and put his money in it, and then he covered it up, and then he strewed pine needles over the ground until he thought no one could see that anything had been done there. But when he went back, the hole was open, and the money was gone."

The Pirate's lips followed the words. A look of terror had come into his face. His fingers picked among the neck hairs of Señor Alec Thompson. The friends exchanged a glance and dropped the subject for the time-being. They turned to the love life of Cornelia Ruiz.

In the night the Pirate crept out of the house, and the dogs crept after him; and Pilon crept after all of them. The Pirate went swiftly into the forest, leaping with sure feet over logs and brush. Pilon floundered behind him. But when they had gone at least two miles, Pilon was winded, and torn by vines. He paused to rest a moment; and then he realized that all sounds ahead of him had ceased. He waited and listened and crept about, but the Pirate had disappeared.

After two hours, Pilon went back again, slowly and tiredly. There was the Pirate in the house, fast asleep among his dogs. The dogs lifted their heads when Pilon entered, and Pilon thought they smiled satirically at him for a moment.

A conference took place in the gulch the next morning.

"It is not possible to follow him," Pilon reported. "He vanished. He sees in the dark. He knows every tree in the forest. We must find some other way."

"Perhaps one is not enough," Pablo suggested. "If all of us should follow him, then one might not lose track of him."

"We will talk again to-night," said Jesus Maria, "only worse. A lady I know is going to give me a little wine," he added modestly. "Maybe if the Pirate has a little wine in him, he will not disappear so easily." So it was left.

Jesus Maria's lady gave him a whole gallon of wine. What could compare with the Pirate's delight that evening when a fruit jar of wine was put into his hand, when he sat with his friends and sipped his wine and listened to the talk? Such joy had come rarely into the Pirate's life. He wished he might clasp these dear people to his breast and tell them how much he loved them. But that was not a thing he could do, for they might think he was drunk. He wished he could do some tremendous thing to show them his love.

"We spoke last night of burying money," said Pilon. "To-day I remembered a cousin of mine, a clever man. If any one in the world could hide money where it would never be found, he could do it. So he took his money and hid it. Perhaps you have seen him, that poor little one who crawls about the wharf and begs fish heads to make soup of. That is my cousin. Some one stole his buried money."

The worry came back into the Pirate's face.

Story topped story, and in each one all manner of evil dogged the footsteps of those who hid their money.

"It is better to keep one's money close, to spend some now and then, to give a little to one's friends," Danny finished.

They had been watching the Pirate narrowly, and in the middle of the worst story they had seen the worry go from his face, and a smile of relief take its place. Now he sipped his wine and his eyes glittered with joy.

The friends were in despair. All their plans had failed. They were sick at heart. After all their goodness and their charity, this had happened. The Pirate had in some way escaped the good they had intended to confer upon him. They finished their wine and went moodily to bed.

Few things could happen in the night without Pilon's knowledge. His ears remained open while the rest of him slept. He heard the stealthy exit of the Pirate and his dogs from the house. He leaped to awaken his friends; and in a moment the four were following the Pirate in the direction of the forest. It was very dark when they entered the pine forest. The four friends ran into trees, tripped on berry vines; but for a long time they could hear the Pirate marching on ahead of them. They followed as far as Pilon had followed the night before, and then, suddenly, silence, and the whispering forest and the vague night wind. They combed the woods and the brush patches, but the Pirate had disappeared again.

At last, cold and disconsolate, they came together and trudged wearily back toward Monterey. The dawn came before they got back. The sun was already shining on the bay. The smoke of the morning fires arose to them out of Monterey.

The Pirate walked out on the porch to greet them, and his face was happy. They passed him sullenly, and filed into the living room. There on the table lay a large canvas bag.

The Pirate followed them in. "I lied to thee, Pilon," he said. "I told thee I had no money, for I was afraid. I did not know about my friends, then. You have told how hidden money is so often stolen, and I am afraid again. Only last night did a way out come to me. My money will be safe with my friends. No one can steal it if my friends guard it for me."

The four men stared at him in horror. "Take thy money back to the woods and hide it," Danny said savagely. "We do not want to watch it."

"No," said the Pirate. "I would not feel safe to hide it. But I will be happy knowing my friends guard it for me. You would not believe it, but the last two nights some one followed me into the forest to steal my money."

Terrible as the blow was, Pilon, that clever man, tried to escape it. "Before this money is put into our hands, maybe you would like to take some out," he suggested smoothly.

The Pirate shook his head. "No. I cannot do that. It is promised. I have nearly a thousand two-bitses. When

118

I have a thousand I will buy a gold candle-stick for San Francisco de Assisi.

"Once I had a nice dog, and that dog was sick; and I promised a gold candle-stick of one thousand days if that dog would get well. And," he spread his great hands, "that dog got well."

"Is it one of these dogs?" Pilon demanded.

"No," said the Pirate. "A truck ran over him a little later."

So it was over, all hope of diverting the money. Danny and Pablo morosely lifted the heavy bag of silver quarters, took it in the other room and put it under the pillow of Danny's bed. In time they would take a certain pleasure in the knowledge that this money lay under the pillow, but now their defeat was bitter. There was nothing in the world they could do about it. Their chance had come, and it had gone.

The Pirate stood before them, and there were tears of happiness in his eyes, for he had proved his love for his friends.

"To think," he said, "all those years I lay in that chicken house, and I did not know any pleasure. But now," he added, "oh, now I am very happy."

# VIII

*How Danny's Friends sought mystic treasure on St. Andrew's Eve. How Pilon found it and later how a pair of serge pants changed ownership twice.*

I F HE had been a hero, the Portagee would have spent a miserable time in the army. The fact that he was Big Joe Portagee, with a decent training in the Monterey jail, not only saved him the misery of patriotism thwarted, but solidified his conviction that as a man's days are rightly devoted half to sleeping and half to waking, so a man's years are rightly spent half in jail and half out. Of the duration of the war, Joe Portagee spent considerably more time in jail than out.

In civilian life, one is punished for things one does; but army codes add a new principle to this—they punish a man for things he does not do. Joe Portagee never did figure this out. He didn't clean his rifle; he didn't shave; and once or twice, on leave, he didn't come back. Coupled with these shortcomings was a propensity Big Joe had for genial argument when he was taken to task.

Ordinarily, he spent half his time in jail; of two years in the army, he spent eighteen months in jail. And he was far from satisfied with prison life in the army. In the Monterey jail he was accustomed to ease and companionship. In the army, he found only work. In Monterey, only one charge was ever brought against him: Drunk and Disorderly Conduct. The charges in the army bewildered him so completely that the effect on his mind was probably permanent.

When the war was over, and all the troops were disbanded, Big Joe still had six months' sentence to serve. The charge had been: "Being drunk on duty. Striking a sergeant with a kerosene can. Denying his identity (he couldn't remember it, so he denied everything). Stealing two gallons of cooked beans, and going A.W.O.L. on the Major's horse."

If the Armistice had not already been signed, Big Joe would probably have been shot. He came home to

Monterey long after the other veterans had arrived and had eaten up all the sweets of victory.

When Big Joe swung down from the train, he was dressed in an army overcoat and tunic and a pair of blue serge trousers.

The town hadn't changed much, except for prohibition; and prohibition hadn't changed Torrelli's. Joe traded his overcoat for a gallon of wine and went out to find his friends.

True friends he found none that night, but in Monterey he found no lack of those vile and false harpies and pimps who are ever ready to lead men into the pit. Joe, who was not very moral, had no revulsion for the pit; he liked it.

Before very many hours had passed, his wine was gone, and he had no money; and then the harpies tried to get Joe out of the pit, and he wouldn't go. He was comfortable there.

When they tried to eject him by force, Big Joe, with a just and terrible resentment, broke all the furniture and all the windows, sent half-clothed girls screaming into the night; and then, as an afterthought, set fire to the house. It was not a safe thing to lead Joe into temptation; he had no resistance to it at all.

A policeman finally interfered and took him in hand. The Portagee sighed happily. He was home again.

After a short and juryless trial, in which he was sentenced to thirty days, Joe lay luxuriously on his leather cot and slept heavily for one tenth of his sentence.

The Portagee liked the Monterey jail. It was a place to meet people. If he stayed there long enough, all his friends were in and out. The time passed quickly. He was a little sad when he had to go, but his sadness was tempered with the knowledge that it was very easy to get back again.

He would have liked to go into the pit again, but he had no money and no wine. He combed the streets for his old friends, Pilon and Danny and Pablo, and could not find them. The police sergeant said he hadn't booked them for a long time.

"They must be dead," said the Portagee.

He wandered sadly to Torrelli's, but Torrelli was not friendly toward men who had neither money nor barterable property, and he gave Big Joe little solace; but Torrelli did say that Danny had inherited a house on

Tortilla Flat, and that all his friends lived there with him.

Affection and a desire to see his friends came to Big Joe. In the evening he wandered up toward Tortilla Flat to find Danny and Pilon. It was dusk as he walked up the street, and on the way he met Pilon, hurrying by in a businesslike way.

"Ai, Pilon. I was just coming to see you."

"Hello, Joe Portagee," Pilon was brusque. "Where you been?"

"In the army," said Joe.

Pilon's mind was not on the meeting. "I have to go on."

"I will go with you," said Joe.

Pilon stopped and surveyed him. "Don't you remember what night it is?" he asked.

"No. What is it?"

"It is St. Andrew's Eve."

Then the Portagee knew; for this was the night when every paisano who wasn't in jail wandered restlessly through the forest. This was the night when all buried treasure sent up a faint phosphorescent glow through the ground. There was plenty of treasure in the woods, too. Monterey had been invaded many times in two hundred years, and each time valuables had been hidden in the earth.

The night was clear. Pilon had emerged from his hard daily shell, as he did now and then. He was the idealist to-night, the giver of gifts. This night he was engaged in a mission of kindness.

"You may come with me, Big Joe Portagee, but if we find any treasure I must decide what to do with it. If you do not agree, you can go by yourself and look for your own treasure."

Big Joe was not an expert at directing his own efforts. "I will go with you, Pilon," he said. "I don't care about the treasure."

The night came down as they walked into the forest. Their feet found the pine-needle beds. Now Pilon knew it for a perfect night. A high fog covered the sky, and behind it, the moon shone so that the forest was filled with a gauze-like light. There was none of the sharp outline we think of as reality. The tree trunks were not black columns of wood, but soft and unsubstantial shadows. The patches of brush were formless and shifting in the queer light. Ghosts could walk freely to-night, without fear of the disbelief of men; for this night was haunted, and it would be an insensitive man who did not know it.

Now and then Pilon and Big Joe passed other searchers who wandered restlessly, zig-zagging among the pines. Their heads were down and they moved silently and passed no greeting. Who could say whether all of them were really living men? Joe and Pilon knew that some were shades of those old folk who had buried the treasures; and who, on Saint Andrew's Eve, wandered back to the earth to see that their gold was undisturbed. Pilon wore his saint's medallion, hung around his neck, outside his clothes; so he had no fear of the spirits. Big Joe walked with his fingers crossed in the Holy Sign. Although they might be frightened, they knew they had protection more than adequate to cope with the unearthly night.

The wind arose as they walked, and drove the fog across the pale moon like a thin wash of gray water color. The moving fog gave shifting form to the forest, so that every tree crept stealthily along and the bushes moved soundlessly, like great dark cats. The tree-tops in the wind talked huskily, told fortunes and foretold deaths. Pilon knew it was not good to listen to the talking of the trees. No good ever came of knowing the future; and besides, this whispering was unholy. He turned the attention of his ears from the trees' talking.

He began a zig-zag path through the forest, and Big Joe walked beside him like a great alert dog. Lone silent men passed them, and went on without a greeting; and the dead passed them noiselessly, and went on without a greeting.

The fog siren began its screaming on the Point, far below them; and it wailed its sorrow for all the good ships that had drowned on the iron reef, and for all those others that would sometime die there.

Pilon shuddered and felt cold, although the night was warm. He whispered a Hail Mary under his breath.

They passed a gray man who walked with his head down, and who gave them no greeting.

An hour went by, and still Pilon and Big Joe wandered as restlessly as the dead who crowded the night.

Suddenly Pilon stopped. His hand found Big Joe's arm. "Do you see?" he whispered.

"Where?"

"Right ahead there."

128

"Ye-s—I think so."

It seemed to Pilon that he could see a soft pillar of blue light that shone out of the ground ten yards ahead of him.

"Big Joe," he whispered, "find two sticks about three or four feet long. I do not want to look away. I might lose it."

He stood like a pointing dog while Big Joe scurried off to find the sticks. Pilon heard him break two small dead limbs from a pine tree. And he heard the snaps as Big Joe broke the twigs from his sticks. And still Pilon stared at the pale shaft of nebulous light. So faint it was that sometimes it seemed to disappear altogether. Sometimes he was not sure he saw it at all. He did not move his eyes when Big Joe put the sticks in his hands. Pilon crossed the sticks at right angles and advanced slowly, holding the cross in front of him. As he came close, the light seemed to fade away, but he saw where it had come from, a perfectly round depression in the pine needles.

Pilon laid his cross over the depression, and he said, "All that lies here is mine by discovery. Go away, all evil spirits. Go away, spirits of men who buried this treasure, *In Nomen Patris et Filius et Spiritu Sancti*," and then he heaved a great sigh and sat down on the ground.

"We have found it, oh my friend, Big Joe," he cried. "For many years I have looked, and now I have found it."

"Let's dig," said Big Joe.

But Pilon shook his head impatiently. "When all the spirits are free? When even to be here is dangerous? You are a fool, Big Joe. We will sit here until morning; and then we will mark the place, and to-morrow night we will dig. No one else can see the light now that we have covered it with the cross. To-morrow night there will be no danger."

The night seemed more fearful now that they sat in the pine needles, but the cross sent out a warmth of holiness and safety, like a little bonfire on the ground. Like a fire, however, it only warmed the front of them. Their backs were to the cold and evil things that wandered about in the forest.

Pilon got up and drew a big circle around the whole place, and he was inside when he closed the circle. "Let no evil thing cross this line, in the Name of the Most

Holy Jesus," he chanted. Then he sat down again. Both he and Big Joe felt better. They could hear the muffled footsteps of the weary wandering ghosts; they could see the little lights that glowed from the transparent forms as they walked by; but their protecting line was impregnable. Nothing bad from this world or from any other world could cross into the circle.

"What are you going to do with the money?" Big Joe asked.

Pilon looked at him with contempt. "You have never looked for treasure, Big Joe Portagee, for you do not know how to go about it. I cannot keep this treasure for myself. If I go after it intending to keep it, then the treasure will dig itself down and down like a clam in the sand, and I shall never find it. No, that is not the way. I am digging this treasure for Danny."

All the idealism in Pilon came out then. He told Big Joe how good Danny was to his friends.

"And we do nothing for him," he said. "We pay no rent. Sometimes we get drunk and break the furniture. We fight with Danny when we are angry with him, and we call him names. Oh, we are very bad, Big Joe. And so all of us, Pablo and Jesus Maria and the Pirate and

I talked and planned. We are all in the woods, to-night, looking for treasure. And the treasure is to be for Danny. He is so good, Big Joe. He is so kind; and we are so bad. But if we take a great sack of treasure to him, then he will be glad. It is because my heart is clean of selfishness that I can find this treasure?"

"Won't you keep any of it?" Big Joe asked, incredulous. "Not even for a gallon of wine?"

Pilon had no speck of the Bad Pilon in him this night. "No, not one scrap of gold! Not one little brown penny! It is all for Danny, every bit."

Joe was disappointed. "I walked all this way, and I won't even get a glass of wine for it," he mourned.

"When Danny has the money," Pilon said delicately, "it may be that he will buy a little wine. Of course I shall not suggest it, for this treasure is Danny's. But I think maybe he might buy a little wine. And then if you were good to him, you might get a glass."

Big Joe was comforted, for he had known Danny a long time. He thought it possible that Danny might buy a great deal of wine.

The night passed on over them. The moon went down and left the forest in muffled darkness. The fog siren screamed and screamed. During the whole night Pilon remained unspotted. He preached a little to Big Joe as recent converts are likely to do.

"It is worth while to be kind and generous," he said. "Not only do such actions pile up a house of joy in Heaven; but there is, too, a quick reward here on earth. One feels a golden warmth glowing like a hot enchilada in one's stomach. The Spirit of God clothes one in a coat as soft as camel's hair. I have not always been a good man, Big Joe Portagee. I confess it freely."

Big Joe knew it perfectly well.

"I have been bad." Pilon continued ecstatically. He was enjoying himself thoroughly. "I have lied and stolen. I have been lecherous. I have committed adultery and taken God's name in vain."

"Me too," said Big Joe happily.

"And what was the result, Big Joe Portagee? I have had a mean feeling. I have known I would go to Hell. But now I see that the sinner is never so bad that he cannot be forgiven. Although I have not yet been to confession, I can feel that the change in me is pleasing to God, for His grace is upon me. If you, too, would change your ways, Big Joe, if you would give up drunkenness and fighting and those girls down at Dora Williams' House, you too might feel as I do."

But Big Joe had gone to sleep. He never stayed awake very long when he was not moving about.

The grace was not quite so sharp to Pilon when he could not tell Big Joe about it, but he sat and watched the treasure place while the sky grayed and the dawn came behind the fog. He saw the pine trees take shape and emerge out of obscurity. The wind died down and the little blue rabbits came out of the brush and hopped about on the pine needles. Pilon was heavy-eyed but happy.

When it was light he stirred Big Joe Portagee with his foot. "It is time to go to Danny's house. The day has come." Pilon threw the cross away, for it was no longer needed, and he erased the circle. "Now," he said, "we must make no mark, but we must remember this by trees and rocks."

"Why don't we dig now?" Big Joe asked.

"And everybody in Tortilla Flat would come to help us," Pilon said sarcastically.

They looked hard at the surroundings, saying, "Now there are three trees together on the right, and two on the left. That patch of brush is down there, and here is a rock." At last they walked away from the treasure, memorizing the way as they went.

At Danny's house they found tired friends. "Did you find any?" the friends demanded.

"No," said Pilon quickly, to forestall Joe's confession.

"Well, Pablo thought he saw the light, but it disappeared before he got to it. And the Pirate saw the ghost of an old woman, and she had his dog with her."

The Pirate broke into a smile. "That old woman told me my dog was happy now," he said.

"Here is Big Joe Portagee, back from the army," announced Pilon.

"Hello, Joe."

"You got a nice place here," said the Portagee, and let himself down easily into a chair.

"You keep out of my bed," said Danny, for he knew that Joe Portagee had come to stay. The way he sat in a chair and crossed his knees had an appearance of permanence.

The Pirate went out, and took his wheelbarrow and started into the forest to cut his kindlings; but the other five men lay down in the sunshine that broke through the fog, and in a little while they were asleep.

It was mid-afternoon before any of them awakened. At last they stretched their arms and sat up and looked listlessly down at the bay below, where a brown oil tanker moved slowly out to sea. The Pirate had left the bags on the table, and the friends opened them and brought out the food the Pirate had collected.

Big Joe walked down the path toward the sagging gate. "See you later," he called to Pilon.

Pilon anxiously watched him until he saw that Big Joe was headed down the hill to Monterey, not up toward the pine forest. The four friends sat down and dreamily watched the evening come.

At dusk Joe Portagee returned. He and Pilon conferred in the yard, out of earshot of the house.

"We will borrow tools from Mrs. Morales," Pilon said. "A shovel and a pick-ax stand by her chicken house."

When it was quite dark they started. "We go to see some girls, friends of Joe Portagee's," Pilon explained. They crept into Mrs. Morales' yard and borrowed the tools. And then, from the weeds beside the road, Big Joe lifted out a gallon jug of wine.

"Thou hast sold the treasure," Pilon cried fiercely. "Thou art a traitor, oh dog of a dog."

Big Joe quieted him firmly. "I did not tell where the treasure was," he said with some dignity. "I told like this, 'We found a treasure,' I said, 'But it is for Danny. When Danny has it, I will borrow a dollar and pay for the wine.'"

Pilon was overwhelmed. "And they believed, and let you take the wine?" he demanded.

"Well—" Big Joe hesitated. "I left something to prove I would bring the dollar."

Pilon turned like lightning and took him by the throat. "What did you leave?"

"Only one little blanket, Pilon," Joe Portagee wailed. "Only one."

Pilon shook at him, but Big Joe was so heavy that Pilon only succeeded in shaking himself. "What blanket," he cried. "Say what blanket it was you stole."

Big Joe blubbered. "Only one of Danny's. Only one. He has two. I took only the little tiny one. Do not hurt me, Pilon. The other one was bigger. Danny will get it back when we find the treasure."

Pilon whirled him around and kicked him with accuracy and fire. "Pig," he said, "dirty thieving cow. You will get the blanket back or I will beat you to ribbons."

Big Joe tried to placate him. "I thought how we are working for Danny," he whispered. "I thought, 'Danny will be so glad, he can buy a hundred new blankets.'"

"Be still," said Pilon. "You will get that same blanket back or I will beat you with a rock." He took up the jug and uncorked it and drank a little to soothe his frayed sensibilities; moreover he drove the cork back and refused the Portagee even a drop. "For this theft you must do all the digging. Pick up those tools and come with me."

Big Joe whined like a puppy, and obeyed. He could not stand against the righteous fury of Pilon.

They tried to find the treasure for a long time. It was late when Pilon pointed to three trees in a row. "There!" he said.

They searched about until they found the depression in the ground. There was a little moonlight to guide them, for this night the sky was free of fog.

Now that he was not going to dig, Pilon developed a new theory for uncovering treasure. "Sometimes the money is in sacks," he said, "and the sacks are rotted. If you dig straight down you might lose some." He drew a generous circle around the hollow. "Now, dig a deep trench around, and then we will come *up* on the treasure."

"Aren't you going to dig?" Big Joe asked.

Pilon broke into fury. "Am I a thief of blankets?" he cried. "Do I steal from the bed of my friend who shelters me?"

"Well, I ain't going to do all the digging," Big Joe said.

Pilon picked up one of the pine limbs that only the night before had served as part of the cross. He advanced ominously toward Big Joe Portagee. "Thief," he snarled. "Dirty pig of an untrue friend. Take up that shovel."

Big Joe's courage flowed away, and he stooped for the shovel on the ground. If Joe Portagee's conscience had not been bad, he might have remonstrated; but his fear of Pilon, armed with a righteous cause and a stick of pine wood, was great.

Big Joe abhorred the whole principle of shoveling. The line of the moving shovel was unattractive. The end to be gained, that of taking dirt from one place and putting it in another, was, to one who held the larger vision, silly and gainless. A whole lifetime of shoveling could accomplish practically nothing. Big Joe's reaction was a little more simple than this. He didn't like to shovel. He had joined the army to fight, and had done nothing but dig.

But Pilon stood over him, and the trench stretched around the treasure place. It did no good to profess sickness, hunger or weakness. Pilon was inexorable, and Joe's crime of the blanket was held against him. Although he whined, complained, held up his hands to show how they were hurt, Pilon stood over him and forced the digging.

Midnight came, and the trench was three feet down. The roosters of Monterey crowed. The moon sank behind the trees. At last Pilon gave the word to move in on the treasure. The bursts of dirt came slowly now; Big Joe was exhausted. Just before daylight, his shovel struck something hard.

"Ai," he cried. "We have it, Pilon."

The find was large and square. Frantically they dug at it in the dark, and they could not see it.

"Careful," Pilon cautioned. "Do not hurt it."

The daylight came before they had it out. Pilon felt metal and leaned down in the gray light to see. It was a good-sized square of concrete. On the top was a round brown plate. Pilon spelled out the words on it:

"United States Geodetic Survey + 1915 + Elevation 600 Feet."

Pilon sat down in the pit and his shoulders sagged in defeat.

"No treasure?" Big Joe asked plaintively.

Pilon did not answer him. The Portagee inspected the cement post and his brow wrinkled with thought. He turned to the sorrowing Pilon. "Maybe we can take this good piece of metal and sell it."

Pilon peered up out of his dejection. "Johnny Pom-pom found one," he said with a quietness of great disappointment. "Johnny Pom-pom took the metal piece and tried to sell it. It is a year in jail to dig one of these up," Pilon mourned. "A year in jail and two thousand dollar fine." In his pain, Pilon wanted only to get away from this tragic place. He stood up, found a weed in which to wrap the wine bottle, and started down the hill.

Big Joe trotted after him solicitously. "Where are we going?" he asked.

"I don't know," said Pilon.

The day was bright when they arrived at the beach; but even there Pilon did not stop. He trudged along the hard sand by the water's edge until Monterey was far behind and only the sand dunes of Seaside and the rippling waves of the bay were there to see his sorrow. At last he sat in the dry sand, with the sun warming him. Big Joe sat beside him, and he felt that in some way he was responsible for Pilon's silent pain.

Pilon took the jug out of its weed and uncorked it and drank deeply, and because sorrow is the mother of a general compassion, he passed Joe's wine to the miscreant Joe.

"How we build," Pilon cried. "How our dreams lead us. I had thought how we would carry bags of gold to Danny. I could see how his face would look. He would be surprised. For a long time he would not believe it." He took the bottle from Joe Portagee and drank colossally. "All this is gone, blown away in the night."

The sun was warming the beach now. In spite of his disappointment, Pilon felt a traitorous comfort stealing over him, a treacherous impulse to discover some good points in the situation.

Big Joe, in his quiet way, was drinking more than his share of the wine. Pilon took it indignantly and drank again and again.

"But after all," he said philosophically, "maybe if we had found gold, it might not have been good for Danny. He has always been a poor man. Riches might make him crazy."

Big Joe nodded solemnly. The wine went down and down in the bottle.

"Happiness is better than riches," said Pilon. "If we try to make Danny happy, it will be a better thing than to give him money."

Big Joe nodded again and took off his shoes. "Make him happy. That's the stuff."

Pilon turned sadly upon him. "You are only a pig, and not fit to live with men," he said gently. "You who stole Danny's blanket should be kept in a sty and fed potato peelings."

They were getting very sleepy in the warm sun. The

little waves whispered along the beach. Pilon took off his shoes.

"Even Stephen," said Big Joe, and they drained the jug to the last drop.

The beach was swaying gently, heaving and falling with a movement like a ground-swell.

"You aren't a bad man," Pilon said. But Big Joe Portagee was already asleep. Pilon took off his coat and laid it over his face. In a few moments, he too was sleeping sweetly.

The sun wheeled over the sky. The tide spread up the beach, and then retreated. A squad of scampering kildeers inspected the sleeping men. A wandering dog sniffed them. Two elderly ladies, collecting seashells, saw the bodies and hurried past lest these men should awaken in passion, pursue and criminally assault them. It was a shame, they agreed, that the police did nothing to control such matters. "They are drunk," one said.

And the other stared back up the beach at the sleeping men. "Drunken beasts," she agreed.

When at last the sun went behind the pines of the hill in back of Monterey, Pilon awakened. His mouth was as dry as alum; his head ached and he was stiff from the hard sand. Big Joe snored on.

"Joe," Pilon cried, but the Portagee was beyond call Pilon rested on his elbow and stared out to sea. "A little wine would be good for my dry mouth," he thought. He tipped up the jug and got not a single drop to soothe his dry tongue. Then he turned out his pockets in the hope that while he slept some miracle had taken place there; but none had. There was a broken pocket knife for which he had been refused a glass of wine at least twenty times. There was a fish-hook in a cork, a piece of dirty string, a dog's tooth and several keys that fit nothing Pilon knew of. In the whole lot was not a thing Torrelli would consider as worth having, even in a moment of insanity.

Pilon looked speculatively at Big Joe. "Poor fellow," he thought. "When Joe Portagee wakes up, he will feel as dry as I do. He will like it if I have a little wine for him." He pushed Big Joe roughly several times; and when the Portagee only mumbled, and then snored again, Pilon looked through his pockets. He found a brass pants button, a little metal disk which said "Good

Eats at the Dutchman," four or five headless matches and a little piece of chewing tobacco.

Pilon sat back on his heels. So it was no use. He must wither here on the beach while his throat called lustily for wine.

He noticed the serge trousers the Portagee was wearing, and stroked them with his fingers. "Nice cloth," he thought. "Why should this dirty Portagee wear such good cloth when all his friends go about in jeans?" Then he remembered how badly the pants fit Big Joe, how tight the waist was even with two fly-buttons undone, how the cuffs missed the shoe tops by inches. "Some one of a decent size would be happy in those pants."

Pilon remembered Big Joe's crime against Danny, and he became an avenging angel. How did this big black Portagee dare to insult Danny so! "When he wakes up I will beat him! But," the more subtle Pilon argued, "his crime was theft. Would it not teach him a lesson to know how it feels to have something stolen? What good is punishment unless something is learned?" It was a triumphant position for Pilon. If, with one action, he could avenge Danny, discipline Big Joe, teach an ethical lesson and get a little wine, who in the world could criticize him?

He pushed the Portagee vigorously, and Big Joe brushed at him as though he were a fly. Pilon deftly removed the trousers, rolled them up and sauntered away into the sand dunes.

Torrelli was out, but Mrs. Torrelli opened the door to Pilon. He was mysterious in his manner, but at last he held up the pants for her inspection.

She shook her head decisively.

"But look," said Pilon. "You are seeing only the spots and the dirt. Look at this fine cloth underneath. Think, señora! You have cleaned the spots off and pressed the trousers! Torrelli comes in! He is silent; he is glum. And then you bring him these fine pants! See how his eyes grow bright! See how happy he is! He takes you on his lap! Look how he smiles at you, señora! Is so much happiness too high at one gallon of red wine?'"

"The seat of the pants is thin," she said.

He held them up to the light. "Can you see through them? No! The stiffness, the discomfort is taken out of them. They are in prime condition."

"No," she said firmly.

"You are cruel to your husband, señora. You deny him happiness. I should not be surprised to see him going to other women, who are not so heartless. For a quart, then?"

Finally her resistance was beaten down and she gave him the quart. Pilon drank it off immediately. "You try to break down the price of pleasure," he warned her. "I should have half a gallon."

Mrs. Torrelli was hard as stone. Not a drop more could Pilon get. He sat there brooding in the kitchen. "Jewess, that's what she is. She cheats me out of Big Joe's pants."

Pilon thought sadly of his friend out there on the beach. What could he do? If he came into town he would be arrested. And what had this harpy done to deserve the pants? She had tried to buy Pilon's friend's pants for a miserable quart of miserable wine. Pilon felt himself dissolving into anger at her.

"I am going away in a moment," he told Mrs. Torrelli. The pants were hung in a little alcove off the kitchen.

"Good-by," said Mrs. Torrelli over her shoulder. She went into her little pantry to prepare dinner.

On his way out Pilon passed the alcove and lifted down not only the pants, but Danny's blanket.

Pilon walked back down the beach, toward the place where he had left Big Joe. He could see a bonfire burning brightly on the sand, and as he drew nearer, a number of small dark figures passed in front of the flame. It was very dark now; he guided himself by the fire. As he came close, he saw that it was a Girl Scout wienie bake. He approached warily.

For a while he could not see Big Joe, but at last he discovered him, lying half covered with sand, speechless with cold and agony. Pilon walked firmly up to him and held up the pants.

"Take them, Big Joe, and be glad you have them back."

Joe's teeth were chattering. "Who stole my pants, Pilon? I have been lying here for hours, and I could not go away because of those girls."

Pilon obligingly stood between Big Joe and the little girls who were running about the bonfire. The Portagee brushed the cold damp sand from his legs and put on his pants. They walked side by side along the dark beach toward Monterey, where the lights hung, necklace above necklace against the hill. The sand dunes crouched along the back of the beach like tired hounds, resting; and the waves gently practiced at striking, and hissed a little. The night was cold and aloof, and its warm life was withdrawn, so that it was full of bitter warnings to man that he is alone in the world, and alone among his fellows; that he has no comfort owing him from anywhere.

Pilon was still brooding, and Joe Portagee sensed the depth of his feeling. At last Pilon turned his head toward his friend. "We learn by this that it is great foolishness to trust a woman," he said.

"Did some woman take my pants?" Big Joe demanded excitedly. "Who was it? I'll kick the hell out of her!"

But Pilon shook his head as sadly as old Jehovah, who, resting on the seventh day, sees that his world is tiresome. "She is punished," Pilon said. "You might say she punished herself, and that is the best way. She had thy pants; she bought them with greed; and now she has them not."

These things were beyond Big Joe. They were mysteries it was better to let alone; and this was as Pilon wished it. Big Joe said humbly, "Thanks for getting my

151

pants back, Pilon." But Pilon was so sunk in philosophy that even thanks were valueless.

"It was nothing," he said. "In the whole matter only the lesson we learn has any value."

They climbed up from the beach and passed the great silver tower of the gas works.

Big Joe Portagee was happy to be with Pilon. "Here is one who takes care of his friends," he thought. "Even when they sleep he is alert to see that no harm comes to them." He resolved to do something nice for Pilon sometime.

# IX

*How Danny was ensnared by a vacuum-cleaner and how Danny's Friends rescued him.*

Dolores Engracia Ramirez lived in her own little house on the upper edge of Tortilla Flat. She did housework for some of the ladies in Monterey, and she belonged to the Native Daughters of the Golden West. She was not pretty, this lean-faced paisana, but there was in her figure a certain voluptuousness of movement; there was in her voice a throatiness some men found indicative. Her eyes could burn behind a mist with a sleepy passion which those men, to whom the flesh is important, found attractive and downright inviting.

In her brusque moments she was not desirable, but an amorous combination came about within her often enough so that she was called Sweets Ramirez on Tortilla Flat.

It was a pleasant thing to see her when the beast in her was prowling. How she leaned over her front gate! How her voice purred drowsily! How her hips moved gently about, now pressing against the fence, now swelling back like a summer beach-wave, and then pressing the fence again! Who in the world could put so much husky meaning into "Ai, amigo. A'onde vas?"

It is true that ordinarily her voice was shrill, her face hard and sharp as a hatchet, her figure lumpy and her intentions selfish. The softer self came into possession only once or twice a week, and then, ordinarily, in the evening.

When Sweets heard that Danny was an heir, she was glad for him. She dreamed of being his lady, as did every other female on Tortilla Flat. In the evenings she leaned over the front gate waiting for the time when he would pass by and fall into her trap. But for a long time her baited trap caught nothing but poor Indians and paisanos who owned no houses, and whose clothes were sometimes fugitive from better wardrobes.

Sweets was not content. Her house was up the hill

from Danny's house, in a direction he did not often take. Sweets could not go looking for him. She was a lady, and her conduct was governed by very strict rules of propriety. If Danny should walk by, now, if they should talk, like the old friends they were, if he should come in for a social glass of wine; and then, if nature proved too strong, and her feminine resistance too weak, there was no grave breach of propriety. But it was unthinkable to leave her web on the front gate.

For many months of evenings she waited in vain, and took such gifts as walked by in jeans. But there are only a limited number of pathways on Tortilla Flat. It was inevitable that Danny should, sooner or later, pass the gate of Dolores Engracia Ramirez; and so he did.

In all the time they had known each other, there had never been an occasion when it was more to Sweets' advantage to have him walk by; for Danny had only that morning found a keg of copper shingle nails, lost by the Central Supply Company. He had judged them jetsam because no member of the company was anywhere near. Danny removed the copper nails from the keg and put them in a sack. Then, borrowing the Pirate's wheelbarrow, and the Pirate to push it, he took his salvage to the Western Supply Company, where he sold the copper for three dollars. The keg he gave to the Pirate.

"You can keep things in it," he said. That made the Pirate very happy.

And now Danny came down the hill, aimed with a fine accuracy toward the house of Torrelli, and the three dollars were in his pocket.

Dolores' voice sounded as huskily sweet as the drone of a bumble-bee. "Ai, amigo, a'onde vas?"

Danny stopped. A revolution took place in his plans. "How are you, Sweets?"

"What difference is it how I am? None of my friends are interested," she said archly. And her hips floated in a graceful and circular undulation.

"What do you mean?" he demanded.

"Well, does my friend Danny ever come to see me?"

"I am here to see thee now," he said gallantly.

She opened the gate a little. "Wilt thou come in for a tiny glass of wine in friendship's name?" Danny went into her house. "What hast thou been doing in the forest?" she cooed.

Then he made an error. He told vaingloriously of his

transaction up the hill, and he boasted of his three dollars.

"Of course I have only enough wine to fill two thimbles," she said.

They sat in Sweets' kitchen and drank a glass of wine. In a little while Danny assaulted her virtue with true gallantry and vigor. He found to his amazement, a resistance out of all proportion to her size and reputation. The ugly beast of lust was awakened in him. He was angry. Only when he was leaving was the way made clear to him.

The husky voice said, "Maybe you would like to come and see me this evening, Danny." Sweets' eyes swam in a mist of drowsy invitation. "One has neighbors," she suggested with delicacy.

Then he understood. "I will come back," he promised.

It was mid-afternoon. Danny walked down the street, re-aimed at Torrelli's; and the beast in him had changed. From a savage and snarling wolf it had become a great, shaggy, sentimental bear. "I will take wine to that nice Sweets," he thought.

On the way down, whom should he meet but Pablo,

and Pablo had two sticks of gum. He gave one to Danny and fell into step. "Where goest thou?"

"It is no time for friendship," Danny said tartly. "First I go to buy a little wine to take to a lady. You may come with me, and have one glass only. I am tired of buying wine for ladies, only to have my friends drink it all up."

Pablo agreed that such a practice was unendurable. For himself, he didn't want Danny's wine, but only his companionship.

They went to Torrelli's. They had a glass of wine out of the new bought gallon. Danny confessed that it was shabby treatment to give his friend only one little glass. Over Pablo's passionate protest they had another. "Ladies," Danny thought, "should not drink too much wine. They were apt to become silly; and besides, it dulled some of those senses one liked to find alert in a lady." They had a few more glasses. Half a gallon of wine was a bountiful present, especially as Danny was about to go down to buy another present. They measured down half a gallon, and drank what was over. Then Danny hid the jug in the weeds in a ditch.

"I would like you to come with me to buy the present, Pablo," he said.

Pablo knew the reason for the invitation. Half of it was a desire for Pablo's company, and half was fear of leaving the wine while Pablo was at large. They walked with studied dignity and straightness down the hill to Monterey.

Mr. Simon, of Simon's Investment, Jewelry and Loan Company, welcomed them into his store. The name of the store defined the outward limits of the merchandise the company sold; for there were saxophones, radios, rifles, knives, fishing-rods and old coins on the counter; all second-hand, but all really better than new because they were just well broken-in.

"Something you would like to see?" Mr. Simon asked.

"Yes," said Danny.

The proprietor named over a tentative list, and then stopped in the middle of a word, for he saw that Danny was looking at a large aluminum vacuum-cleaner. The dust-bag was blue and yellow checks. The electric cord was long and black and slick. Mr. Simon went to it and rubbed it with his hand, and stood off and admired it. "Something in a vacuum-cleaner?" he asked.

"How much?"

"For this one, fourteen dollars." It was not a price so much as an endeavor to find out how much Danny had. And Danny wanted it, for it was large and shiny. No woman of Tortilla Flat had one. In this moment he forgot there was no electricity on Tortilla Flat. He laid his two dollars on the counter and waited while the explosion took place; the fury, the rage, the sadness, the poverty, the ruin, the cheating. The polish was invoked, the color of the bag, the extra long cord, the value of the metal alone. And when it was all over, Danny went out carrying the vacuum-cleaner.

Often as a pasatiempo in the afternoon, Sweets brought out the vacuum-cleaner and leaned it against a chair. While her friends looked on, she pushed it back and forth to show how easily it rolled. And she made a humming with her voice to imitate a motor.

"My friend is a rich man," she said. "I think pretty soon there will be wires full of electricity coming right into the house, and then zip and zip and zip! And you have the house clean!"

Her friends tried to belittle the present, saying, "It is too bad you can't run this machine." And, "I have always held that a broom and dust-pan, *properly* used, are more thorough."

But their envy could do nothing against the vacuum. Through its possession, Sweets climbed to the peak of the social scale of Tortilla Flat. People who did not remember her name referred to her as "that one with

the sweeping-machine." Often when her enemies passed the house, Sweets could be seen through the window, pushing the cleaner back and forth, while a loud humming came from her throat. Indeed, after she had swept her house every day, she pushed the cleaner about on the theory that of course it would clean better with electricity, but one could not have everything.

She excited envy in many houses. Her manner became dignified and gracious, and she held her chin high as befitted one who had a sweeping-machine. In her conversation she included it. "Ramon passed this morning, while I was pushing the sweeping-machine." "Louise Meater cut her hand this morning, not three hours after I had been pushing the sweeping-machine."

But in her elevation she did not neglect Danny. Her voice growled with emotion when he was about. She swayed like a pine tree in the wind. And he spent every evening at the house of Sweets.

At first his friends ignored his absence, for it is the right of every man to have these little affairs. But as the weeks went on, and as a rather violent domestic life began to make Danny listless and pale, his friends became convinced that Sweets' gratitude for the sweeping-machine was not to Danny's best physical interests. They were jealous of a situation that was holding his attention so long.

Pilon and Pablo and Jesus Maria Corcoran in turn assaulted the nest of his affections during his absence; but Sweets, while she was sensible of the compliment, remained true to the man who had raised her position to such a gratifying level. She tried to keep their friendship for a future time of need, for she knew how fickle fortune is; but she stoutly refused to share with Danny's friends that which was dedicated for the time being to Danny.

Wherefore the friends, in despair, organized a group, formed for and dedicated to her destruction.

It may be that Danny, deep in his soul, was beginning to tire of Sweets' affection and the duty of attendance it demanded. If such a change were taking place, he did not admit it to himself.

At three o'clock one afternoon, Pilon and Pablo and Jesus Maria, followed vaguely by Big Joe Portagee, returned triumphant from three-quarters of a day of strenuous effort. Their campaign had called into play and taxed to the limit the pitiless logic of Pilon, the artistic ingenuousness of Pablo and the gentleness and humanity of Jesus Maria Corcoran. Big Joe had contributed nothing.

But now, like four hunters, they returned from the chase more happy because their victory had been a difficult one. And in Monterey, a poor puzzled Italian came gradually to the conviction that he had been swindled.

Pilon carried a gallon jug of wine concealed in a bundle of ivy. They marched joyfully into Danny's house and Pilon set the gallon on the table.

Danny, awakened out of a sound sleep, smiled quietly, got up from bed and laid out the fruit jars. He poured the wine. His four friends fell into chairs, for it had been an exhausting day.

They drank quietly in the late afternoon, that time of curious intermission. Nearly every one in Tortilla Flat stops then and considers those things that have taken place in the day just past, and thinks over the possibilities of the evening. There are many things to discuss in an afternoon.

"Cornelia Ruiz got a new man this morning," Pilon observed. "He has a bald head. His name is Kilpatrick. Cornelia says her other man didn't come home three nights last week. She didn't like that."

"Cornelia is a woman who changes her mind too quickly," said Danny. He thought complacently of his own sure establishment, built on the rock of the vacuum-cleaner.

"Cornelia's father was worse," said Pablo. "He could not tell the truth. Once he borrowed a dollar from me. I have told Cornelia about it, and she does nothing."

"Two of one blood. 'Know the breed and know the dog,'" Pilon quoted virtuously.

Danny poured the jars full of wine again, and the gallon was exhausted. He looked ruefully at it.

Jesus Maria, that lover of the humanities, spoke up quietly. "I saw Susie Francisco, Pilon. She said the recipe worked fine. She has been out riding with Charlie Guzman on his motorcycle three times. The first two times she gave him the love medicine it made him sick. She thought it was no good. But now Susie says you can have some cookies any time."

"What was in that potion?" Pablo asked.

Pilon became secretive. "I cannot tell all of it. I guess it must have been the poison oak in it that made Charlie Guzman sick."

The gallon of wine had gone too quickly. Each of the six friends was conscious of a thirst so sharp that it was a pain of desire. Pilon looked at his friends with drooped eyes, and they looked back at him. The conspiracy was ready.

Pilon cleared his throat. "What hast thou done, Danny, to set the whole town laughing at thee?"

Danny looked worried. "What do you mean?"

Pilon chuckled. "It is said by many that you bought a sweeping-machine for a lady, and that machine will not work unless wires are put into the house. Those wires cost a great deal of money. Some people find this present very funny."

Danny grew uncomfortable. "That lady likes the sweeping-machine," he said defensively.

"Why not?" Pablo agreed. "She has told some people that you have promised to put wires into her house so the sweeping-machine will work."

Danny looked even more perturbed. "Did she say that?"

"So I was told."

"Well, I will not," Danny cried.

"If I did not think it funny, I should be angry to hear my friend laughed at," Pilon observed.

"What will you do when she asks for those wires?" Jesus Maria asked.

"I will tell her no," said Danny.

Pilon laughed. "I wish I could be there. It is not such a simple thing to tell that lady 'no.' "

Danny felt that his friends were turning against him. "What shall I do?" he asked helplessly.

Pilon gave the matter his grave consideration and brought his realism to bear on the subject. "If that lady did not have the sweeping-machine, she would not want those wires," he said.

The friends nodded in agreement.

"Therefore," Pilon continued, "the thing to do is to remove the sweeping-machine."

"Oh, she wouldn't let me take it," Danny protested.

"Then we will help you," said Pilon. "I will take the machine, and in return you can take the lady a present of a gallon of wine. She will not even know where the sweeping-machine has gone."

"Some neighbor will see you take it."

"Oh, no," said Pilon. "You stay here, Danny. I will get the machine."

Danny sighed with relief that his problem was assumed by his good friends.

There were few things going on in Tortilla Flat that

Pilon did not know. His mind made sharp little notes of everything that his eyes saw or his ears heard. He knew that Sweets went to the store at four-thirty every afternoon. He depended upon this almost invariable habit to put his plan into effect.

"It is better that you do not know anything about it," he told Danny.

In the yard Pilon had a gunny sack in readiness. With his knife he cut a generous branch from the rose bush and pushed it into the sack.

At Sweets' house, he found her absent, as he had expected and hoped she would be. "It is really Danny's machine," he told himself.

It was a moment's work to enter the house, to put the vacuum-cleaner in the sack and to arrange the rose branch artistically in the sack's mouth.

As he came out of the yard, he met Sweets. Pilon took off his hat politely. "I stepped in to pass the time," he said.

"Will you stop now, Pilon?"

"No. I have business down in Monterey. It is late."

"Where do you go with this rose bush?"

"A man in Monterey is to buy it. A very fine rose bush. See how strong it is."

"Stop in some other time, Pilon."

He heard no cry of anger as he walked sedately down the street. "Perhaps she will not miss it for a while," he thought.

Half the problem was solved, but half was yet to be approached. "What can Danny do with this sweeping-machine?" Pilon asked himself. "If he has it, Sweets will know he has taken it. Can I throw it away? No, for it is valuable. The thing to do would be to get rid of it, and still to reap the benefit of its value."

Now the whole problem was solved. Pilon headed down the hill toward Torrelli's house.

It was a large and shining vacuum-cleaner. When Pilon came again up the hill, he had a gallon of wine in each hand.

The friends received him in silence when he entered Danny's house. He set one jug on the table and the other on the floor.

"I have brought you a present to take to the lady, he told Danny. "And here is a little wine for us."

They gathered happily, for their thirst was a raging fire. When the first gallon was far gone, Pilon held his glass to the candle-light and looked through it. "Things that happen are of no importance," he said. "But from everything that happens, there is a lesson to be learned. By this we learn that a present, especially to a lady, should have no quality that will require a further present. Also we learn that it is sinful to give presents of too great value, for they may excite greed."

The first gallon was gone. The friends looked at Danny to see how he felt about it. He had been very quiet, but now he saw that his friends were waiting on him.

"That lady was lively," he said judiciously. "That lady had a very sympathetic nature. But God damn it!" he said, "I'm sick of it!" He went to the second jug and drew the cork.

The Pirate, sitting in the corner among his dogs, smiled to himself and whispered in admiration, " 'God damn it, I'm sick of it.' " That, thought the Pirate, was very fine.

They had not more than half finished the second jug, indeed they had sung only two songs, when young

Johnny Pom-pom came in. "I was at Torelli's," Johnny said. "Oh, that Torrelli is mad! He is shouting! He is beating on the table with his fists."

The friends looked up with mild interest. "Something has happened. It is probable Torrelli deserves it."

"Often he has refused his good customers a little glass of wine."

"What is the matter with Torrelli?" Pablo asked.

Johnny Pom-pom accepted a jar of wine. "Torrelli says he bought a sweeping-machine from Pilon, and when he hooked it up to his light wire, it would not work. So he looked on the inside, and it had no motor. He says he will kill Pilon."

Pilon looked shocked. "I did not know this machine was at fault," he said. "But did I not say Torrelli deserved what was the matter with him. That machine was worth three or four gallons of wine, but that miser Torrelli would give no more than two."

Danny still felt a glow of gratitude toward Pilon. He smacked his lips on his wine. "This stuff of Torrelli's is getting worse and worse," he said. "At its best, it is swill the pigs leave, but lately it is so bad that Charlie Marsh even would not drink it."

They all felt a little bit revenged on Torrelli then.

"I think," said Danny, "that we will buy our wine some place else, if Torrelli does not look out."

# X

*How the Friends solaced a Corporal and in return received a lesson in paternal ethics.*

Jesus Maria Corcoran was a pathway for the humanities. Suffering he tried to relieve; sorrow he tried to assuage; happiness he shared. No hard nor haunted Jesus Maria existed. His heart was free for the use of any one who had a use for it. His resources and wits were at the disposal of any one who had less of either than had Jesus Maria.

He it was who carried José de la Nariz four miles when José's leg was broken. When Mrs. Palochico lost the goat of her heart, the good goat of milk and cheese, it was Jesus Maria who tracked that goat to Big Joe Portagee and halted the murder and made Big Joe give it back. It was Jesus Maria who once picked Charlie Marsh out of a ditch where he lay in his own filth, a deed which required not only a warm heart, but a strong stomach.

Together with his capacity for doing good, Jesus Maria had a gift for coming in contact with situations where good wanted doing.

Such was his reputation that Pilon had once said, "If that Jesus Maria had gone into the Church, Monterey would have had a saint for the calendar, I tell you."

Out of some deep pouch in his soul, Jesus Maria drew kindness that renewed itself by withdrawal.

It was Jesus Maria's practice to go to the post office every day, first because there he could see many people whom he knew, and second because on that windy post office corner he could look at the legs of a great many girls. It must not be supposed that in this latter interest there was any vulgarity. As soon criticize a man who goes to art galleries or to concerts. Jesus Maria liked to look at girls' legs.

One day when he had leaned against the post office for two hours with very little success, he was witness to a pitiful scene. A policeman came along the sidewalk leading a young boy of about sixteen, and the boy carried a little baby, wrapped in a piece of gray blanket.

The policeman was saying, "I don't care if I can't understand you. You can't sit in the gutter all day. We'll find out about you."

And the boy, in Spanish, with a peculiar inflection,

said, "But señor, I do nothing wrong. Why do you take me away?"

The policeman saw Jesus Maria. "Hey paisano," he called. "What's this cholo talking about?"

Jesus Maria stepped out and addressed the boy. "Can I be of service to you?"

The boy broke into a relieved flood. "I came here

to work. Some Mexican men said there would be work here, and there was none. I was sitting down resting when this man came to me and dragged me away."

Jesus Maria nodded and turned back to the policeman. "Has he done some crime, this little one?"

"No, but he's been sitting in the gutter on Alvarado Street for about three hours."

"He is a friend of mine," Jesus Maria said. "I will take care of him."

"Well, keep him out of the gutter."

Jesus Maria and his new friend walked up the hill. "I will take you to the house where I live. There you will have something to eat. What baby is this?"

"It is my baby," said the boy. "I am a caporál, and he is my baby. He is sick now; but when he grows up, he is going to be a generál."

"What is he sick from, Señor Caporál?"

"I don't know. He is just sick." He showed the baby's face, and it looked very ill indeed.

The sympathies of Jesus Maria mounted. "The house where I live is owned by my friend Danny, and there is a good man, Señor Caporál. There is one to appeal to when trouble is upon one. Look, we will go there, and that Danny will give us shelter. My friend Mrs. Palochico has a goat. We will borrow a little milk for the baby."

The corporal's face for the first time wore a smile of comfort. "It is good to have friends," he said. "In Torreón I have many friends who would make themselves beggars to help me." He boasted a little to Jesus Maria. "I have rich friends, but of course they do not know my need."

Pilon pushed open the gate of Danny's yard, and they entered together. Danny and Pablo and Big Joe were sitting in the living room, waiting for the daily miracle of food. Jesus Maria pushed the boy into the room.

"Here is a young soldier, a caporál," he explained. "He has a baby here with him, and that baby is sick."

The friends arose with alacrity. The corporal threw back the gray blanket from the baby's face.

"He is sick, all right," Danny said. "Maybe we should get a doctor."

But the soldier shook his head. "No doctors. I do not like doctors. This baby does not cry, and he will not eat much. Maybe when he rests, then he will be well again."

At this moment Pilon entered and inspected the child. "This baby is sick," he said.

Pilon immediately took control. Jesus Maria he sent to Mrs. Palochico's house to borrow goat milk; Big Joe and Pablo to get an apple box, pad it with dry grass and line it with a sheepskin coat. Danny offered his bed, but it was refused. The corporal stood in the living room and smiled gently on these good people. At last the baby lay in its box, but its eyes were listless and it refused the milk.

The Pirate came in, bearing a bag of mackerels. The friends cooked the fish and had their dinner. The baby would not even eat mackerel. Every now and then one of the friends jumped up and ran to look at the baby. When supper was over, they sat about the stove and prepared for a quiet evening.

The corporal had been silent, had given no account of himself. The friends were a little hurt at this, but they knew he would tell them in time. Pilon, to whom knowledge was as gold to be mined, made a few tentative drills into the corporal's reticence.

"It is not often that one sees a young soldier with a baby," he suggested delicately.

The corporal grinned with pride.

Pablo added, "This baby was probably found in the garden of love. And that is the best kind of babies, for only good things are in it."

"We too have been soldiers," said Danny. "When we die, we will go to the grave on a gun carriage, and a firing squad will shoot over us."

They waited to see whether the corporal would improve upon the opportunity they had offered. The corporal looked his appreciation. "You have been good to me," he said. "You have been as good and kind as my friends in Torreón would be. This is my baby, the baby of my wife."

"And where is your wife?" Pilon asked.

The corporal lost his smile. "She is in Mexico," he said. Then he grew vivacious again. "I met a man, and he told me a curious thing. He said we can make of babies what we will. He said, 'You tell the baby often what you want him to do, and when he grows up he will do that.' Over and over I tell this baby, 'You will be a generál.' Do you think it will be so?"

The friends nodded politely. "It may be," said Pilon. "I have not heard of this practice."

"I say twenty times a day, 'Manuel, you will be a generál some day. You will have big epaulets and a sash. Your sword will be gold. You will ride a palamino horse. What a life for you, Manuel!' The man said he surely will be a generál if I say it so."

Danny got up and went to the apple box. "You will be a generál," he said to the baby. "When you grow up you will be a great generál."

The others trooped over to see whether the formula had had any effect.

The Pirate whispered, "You will be a generál," and he wondered whether the same method would work on a dog.

"This baby is sick all right," Danny said. "We must keep him warm."

They went back to their seats.

"Your wife is in Mexico—" Pilon suggested.

The corporal wrinkled his brows and thought for a while, and then he smiled brilliantly. "I will tell you. It is not a thing to tell to strangers, but you are my friends. I was a soldier in Chihuahua, and I was diligent and clean and kept oil in my rifle, so that I became a caporál. And then I was married to a beautiful girl. I do not say that it was not because of the chevrons that she married me. But she was very beautiful and young. Her eyes were bright, she had good white teeth and her hair was long and shining. So pretty soon this baby was born."

"That is good," said Danny. "I should like to be you. There is nothing so good as a baby."

"Yes," said the corporal, "I was glad. And we went in to the baptism, and I wore a sash, although the book of the army did not mention it. And when we came out of that church, a capitán with epaulets and a sash and a silver sword saw my wife. Pretty soon my wife went away. Then I went to that capitán and I said, 'Give me back my wife,' and he said, 'You do not value your life, to talk this way to your superior.'" The corporal spread his hands and lifted his shoulders in a gesture of caged resignation.

"Oh, that thief!" cried Jesus Maria.

"You gathered your friends. You killed that capitán," Pablo anticipated.

The corporal looked self-conscious. "No. There was

nothing to do. The first night, some one shot at me through the window. The second day a field gun went off by mistake and it came so close to me that the wind knocked me down. So, I went away from there, and I took the baby with me."

There was fierceness in the faces of the friends, and their eyes were dangerous. The Pirate, in his corner, snarled, and all the dogs growled.

"We should have been there," Pilon cried. "We would have made that capitán wish he had never lived. My grandfather suffered at the hands of a priest, and he tied that priest naked to a post in a corral and turned a little calf in with him. Oh, there are ways."

"I was only a caporál," said the boy. "I had to run away." Tears of shame were in his eyes. "There is no help for a caporál when a capitán is against him; so I ran away, with the baby Manuel. In Fresno I met this wise man, and he told me I could make Manuel be what I wished. I tell that baby twenty times every day, 'You will be a generál. You will wear epaulets and carry a golden sword.'"

Here was drama that made the experiments of Cornelia Ruiz seem uninteresting and vain. Here was a

182

situation which demanded the action of the friends. But its scene was so remote that action was impossible. They looked in admiration at the corporal. He was so young to have had such an adventure!

"I wish," Danny said wickedly, "that we were in Torreón now. Pilon would make a plan for us. It is too bad we cannot go there."

Big Joe Portagee had stayed awake, a tribute to the fascination of the corporal's story. He went to the apple box and looked in. "You going to be a general," he said. And then, "Look! This baby is moving funny." The friends crowded around. The spasm had already started. The little feet kicked down and then drew up. The hands clawed about helplessly, and then the baby scrabbled and shuddered.

"A doctor," Danny cried. "We must have a doctor." But he and every one knew it was no use. Approaching death wears a cloak no one ever mistakes. While they watched, the baby stiffened and the struggle ended. The mouth dropped open, and the baby was dead. In kindness, Danny covered the apple box with a piece of blanket. The corporal stood very straight and stared before him, so shocked that he could not speak nor think.

Jesus Maria laid a hand on his shoulder and led him to a chair. "You are so young," he said. "You will have many more babies."

The corporal moaned, "Now he is dead. Now he will never be a generál with that sash and that sword."

There were tears in the eyes of the friends. In the corner, all the dogs whined miserably. The Pirate buried his big head in the fur of Señor Alec Thompson.

In a soft tone, almost a benediction, Pilon said, "Now you yourself must kill the capitán. We honor you for a noble plan of revenge; but that is over and you must take your own vengeance, and we will help you, if we can."

The corporal turned dulled eyes to him. "Revenge?" he asked. "Kill the capitán? What do you mean?"

"Why, it was plain what your plan was," Pilon said. "This baby would grow up, and he would be a generál; and in time he would find that capitán, and he would kill him slowly. It was a good plan. The long waiting, and then the stroke. We, your friends, honor you for it."

The corporal was looking bewilderedly at Pilon.

"What is this?" he demanded. "I have nothing to do with this capitán. He is the capitán."

The friends sat forward.

Pilon cried, "Then what was this plan to make the baby be a generál? Why was that?"

The corporal was a little embarrassed then. "It is the duty of a father to do well by his child. I wanted Manuel to have more good things than I had."

"Is that all?" Danny cried.

"Well," said the corporal, "my wife was so pretty, and she was not any *puta,* either. She was a good woman, and that capitán took her. He had little epaulets, and a little sash, and his sword was only of a silver color. Consider," said the corporal; and he spread out his hands, "if that capitán, with the little epaulets and the little sash could take my wife, imagine what a generál with a big sash and a gold sword could take!"

There was a long silence while Danny and Pilon and Pablo and Jesus Maria and the Pirate and Big Joe Portagee digested the principle. And when it was digested, they waited for Danny to speak.

"It is to be pitied," said Danny at last, "that so few parents have the well-being of their children at heart.

Now we are more sorry than ever that the baby is gone, for with such a father, what a happy life he has missed."

All of the friends nodded solemnly.

"What will you do now?" asked Jesus Maria, the discoverer.

"I will go back to Mexico," said the corporal. "I am a soldier in my heart. It may be, if I keep oiling my rifle, I myself may be an officer some day. Who can tell?"

The six friends looked at him admiringly. They were proud to have known such a man.

# XI

*How, under the most adverse circumstances, love came to Big Joe Portagee.*

For Big Joe Portagee, to feel love was to do something about it. And this is the history of one of his love affairs.

It had been raining in Monterey; from the tall pines the water dripped all day. The paisanos of Tortilla Flat did not come out of their houses, but from every chimney a blue column of pine wood smoke drifted so that the air smelled clean and fresh and perfumed.

At five o'clock in the afternoon, the rain stopped for a few moments and Big Joe Portagee, who had been under a rowboat on the beach most of the day, came out and started up the hill toward Danny's house. He was cold and hungry.

When he came to the very edge of Tortilla Flat, the

skies opened and the rain poured down. In an instant Big Joe was soaked through. He ran into the nearest house to get out of the rain, and that house was inhabited by Tia Ignacia.

The lady was about forty-five, a widow of long standing and some success. Ordinarily she was taciturn and harsh, for there was in her veins more Indian blood than is considered decent in Tortilla Flat.

When Big Joe entered, she had just opened a gallon of red wine and was preparing to pour out a glass for her stomach's sake. Her attempt to push the jug under a chair was unsuccessful. Big Joe stood in her doorway dripping water on the floor.

"Come in and get dry," said Tia Ignacia. Big Joe, watching the bottle as a terrier watches a bug, entered the room. The rain roared down on the roof. Tia Ignacia poked up a blaze in her air-tight stove.

"Would you care for a glass of wine?"

"Yes," said Big Joe. Before he had finished his first glass, Big Joe's eyes had refastened themselves on the jug. He drank three glasses before he consented to say a word, and before the wolfishness went out of his eyes.

Tia Ignacia had given her new jug of wine up for

lost. She drank with him as the only means to preserve a little of it to her own use. It was only when the fourth glass of wine was in his hand that Big Joe relaxed and began to enjoy himself.

"This is not Torrelli's wine," he said.

"No, I get it from an Italian lady who is my friend." She poured out another glass.

The early evening came. Tia Ignacia lighted a kerosene lamp and put some wood in the fire. As long as the wine must go, it must go, she thought. Her eyes dwelt on the huge frame of Big Joe Portagee with critical appraisal. A little flush warmed her chest.

"You have been working out in the rain, poor man," she said. "Here, take off your coat and let it dry."

Big Joe rarely told a lie. His mind didn't work

quickly enough. "I been on the beach under a row-boat, asleep," he said.

"But you are all wet, poor fellow." She inspected him for some response to her kindness, but on Big Joe's face nothing showed except gratification at being out of the rain and drinking wine. He put out his glass to be filled again. Having eaten nothing all day, the wine was having a profound effect on him.

Tia Ignacia addressed herself anew to the problem. "It is not good to sit in a wet coat. You will be ill with cold. Come, let me help you to take off your coat."

Big Joe wedged himself comfortably into his chair. "I'm all right," he said stubbornly.

Tia Ignacia poured herself another glass. The fire made a rushing sound to counteract with comfort the drumming of water on the roof.

Big Joe made absolutely no move to be friendly, to be gallant, even to recognize the presence of his hostess. He drank his wine in big swallows. He smiled stupidly at the stove. He rocked himself a little in the chair.

Anger and despair arose in Tia Ignacia. "This pig," she thought, "this big and dirty animal. It would be better for me if I brought some cow in the house out of the rain. Another man would say some little friendly word, at least."

Big Joe stuck out his glass to be filled again.

Now Tia Ignacia strove heroically. "In a little warm house there is happiness on such a night," she said, "when the rain is dripping and the stove burns sweetly, then is a time for people to feel friendly. Don't you feel friendly?"

"Sure," said Big Joe.

"Perhaps the light is too bright in your eyes," she said coyly. "Would you like me to blow out the light?"

"It don't bother me none," said Big Joe, "if you want to save oil, go ahead."

She blew down the lamp chimney, and the room leaped to darkness. Then she went back to her chair and waited for his gallantry to awaken. She could hear the gentle rocking of his chair. A little light came from the cracks of the stove and struck the shiny corners of the furniture. The room was nearly luminous with warmth. Tia Ignacia heard his chair stop rocking and braced herself to repel him. Nothing happened.

"To think," she said, "you might be out in this storm, shivering in a shed or lying on the cold sand under a boat. But no; you are sitting in a good chair, drinking good wine, in the company of a lady who is your friend."

There was no answer from Big Joe. She could neither hear him nor see him. Tia Ignacia drank off her glass. She threw virtue to the winds. "My friend Cornelia Ruiz has told me that some of her best friends came to her out of the rain and cold. She comforted them, and they were her good friends."

The sound of a little crash came from the direction of Big Joe. She knew he had dropped his glass, but no movement followed the crash. "Perhaps he is ill," she thought. "Maybe he has fainted." She jumped up, lighted a match and set it to the lamp wick. And then she turned to her guest.

Big Joe was mountainously asleep. His feet stuck out ahead of him. His head was back and his mouth wide open. While she looked, amazed and shocked, a tremendous rattling snore came from his mouth. Big Joe simply could not be warm and comfortable without going to sleep.

It was a moment before Tia Ignacia could move all her crowding emotions into line. She inherited a great deal of Indian blood. She did not cry out. No, shivering with rage although she was, she walked to her wood basket, picked out a likely stick, weighed it, put it down and picked out another one. And then she turned slowly on Big Joe Portagee. The first blow caught him on the shoulder and knocked him out of the chair.

"Pig!" Tia Ignacia screamed. "Big dirty garbage! Out in the mud with you!"

Joe rolled over on the floor. The next blow made a muddy identation on the seat of his pants. Big Joe was waking up rapidly now.

"Huh?" he said. "What's the matter? What you doing?"

"I'll show you," she screamed. She flung open her door and ran back to him. Big Joe staggered to his feet under the beating. The stick hammered at his back and shoulders and head. He ran out of the door, protecting his head with his hands.

"Don't," he pleaded. "Now don't do that. What's the matter?"

The fury followed him like a hornet, down the garden path and into the muddy street. Her rage was terrible. She followed him along the street, still beating him.

"Hey," he cried. "Now don't." He grabbed her and held her while her arms struggled violently to be free to continue the beating.

"Oh, great garbage pig!" she cried. "Oh, cow!"

He could not let her go without more beating, so he held her tightly; and as he stood there, love came to Big Joe Portagee. It sang in his head; it roared through his body like a great freshet; it shook him as a tropical storm shakes a forest of palms. He held her tightly for a moment, until her anger relaxed.

In the night, in Monterey, a policeman patrols the streets on a motorcycle to see that good things come to no evil. Jake Lake rode about now, his slicker shining dully, like basalt. He was unhappy and uncomfortable. It was not so bad on the paved streets, but part of his route lay through the mud paths of Tortilla Flat, and there the yellow mud splashed nastily. His little light flashed about. The motor coughed with effort.

All of a sudden Jake Lake cried out in astonishment and stopped his motor. "What the devil! Say, what the hell is this?"

Big Joe twisted his neck. "Oh, is that you, Jake? Say, Jake, as long as you're going to take us to jail anyway, can't you just wait a minute?"

The policeman turned his motor around. "You get out of the street," he said. "Somebody'll come along and run over you."

His motor roared in the mud, and the flicker of his little headlight disappeared around the corner. The rain pattered gently among the trees of Tortilla Flat.

# XII

*How Danny's Friends assisted the Pirate to keep a*
*vow, and how as a reward for merit the Pirate's*
*dogs saw an holy vision.*

Every afternoon the Pirate
pushed his empty wheelbarrow up the hill and into
Danny's yard. He leaned it against the fence and covered it with a sack; then he buried his ax in the ground,
for, as every one knows, it makes steel much harder to
be buried. Last, he went into the house, reached into a
Bull Durham bag which hung around his neck on a
string, took out the day's quarter dollar and gave it to
Danny. Then Danny and the Pirate and any other of
the friends who happened to be in the house went
solemnly into the bedroom, stepping over the bedding
that littered the floor. While the paisanos looked on,
Danny reached under his pillow, brought out the can-

vas bag and deposited the new quarter. This practice had continued for a long time.

The bag of money had became the symbolic center of the friendship, the point of trust about which the fraternity revolved. They were proud of the money, proud that they had never tampered with it. About the guardianship of the Pirate's money there had grown a structure of self-respect and not a little complacency. It is a fine thing for a man to be trusted. This money had long ceased, in the minds of the friends, to be currency. It is true that for a time they had dreamed of how much wine it would buy, but after a while they lost the conception of it as legal tender. The hoard was aimed at a gold candlestick, and this potential candlestick was the property of San Francisco de Assisi. It is far worse to defraud a saint than it is to take liberties with the law.

One evening, by that quick and accurate telegraph no one understands, news came in that a coast guard cutter had gone on the rocks near Carmel. Big Joe Portagee was away on business of his own, but Danny and Pablo and Pilon and Jesus Maria and the Pirate and his dogs joyfully started over the ridge; for if there was anything they loved, it was to pick up useable articles on the beach. This they thought the most exciting thing in the world. Although they arrived a little late, they made up for lost time. All night the friends scurried about the beach, and they accumulated a good pile of flotsam, a five-pound can of butter, several cases of canned goods, a water-soaked Bowditch, two pea jackets, a water barrel from a life boat and a machine gun. When daylight came, they had a goodly pile under guard.

They accepted a lump sum of five dollars for the lot from one of the spectators, for it was out of the question to carry all those heavy things over six miles of steep hillside to Tortilla Flat.

Because he had not cut his day's wood, the Pirate received a quarter from Danny, and he put it in his Bull Durham bag. Then they started tiredly, but with a warm and expectant happiness, straight over the hills to Monterey.

It was afternoon when they got back to Danny's house. The Pirate ritualistically opened his bag and gave the quarter to Danny. The whole squad trooped into the other room. Danny reached under the pillow—and his hand came out empty. He threw the pillow back, threw the mattress back, and then he turned slowly to his friends, and his eyes had become as fierce as a tiger's eyes. He looked from face to face, and on every one saw horror and indignation that could not be simulated.

"Well," he said, "—well." The Pirate began to cry. Danny put his arm around his shoulder. "Do not cry, little friend," he said ominously. "Thou wilt have thy money again."

The paisanos went silently out of the room. Danny walked out into the yard and found a heavy pine stick three feet long, and swung it experimentally. Pablo went into the kitchen and returned bearing an ancient can-opener with a vicious blade. Jesus Maria from under the house pulled out a broken pick handle. The Pirate watched them bewilderedly. They all came back to the house and sat quietly down.

The Pirate aimed down the hill with his thumb. "Him?" he asked.

Danny nodded slowly. His eyes were veiled and deadly. His chin stuck out, and, as he sat in the chair, his whole body weaved a little, like a rattlesnake aiming to strike.

The Pirate went into the yard and dug up his ax.

For a long time they sat in the house. No words were spoken, but a wave of cold fury washed and crouched in the room. The feeling in the house was the feeling of a rock when the fuse is burning in toward the dynamite.

The afternoon waned; the sun went behind the hill. The whole of Tortilla Flat seemed hushed and expectant.

They heard his footsteps on the street and their hands tightened on their sticks. Joe Portagee walked uncertainly up on the porch and in at the front door. He had a gallon of wine in his hand. His eyes went uneasily from face to face, but the friends sat still and did not look directly at him.

"Hello," said Big Joe.

"Hello," said Danny. He stood up and stretched lazily. He did not look at Big Joe; he did not walk directly toward him, but at an angle, as though to pass him. When he was abreast, he struck with the speed of a striking snake. Fair on the back of Big Joe's head the stick crashed, and Big Joe went down, completely out.

Danny thoughtfully took a string of rawhide from

his pocket and tied the Portagee's thumbs together. "Now water," he said.

Pablo threw a bucket of water in Big Joe's face. He turned his head and stretched his neck like a chicken, and then he opened his eyes and looked dazedly at his friends. They did not speak to him at all. Danny measured his distance carefully, like a golfer addressing the ball. His stick smashed on Big Joe's shoulder; then the friends went about the business in a cold and methodical manner. Jesus Maria took the legs, Danny the shoulders and chest. Big Joe howled and rolled on the floor. They covered his body from the neck down. Each blow found a new space and welted it. The shrieks were deafening. The Pirate stood helplessly by, holding his ax.

At last, when the whole front of the body was one bruise, they stopped. Pablo knelt at Big Joe's head with his can-opener. Pilon took off the Portagee's shoes and picked up his stick again.

Then Big Joe squalled with fear. "It's buried out by the front gate," he cried. "For the love of Christ don't kill me!"

Danny and Pilon went out the front door and in a

few minutes they came back, carrying the canvas bag. "How much did you take out?" Danny asked. There was no inflection in his voice at all.

"Only four, Honest to God. I only took four, and I'll work and put them back."

Danny leaned down, took him by the shoulder and rolled him over on his face. Then the friends went over his back with the same deadly precision. The cries grew weaker, but the work only stopped when Big Joe was beaten into unconsciousness. Then Pilon tore off the blue shirt and exposed the pulpy raw back. With the can-opener he cross-hatched the skin so deftly that a little blood ran from each line. Pablo brought the salt to him and helped him to rub it in all over the torn back. At last Danny threw a blanket over the unconscious man.

"I think he will be honest now," said Danny.

"We should count the money," Pilon observed. "We have not counted it for a long time." They opened Big Joe's gallon of wine and poured the fruit jars full, for they were tired from their work, and their emotions were exhausted.

Then they counted the quarters out in piles of ten,

and excitedly counted again. "Pirate," Danny cried, "there are seven over a thousand! Thy time is done! The day is come for thee to buy thy candlestick for San Francisco!"

The day had been too full for the Pirate. He went into the corner with his dogs, and he put his head down on Fluff and burst into hysterical sobs. The dogs moved uneasily about, and they licked his ears and pushed at his head with their noses; but Fluff, sensible of the honor of being chosen, lay quietly and nuzzled the thick hair on the Pirate's neck.

Danny put all the money back in the bag, and the bag under his pillow again.

Now Big Joe came to and groaned, for the salt was working into his back. The paisanos paid no attention to him until at last Jesus Maria, that prey to the humanities, untied Big Joe's thumbs and gave him a jar of wine. "Even the enemies of our Saviour gave him a little comfort," he excused himself.

That action broke up the punishment. The friends gathered tenderly about Big Joe. They laid him on Danny's bed and washed the salt out of his wounds. They put cold cloths on his head and kept his jar full of wine. Big Joe moaned whenever they touched him. His morals were probably untouched, but it would have been safe to prophesy that never again would he steal from the paisanos of Danny's house.

The Pirate's hysteria was over. He drank his wine and his face shone with pleasure while he listened to Danny make plans for him.

"If we take all this money into town, to the bank, they will think we have stolen it from a slot machine. We must take this money to Father Ramon and tell him about it. Then he will buy the gold candlestick, and he will bless it, and the Pirate will go into the church. Maybe Father Ramon will say a word about him on Sunday. The Pirate must be there to hear."

Pilon looked distastefully at the Pirate's dirty, ragged clothes. "To-morrow," he said sternly, "you must take the seven extra two-bitses and buy some decent clothes. For ordinary times these may be all right, but on such an occasion as this you cannot go into the church looking like such a gutter rat. It will not be a compliment to your friends."

The Pirate beamed at him. "To-morrow I will do it," he promised.

The next morning, true to his promise, he went down to Monterey. He shopped carefully, and bargained with an astuteness that seemed to belie the fact that he had bought nothing in over two years. He came back to Danny's house in triumph, bearing a huge silk handkerchief in purple and green and also a broad belt studded profusely with colored glass jewels. His friends admired his purchases.

"But what are you going to wear?" Danny asked despairingly. "Two toes are out of your shoes where you cut holes to ease your bunions. You have only ragged overalls and no hat."

"We will have to lend him clothes," said Jesus Maria. "I have a coat and vest. Pilon has his father's good hat. You, Danny, have a shirt and Big Joe has those fine blue pants."

"But then we can't go," Pilon protested.

"It is not our candlestick," said Jesus Maria. "Father Ramon is not likely to say anything nice about us."

That afternoon they convoyed the treasure to the priest's house. He listened to the story of the sick dog, and his eyes softened. "—and then, Father," said the Pirate, "there was that good little dog, and his nose was dry, and his eyes were like the glass of bottles out of the sea, and he groaned because he hurt inside. And then, Father, I promised the gold candlestick of one thousand days to San Francisco. He is really my patron, Father. And then there was a miracle! For that dog wagged his tail three times, and right away he started to get well. It was a miracle from San Francisco, Father, wasn't it?"

The priest nodded his head gravely. "Yes," he said. "It was a miracle sent by our good Saint Francis. I will buy the candlestick for thee."

The Pirate was very glad, for it is no little thing to have one's prayer answered with a true miracle. If it were noised about, the Pirate would have a higher station on Tortilla Flat. Already his friends looked at him with a new respect. They thought no more of his intelligence than they had before, but they knew now that his meager wits were supplemented with all the power of Heaven and all the strength of the saints.

They walked back up to Danny's house, and the dogs walked behind them. The Pirate felt that he had been washed in a golden fluid of beatitude. Little chills and fevers of pleasure chased one another through his body.

The paisanos were glad they had guarded his money, for even they took a little holiness from the act. Pilon was relieved that he had not stolen the money in the first place. What terrible things might not have happened if he had taken the two-bitses belonging to a saint! All of the friends were as subdued as though they were in church.

The five dollars from the salvage had lain like fire in Danny's pocket, but now he knew what to do with it. He and Pilon went to the market and bought seven pounds of hamburger and a bag of onions and bread and a big paper of candy. Pablo and Jesus Maria went to Torrelli's for two gallons of wine, and not a drop did they drink on the way home, either.

That night when the fire was lighted and two candles burned on the table, the friends feasted themselves to repletion. It was a party in the Pirate's honor. He behaved himself with a great deal of dignity. He smiled and smiled when he should have been grave, though. But he couldn't help that.

After they had eaten enormously, they sat back and sipped wine out of the fruit jars. "Our little friend," they called the Pirate.

Jesus Maria asked, "How did you feel when it happened? When you promised the candlestick and the dog began to get well, how did you feel? Did you see any holy vision?"

The Pirate tried to remember. "I don't think so— Maybe I saw a little vision—maybe I saw San Francisco in the air and he was shining like the sun——"

"Wouldn't you remember that?" Pilon demanded.

"Yes—I think I remember—San Francisco looked on me—and he smiled, like the good saint he is. Then I knew the miracle was done. He said, 'Be good to little doggies, you dirty man.'"

"He called you that?"

"Well, I was, and he is not a saint to be telling lies."

"I don't think you remember that at all," said Pablo.

"Well—maybe not. I think I do, though," The Pirate was drunk with happiness from the honor and the attention.

"My grandmother saw the Holy Virgin," said Jesus Maria. "She was sick to death, and I myself heard her cry out. She said, 'Ohee. I see the Mother of God. Ohee. My dear Mary, full of grace.'"

"It is given to some to see these things," said Danny.

"My father was not a very good man, but he sometimes saw saints, and sometimes he saw bad things. It depended on whether he was good or bad when he saw them. Have you ever seen any other visions, Pirate?"

"No," said the Pirate. "I would be afraid to see any more."

It was a decorous party for a long time. The friends knew that they were not alone this night. Through the walls and the windows and the roof they could feel the eyes of the holy saints looking down upon them.

"On Sunday your candlestick will be there," said Pilon. "We cannot go, for you will be wearing our clothes. I do not say Father Ramon will mention you by name, but maybe he will say something about the candlestick. You must try to remember what he says, Pirate, so you can tell us."

Then Pilon grew stern. "To-day, my little friend, there were dogs all over Father Ramon's house. That was all right for to-day, but you must remember not to take them to the church on Sunday. It is not fitting that dogs should be in the church. Leave the dogs at home."

The Pirate looked disappointed. "They want to go,"

he cried. "How can I leave them? Where can I leave them?"

Pablo was shocked. "In this affair so far thou hast conducted thyself with merit, little Pirate. Right at the last do you wish to commit sacrilege?"

"No," said the Pirate humbly.

"Then leave thy dogs here, and we will take care of them. It will be a sacrilege to take them into the church."

It was curious how soberly they drank that night. It was three hours before they sang even an obscene song. And it was late before their thoughts strayed to light women. And by the time their minds turned to fighting they were almost too sleepy to fight. This evening was a great good marker in their lives.

On Sunday morning the preparation was violent. They washed the Pirate and inspected his ears and his nostrils. Big Joe, wrapped in a blanket, watched the Pirate put on his blue serge trousers. Pilon brought out his father's hat. They persuaded the Pirate not to wear his jewel-studded belt outside his coat, and showed him how he could leave his coat open so that the jewels flashed now and then. The item of shoes gave the most trouble.

Big Joe had the only shoes big enough for the Pirate, and his were worse even than the Pirate's. The difficulty lay in the holes cut for the comfort of bunions, where the toes showed through. Pilon solved it finally with a little soot from the inside of the stove. Well rubbed into the skin, the soot made it quite difficult to see the bunion holes.

At last he was ready; Pilon's father's hat rakishly on his head, Danny's shirt, Big Joe's pants, the huge handkerchief around his neck, and at intervals, the flashing of the jeweled belt. He walked, for the friends to inspect him, and they looked on critically.

"Pick up your feet, Pirate."

"Don't drag your heels."

"Stop picking at your handkerchief."

"Those people who see you will think you are not in the habit of good clothes."

At last the Pirate turned to his friends. "If those dogs could only come with me," he complained. "I would tell them they must not come in the church."

But the paisanos were firm. "No," said Danny. "They might get in some way. We will keep them here in the house for you."

"They won't like it," said the Pirate helplessly. "They will be lonely, maybe." He turned to the dogs in the corner. "You must stay here," he said. "It would not be good for you to go to church. Stay with my friends until I come back again." And then he slipped out and closed the door behind him. Instantly a wild clamor of barking and howling broke out in the house. Only his faith in the judgment of his friends prevented the Pirate's relenting.

As he walked down the street, he felt naked and unprotected without his dogs. It was as though one of his senses were gone. He was frightened to be out alone. Any one might attack him. But he walked bravely on, through the town and out to the Church of San Carlos.

Now, before the service began, the swinging doors were open. The Pirate dipped Holy Water out of the marble font, crossed himself, genuflected before the Virgin, went into the church, did his duty to the altar and sat down. The long church was rather dark, but the high altar was on fire with candles. And in front of the images at the sides, the votive lights were burning. The old and sweet incense perfumed the church.

For a time the Pirate sat looking at the altar, but it

was too remote, too holy to think about very much, too unapproachable by a poor man. His eyes sought something warmer, something that would not frighten him. And there, in front of the figure of Saint Francis, was a beautiful golden candlestick, and in it a tall candle was burning.

The Pirate sighed with excitement. And although the people came in, and the swinging doors were shut and the service began and the Pirate went through the form, he could not stop looking at his saint and at the candlestick. It was so beautiful. He could not believe that he, the Pirate, had given it. He searched the face of the saint to see whether St. Francis liked the candlestick. He was sure the image smiled a little now and then, the recurring smile of one who thinks of pleasant things.

At last the sermon began. "There is a new beauty in the church," Father Ramon said. "One of the children of the church has given a golden candlestick to the glory of Saint Francis." He told the story of the dog, then, told it rather baldly on purpose. His eyes searched the faces of the parishioners until he saw little smiles appear there. "It is not a thing to be considered funny," he said. "Saint Francis loved the beasts so much that he preached to them." Then Father Ramon told the story of the bad wolf of Gubbio and he told of the wild turtle-doves and of the sister larks. The Pirate looked at him in wonder as the sermon went on.

Suddenly a rushing sound came from the door. A furious barking and scratching broke out. The doors swung wildly and in rushed Fluff and Rudolph, Enrique, Pajarito and Señor Alec Thompson. They raised their noses, and then darted in a struggling squad to the Pirate. They leaped upon him with little cries and whinings. They swarmed over him.

The priest stopped talking and looked sternly down toward the commotion. The Pirate looked back helplessly, in agony. So it was in vain, and the sacrilege was committed.

Then Father Ramon laughed, and the congregation laughed. "Take the dogs outside," he said. "Let them wait until we are through."

The Pirate, with embarrassed, apologetic gestures, conducted his dogs outside. "It is wrong," he said to them. "I am angry with you. Oh, I am ashamed of you." The dogs cringed to the ground and whined piteously. "I know what you did," said the Pirate. "You bit my friends, you broke a window, and you came. Now stay here and wait, oh, wicked dogs; oh, dogs of sacrilege."

He left them stricken with grief and repentance and went back into the church. The people, still laughing, turned and looked at him, until he sank into his seat and tried to efface himself.

"Do not be ashamed," Father Ramon said. "It is no sin to be loved by your dogs, and no sin to love them. See how Saint Francis loved the beasts." Then he told more stories of that good saint.

The embarrassment left the Pirate. His lips moved. "Oh," he thought, "if the dogs could only hear this. They would be glad if they could know all this." When the sermon was over, his ears still rang with the stories. Automatically he followed the ritual, but he did not hear the service. And when it was over, he rushed for the door. He was first out of the church. The dogs, still sad and diffident, crowded about him.

"Come," he cried. "I have some things to tell you."

He started at a trot up the hill toward the pine forest, and the dogs galloped and bounced about him. He came at last to the shelter of the woods, and still he went on, until he found a long aisle among the pines, where the branches met overhead, where the tree trunks were near together. For a moment he looked helplessly about.

"I want it to be the way it was," he said. "If only you could have been there, and heard the father say it." He laid one big stone on top of another. "Now here is the image," he told the dogs. He stuck a little stick in the ground. "Right here is the candlestick, with a candle in it."

It was dusky in the glade, and the air was sweet with pine resin. The trees whispered softly in the breeze. The Pirate said with authority, "Now, Enrique, you sit here. And you, Rudolph, here. I want Fluff here because he is the littlest. Pajarito, thou great fool, sit here and make no trouble. Señor Alec Thompson, you may *not* lie down."

Thus he arranged them in two rows, two in the front line and three in the back.

"I want to tell you how it was," he said. "You are forgiven for breaking into the church. Father Ramon said it was no sacrilege this time. Now, attention. I have things to tell."

The dogs sat in their places and watched him earnestly. Señor Alec Thompson flapped his tail, until the

Pirate turned to him. "Here is no place for that," he said. "Saint Francis would not mind, but I do not like you to wag your tail while you listen. Now, I am going to tell you about Saint Francis."

That day his memory was inspired. The sun found

interstices in the foliage and threw brilliant patterns on the pine-needle carpet. The dogs sat patiently, their eyes on the Pirate's lips. He told everything the priest had told, all the stories, all the observations. Hardly a word was out of its place.

When he was done, he regarded the dogs solemnly. "Saint Francis did all that," he said.

The trees hushed their whispering. The forest was silent and enchanted.

Suddenly there was a tiny sound behind the Pirate. All the dogs looked up. The Pirate was afraid to turn his head. A long moment passed.

And then the moment was over. The dogs lowered their eyes. The tree-tops stirred to life again and the sunlight patterns moved bewilderingly.

The Pirate was so happy that his heart pained him. "Did you see him?" he cried. "Was it San Francisco? Oh! What good dogs you must be to see a vision."

The dogs leaped up at his tone. Their mouths opened and their tails threshed joyfully.

# XIII

*How Danny's Friends threw themselves to the aid*
*of a distressed lady.*

Señora Teresina Cortez and her eight children and her ancient mother lived in a pleasant cottage on the edge of the deep gulch that defines the southern frontier of Tortilla Flat. Teresina was a good figure of a mature woman, nearing thirty. Her mother, that ancient, dried, toothless one, relict of a past generation, was nearly fifty. It was long since any one had remembered that her name was Angelica.

During the week work was ready to this vieja's hand, for it was her duty to feed, punish, cajole, dress and bed down seven of the eight children. Teresina was busy with the eighth, and with making certain preparations for the ninth.

On Sunday, however, the vieja, clad in black satin

more ancient even than she, hatted in a grim and dura-
ble affair of black straw, on which were fastened two
true cherries of enameled plaster, threw duty to the
wind and went firmly to church, where she sat as motionless as the saints in their niches. Once a month, in
the afternoon, she went to confession. It would be interesting to know what sins she confessed, and where
she found the time to commit them, for in Teresina's
house there were creepers, crawlers, stumblers, shriek-
ers, cat-killers, fallers-out-of-trees; and each one of these
charges could be trusted to be ravenous every two
hours.

Is it any wonder that the vieja had a remote soul and
nerves of steel? Any other kind would have gone screaming out of her body like little skyrockets.

Teresina was a mildly puzzled woman, as far as her
mind was concerned. Her body was one of those perfect
retorts for the distillation of children. The first baby,
conceived when she was fourteen, had been a shock to
her; such a shock, that she delivered it in the ball park
at night, wrapped it in newspaper and left it for the
night watchman to find. This is a secret. Even now
Teresina might get into trouble if it were known.

When she was sixteen, Mr. Alfred Cortez married her and gave her his name and the two foundations of her family, Alfredo and Ernie. Mr. Cortez gave her that name gladly. He was only using it temporarily anyway. His name, before he came to Monterey and after he left, was Guggliemo. He went away after Ernie was born. Perhaps he foresaw that being married to Teresina was not going to be a quiet life.

The regularity with which she became a mother always astonished Teresina. It occurred sometimes that she could not remember who the father of the impending baby was; and occasionally she almost grew convinced that no lover was necessary. In the time when she had been under quarantine as a diphtheria carrier she conceived just the same. However, when a question became too complicated for her mind to unravel, she usually laid that problem in the arms of the Mother of Jesus, who, she knew, had more knowledge of, interest in and time for such things than she.

Teresina went often to confession. She was the despair of Father Ramon. Indeed he had seen that while her knees, her hands and her lips did penance for an old sin, her modest and provocative eyes, flashing under drawn lashes, laid the foundations for a new one.

During the time I have been telling this, Teresina's ninth child was born, and for the moment she was un-engaged. The vieja received another charge; Alfredo entered his third year in the first grade, Ernie his second, and Panchito went to school for the first time.

At about this time in California it became the stylish thing for school nurses to visit the classes and to cate-chize the children on intimate details of their home life. In the first grade, Alfredo was called to the principal's office, for it was thought that he looked thin.

The visiting nurse, trained in child psychology, said kindly, "Freddie, do you get enough to eat?"

"Sure," said Alfredo.

"Well, now. Tell me what you have for breakfast."

"Tortillas and beans," said Alfredo.

The nurse nodded her head dismally to the principal. "What do you have when you go home for lunch?"

"I don't go home."

"Don't you eat at noon?"

"Sure. I bring some beans wrapped up in a tortilla."

Actual alarm showed in the nurse's eyes, but she con-

trolled herself. "At night what do you have to eat?"

"Tortillas and beans."

Her psychology deserted her. "Do you mean to stand there and tell me you eat nothing but tortillas and beans?"

Alfredo was astonished. "Jesus Christ," he said, "what more do you want?"

In due course the school doctor listened to the nurse's horrified report. One day he drove up to Teresina's house to look into the matter. As he walked through the yard the creepers, the crawlers and the stumblers were shrieking one terrible symphony. The doctor stood in the open kitchen door. With his own eyes he saw the vieja go to the stove, dip a great spoon into a kettle and sow the floor with boiled beans. Instantly the noise ceased. Creepers, crawlers and stumblers went to work with silent industry, moving from bean to bean, pausing only to eat them. The vieja went back to her chair for a few moments of peace. Under the bed, under the chairs, under the stove the children crawled with the intentness of little bugs. The doctor stayed two hours, for his scientific interest was piqued. He went away shaking his head.

He shook his head incredulously while he made his report. "I gave them every test I know of," he said, "teeth, skin, blood, skeleton, eyes, co-ordination. Gentlemen, they are living on what constitutes a slow poison, and they have from birth. Gentlemen, I tell you I have never seen healthier children in my life!" His emotion overcame him. "The little beasts," he cried. "I never saw such teeth in my life. I *never* saw such teeth!"

You will wonder how Teresina procured food for her family. When the bean threshers have passed, you will see, where they have stopped, big piles of bean chaff. If you will spread a blanket on the ground, and, on a windy afternoon, toss the chaff in the air over the blanket, you will understand that the threshers are not infallible. For an afternoon of work you may collect twenty or more pounds of beans.

In the autumn the vieja and those children who could walk went into the fields and winnowed the chaff. The landowners did not mind, for she did no harm. It was a bad year when the vieja did not collect three or four hundred pounds of beans.

When you have four hundred pounds of beans in the house, you need have no fear of starvation. Other things, delicacies such as sugar, tomatoes, peppers, coffee, fish or meat may come sometimes miraculously, through the intercession of the Virgin, sometimes through industry or cleverness; but your beans are there, and you are safe. Beans are a roof over your stomach. Beans are a warm cloak against economic cold.

Only one thing could threaten the lives and happiness of the family of the Señora Teresina Cortez; that was a failure of the bean crop.

When the beans are ripe, the little bushes are pulled and gathered into piles, to dry crisp for the threshers. Then is the time to pray that the rain may hold off. When the little piles of beans lie in lines, yellow against the dark fields, you will see the farmers watching the sky, scowling with dread at every cloud that sails over; for if a rain comes, the bean piles must be turned over to dry again. And if more rain falls before they are dry, they must be turned again. If a third shower falls, mildew and rot set in, and the crop is lost.

When the beans were drying, it was the vieja's custom to burn a candle to the Virgin.

In the year of which I speak, the beans were piled

and the candle had been burned. At Teresina's house, the gunny sacks were laid out in readiness.

The threshing machines were oiled and cleaned.

A shower fell.

Extra hands rushed to the fields and turned the sodden hummocks of beans. The vieja burned another candle.

More rain fell.

Then the vieja bought two candles with a little gold piece she had kept for many years. The field hands turned over the beans to the sun again; and then came a downpour of cold streaking rain. Not a bean was harvested in all Monterey County. The soggy lumps were turned under by the plows.

Oh, then distress entered the house of Señora Teresina Cortez. The staff of life was broken; the little roof destroyed. Gone was that eternal verity, beans. At night the children cried with terror at the approaching starvation. They were not told, but they knew. The vieja sat in church, as always, but her lips drew back in a sneer when she looked at the Virgin. "You took my candles," she thought. "Ohee, yes. Greedy you are for candles. Oh, thoughtless one." And sullenly she transferred her allegiance to Santa Clara. She told Santa Clara of the injustice that had been done. She permitted herself a little malicious thought at the Virgin birth. "You know, sometimes Teresina can't remember either," she told Santa Clara viciously.

It has been said that Jesus Maria Corcoran was a great-hearted man. He had also that gift some humanitarians possess of being inevitably drawn toward those spheres where his instinct was needed. How many times had he not come upon young ladies when they needed comforting. Toward any pain or sorrow he was irresistibly drawn. He had not been to Teresina's house for many months. If there is no mystical attraction between pain and humanitarianism, how did it happen that he went there to call on the very day when the last of the old year's beans was put in the pot?

He sat in Teresina's kitchen, gently brushing children off his legs. And he looked at Teresina with polite and pained eyes while she told of the calamity. He watched, fascinated, when she turned the last bean sack inside out to show that not one single bean was left. He nodded sympathetically when she pointed out the children, so soon to be skeletons, so soon to die of starvation.

Then the vieja told bitterly how she had been tricked by the Virgin. But upon this point, Jesus Maria was not sympathetic.

"What do you know, old one?" he said sternly. "Maybe the Blessed Virgin had business some place else."

"But four candles I burned," the vieja insisted shrilly.

Jesus Maria regarded her coldly. "What are four candles to Her?" he said. "I have seen one church where She had hundreds. She is no miser of candles."

But his mind burned with Teresina's trouble. That evening he talked mightily and piteously to the friends at Danny's house. Out of his great heart he drew a compelling oratory, a passionate plea for those little children who had no beans. And so telling was his speech that the fire in his heart ignited the hearts of his friends. They leaped up. Their eyes glowed.

"The children shall not starve," they cried. "It shall be our trust!"

"We live in luxury," Pilon said.

"We shall give of our substance," Danny agreed. "And if they needed a house, they could live here."

"To-morrow we shall start," Pablo exclaimed. "No more laziness! To work! There are things to be done!"

Jesus Maria felt the gratification of a leader with followers.

Theirs was no idle boast. Fish they collected. The vegetable patch of the Hotel Del Monte they raided. It was a glorious game. Theft robbed of the stigma of theft, crime altruistically committed— What is more gratifying?

The Pirate raised the price of kindlings to thirty cents and went to three new restaurants every morning. Big Joe stole Mrs. Palochico's goat over and over again, and each time it went home.

Now food began to accumulate in the house of Teresina. Boxes of lettuce lay on her porch, spoiled mackerel filled the neighborhood with a strong odor. And still the flame of charity burned in the friends.

If you could see the complaint book at the Monterey Police Department, you would notice that during this time there was a minor crime wave in Monterey. The police car hurried from place to place. Here a chicken was taken, there a whole patch of pumpkins. Paladini Company reported the loss of two one-hundred-pound cases of abalone steaks.

Teresina's house was growing crowded. The kitchen was stacked high with food. The back porch overflowed with vegetables. Odors like those of a packing house permeated Tortilla Flat. Breathlessly the friends dashed about at their larcenies, and long they talked and planned with Teresina.

At first Teresina was maddened with joy at so much food, and her head was turned by the compliment. After a week of it, she was not so sure. The baby was down with colic, Ernie had some kind of bowel trouble, Alfredo's face was flushed. The creepers and crawlers cried all the time. Teresina was ashamed to tell the friends what she must tell them. It took her several days to get her courage up; and during that time there arrived fifty pounds of celery and a crate of cantaloupes. At last she had to tell them. The neighbors were beginning to look at her with lifted brows.

She asked all of Danny's friends into her kitchen, and

then she informed them of the trouble, modestly and carefully, that their feelings might not be hurt.

"Green things and fruit are not good for children," she explained. "Milk is constipating to a baby after it is weaned." She pointed to the flushed and irritable children. See, they were all sick. They were not getting the proper food.

"What is the proper food?" Pilon demanded.

"Beans," she said. "There you have something to trust, something that will not go right through you."

The friends went silently away. They pretended to themselves to be disheartened, but they knew that the first fire of their enthusiasm had been lacking for several days.

At Danny's house they held a conference.

This must not be told in some circles, for the charge might be serious.

Long after midnight, four dark forms who shall be nameless, moved like shadows through the town. Four indistinct shapes crept up on the Western Warehouse Company platform. The watchman said, afterward, that he heard sounds, investigated and saw nothing. He could not say how the thing was done, how a lock was broken and the door forced. Only four men know that the watchman was sound asleep, and they will never tell on him.

A little later the four shadows left the warehouse, and now they were bent under tremendous loads. Pantings and snortings came from the shadows.

At three o'clock in the morning Teresina was awakened by hearing her back door open. "Who is there?" she cried.

There was no answer, but she heard four great thumps that shook the house. She lighted a candle and went to the kitchen in her bare feet. There, against the wall, stood four one-hundred-pound sacks of pink beans.

Teresina rushed in and awakened the vieja. "A miracle!" she cried. "Come look in the kitchen."

The vieja regarded with shame the plump full sacks. "Oh, miserable dirty sinner am I," she moaned. "Oh, Holy Mother, look with pity on an old fool. Every month thou shalt have a candle, as long as I live."

At Danny's house, four friends were lying happily in their blankets. What pillow can one have like a good conscience? They slept well into the afternoon, for their work was done.

And Teresina discovered, by a method she had found to be infallible, that she was going to have a baby. As she poured a quart of the new beans into the kettle, she wondered idly which one of Danny's friends was responsible.

# XIV

*Of the good life at Danny's House, of a gift pig, of the pain of Tall Bob, and of the thwarted love of the Viejo Ravanno.*

Clocks and watches were not used by the paisanos of Tortilla Flat. Now and then one of the friends acquired a watch in some extraordinary manner, but he kept it only long enough to trade it for something he really wanted. Watches were in good repute at Danny's house, but only as media of exhange. For practical purposes, there was the great golden watch of the sun. It was better than a watch, and safer, for there was no way of diverting it to Torrelli.

In the summer, when the hands of a clock point to seven, it is a nice time to get up, but in winter the same time is of no value whatever. How much better is the sun! When he clears the pine tops and clings to the front porch, be it summer or winter, that is the sensible time to get up. That is a time when one's hands do not quiver nor one's belly quake with emptiness.

The Pirate and his dogs slept in the living room, secure and warm in their corner. Pilon and Pablo and Jesus Maria and Danny and Big Joe Portagee slept in the bedroom. For all his kindness, his generosity, Danny never allowed his bed to be occupied by any one but himself. Big Joe tried it twice, and was smacked across the soles of the feet with a stick; so that even he learned the inviolable quality of Danny's bed.

The friends slept on the floor, and their bedding was unusual. Pablo had three sheepskins stitched together. Jesus Maria retired by putting his arms through the sleeves of one old overcoat, and his legs through the sleeves of another. Pilon wrapped himself in a big strip of carpet. Most of the time Big Joe simply curled up like a dog, and slept in his clothes. Big Joe, while he had no ability to keep any possession for very long, had a well-developed genius for trading everything that came into his hands for some little measure of wine. Thus they slept, noisily sometimes, but always comfortably. On one cold night, Big Joe tried to borrow a dog for his feet, and got well bitten, for the Pirate's dogs were not lendable.

No curtains covered the windows, but a generous Nature had obscured the glass with cobwebs, with dust and with the neat marks of raindrops.

"It would be nice to clean that window with soap and water," Danny said one time.

Pilon's sharp mind leaped to the problem with energy, but it was too easy for him. It did not require a decent quota of his powers. "More light would get in," he said. "We would not spend so much time out in the air if it were light in here. And at night, when the air is poisonous, we have no need for light."

Danny retired from the field, for if one little mention brought such clear and quick refutation of his project, what crushing logic would insistence bring forth? The window remained as it was; and as time passed, as fly after fly went to feed the spider family with his blood and left his huskish body in the webs against the glass, as dust adhered to dust, the bedroom took on a pleasant obscurity which made it possible to sleep in a dusky light even at noonday.

They slept peacefully, the friends; but when the sun

struck the window in the morning and, failing to get in, turned the dust to silver and shone on the iridescence of the blue-bottle flies, then the friends awakened and stretched and looked about for their shoes. They knew the front porch was warm when the sun was on the window.

They did not awaken quickly, nor fling about nor shock their systems with any sudden movement. No, they arose from slumber as gently as a soap bubble floats out from its pipe. Down into the gulch they trudged, still only half awake. Gradually their wills coagulated. They built a fire and boiled some tea and drank it from the fruit jars, and at last they settled in the sun on the front porch. The flaming flies made halos about their heads. Life took shape about them, the shape of yesterday and of to-morrow.

Discussion began slowly, for each man treasured the little sleep he still possessed. From this time until well after noon, intellectual comradeship came into being. Then roofs were lifted, houses peered into, motives inspected, adventures recounted. Ordinarily their thoughts went first to Cornelia Ruiz, for it was a rare day and night during which Cornelia had not some curious and interesting adventure. And it was an unusual adventure from which no moral lesson could be drawn.

The sun glistened in the pine needles. The earth smelled dry and good. The rose of Castile perfumed the world with its flowers. This was one of the best of times for the friends of Danny. The struggle for existence was remote. They sat in judgment on their fellows, judging not for morals, but for interest. Any one having a good thing to tell saved it for recounting at this time. The big brown butterflies came to the rose and sat on the flowers and waved their wings slowly, as though they pumped honey out by wing power.

"I saw Albert Rasmussen," said Danny. "He came from Cornelia's house. What trouble that Cornelia has. Every day some trouble."

"It is her way of life," said Pablo. "I am not one to cast stones, but sometimes I think Cornelia is a little too lively. Two things only occur to Cornelia, love and fighting."

"Well," said Pilon. "What do you want?"

"She never has any peace," Jesus Maria said sadly.

"She doesn't want any," said Pilon. "Give peace to that Cornelia, and she will die. Love and fighting. That is good, what you said, Pablo. Love and fighting, and a little wine. Then you are always young, always happy. What happened to Cornelia yesterday?"

Danny looked in triumph at Pilon. It was an unusual thing for Pilon not to know everything that happened. And now Danny could tell by the hurt and piqued look on Pilon's face that he did not know this one.

"All of you know Cornelia," he began. "Sometimes men take presents to Cornelia, a chicken or a rabbit or a cabbage. Just little things, and Cornelia likes those things. Well, yesterday Emilio Murietta took to Cornelia a little pig, only so long; a nice little pink pig. Emilio found that pig in the gulch. The sow chased him when he picked it up, but he ran fast, and he came to Cornelia's house with that pig.

"This Emilio is a great talker. He said to Cornelia, 'There is nothing nicer to have than a pig. He will eat anything. He is a nice pet. You get to love that little pig. But then that pig grows up and his character changes. That pig becomes mean and evil-tempered, so

242

that you do not love him any more. Then one day that pig bites you, and you are angry. And so you kill that pig and eat him.' "

The friends nodded gravely, and Pilon said, "In some ways Emilio is not a dull man. See how many satisfactions he has made with his pig—affection, love, revenge and food. I must go to talk with Emilio sometime.". But the friends could see that Pilon was jealous of a rival logician.

"Go on with this pig," said Pablo.

"Well," said Danny, "Cornelia took that little pig, and she was nice to Emilio. She said that when the time came, and she was angry at that pig, Emilio could have some of it to eat. Well, then Emilio went away. Cornelia made a little box for that pig to sleep in, by the stove.

"Some ladies came in to see her, then, and Cornelia let them hold the little pig and pet it. After a while Sweets Ramirez stepped on that pig's tail. Oh! It squealed like a steam whistle. The front door was open. That big sow she came in for her little pig again. All the tables and all the dishes were smashed. All the chairs, they were broken. And that big sow bit Sweets Ramirez, and pulled off Cornelia's skirt, and then, when those ladies were in the kitchen and the door locked, the sow went away, and that little pig went too. Now Cornelia is furious. She says she will beat Emilio."

"There it is," said Pablo. "That is the way life goes,

never the way you planned. It was that way when Tall Bob Smoke went to kill himself."

The faces of the friends swung appreciatively toward Pablo.

"You will know Bob Smoke," Pablo began. "He looks the way a vaquero should look, long legs, thin body; but he cannot ride very well. At the rodeo he is often in the dust. Now this Bob is one who wants to be admired. When there is a parade he likes to carry the flag. When there is a fight he wants to be referee. At the show he is always the first one to say 'Down in front!' Yes, there is a man who wants to be a great man, and to have people see him, and admire him. And something you do not know, perhaps, he wants people to love him, too.

"Poor unfortunate one, he is a man born to be laughed at. Some people pity him, but most of them just laugh at him. And laughter stabs that Tall Bob Smoke.

"Maybe you remember that time in the parade when he carried the flag. Very straight Bob sat, on a big white horse. Right in front of the place where the judges sat, that big stupid horse fainted from the heat. Bob went flying right over that horse's head, and the flag sailed through the air like a spear and stuck in the ground, upside down.

"That is how it is with him. Whenever he tries to be a great man, something happens and everybody laughs. You remember when he was poundmaster he tried all afternoon to lasso a dog. Everybody in town came to see. He threw the rope and the dog squatted down and the rope slipped off and the dog ran away. Oh, the people laughed. Bob was so ashamed that he thought, 'I will kill myself, and then people will be sad. They will be sorry they laughed.' And then he thought, 'But I will be dead. I will not know how sorry they are.' So he made this plan, 'I will wait until I hear some one coming to my room. I will point a pistol at my head. Then that friend will argue with me. He will make me promise not to shoot myself. The people will be sorry then that they drove me to kill myself.' That is the way he thought it.

"So he walked home to his little house, and everybody he passed called out, 'Did you catch the dog, Bob?' He was very sad when he got home. He took a pistol and put cartridges in it, and then he sat down and waited for some one to come.

"He planned how it would be, and he practiced it with a pistol. The friend would say, 'Ai, what you doing? Don't shoot yourself, poor fellow.' Then Bob would say how he didn't want to live any more because every one was so mean.

"He thought about it over and over, but no one

came. And the next day he waited, and no one came. But that next night Charlie Meeler came. Bob heard him on the porch and put the pistol to his head. And he cocked it to make it look more real. 'Now he will argue with me, and I will let him persuade me,' Bob thought.

"Charlie Meeler opened the door. He saw Bob holding that pistol to his head. But he did not shout; no, Charlie Meeler jumped and grabbed that gun and that gun went off and shot away the end of Bob's nose. And then the people laughed even more. There were pieces in the paper about it. The whole town laughed.

"You have all seen Bob's nose, with the end shot off. The people laughed; but it was a hard kind of laughing, and they felt bad to laugh. And ever since then, they let Tall Bob carry the flag in every parade there is. And the city bought him a net to catch dogs with.

"But he is not a happy man, with his nose like that." Pablo fell silent and picked up a stick from the porch and whipped his leg a little.

"I remember his nose, how it was," said Danny. "He is not a bad one, that Bob. The Pirate can tell you,

247

when he gets back. Sometimes the Pirate puts all his dogs in Bob's wagon and then the people think Bob has caught them, and the people say, 'There is a pound-man for you.' It is not so easy to catch dogs when it is your business to catch dogs."

Jesus Maria had been brooding, with his head back against the wall. He observed, "It is worse than whipping to be laughed at. Old Tomas, the rag sucker, was laughed right into his grave. And afterwards the people were sorry they laughed.

"And," said Jesus Maria, "there is another kind of laughing, too. That story of Tall Bob is funny; but when you open your mouth to laugh, something like a hand squeezes your heart. I know about old Mr. Ravanno who hanged himself last year. And there is a funny story too, but it is not pleasant to laugh at."

"I heard something about it," said Pilon, "but I do not know that story."

"Well," said Jesus Maria. "I will tell you that story, and you will see if you can laugh. When I was a little boy, I played games with Petey Ravanno. A good quick little boy, that Petey, but always in trouble. He had two brothers and four sisters, and there was his father,

Old Pete. All that family is gone now. One brother is in San Quentin, the other was killed by a Japanese gardener for stealing a wagonload of watermelons. And the girls, well, you know how girls are; they went away. Susy is in Old Jenny's house in Salinas right now.

"So there was only Petey and the old man left. Petey grew up, and always he was in trouble. He went to reform school for a while, and then he came back. Every Saturday he was drunk, and every time he went to jail until Monday. His father was a kind of a friendly man. He got drunk every week with Petey. Nearly always they were in jail together. Old man Ravanno was lonely when Petey was not there with him. He liked that boy Petey. Whatever Petey did, that old man did, even when he was sixty years old.

"Maybe you remember that Gracie Montez?" Jesus Maria asked. "She was not a very good girl. When she was only twelve years old, the fleet came to Monterey, and Gracie had her first baby, so young as that. She was pretty, you see, and quick, and her tongue was sharp. Always she seemed to run away from men, and men ran fast after her. And sometimes they caught her. But you could not get close to her. Always that Gracie seemed to have something nice that she did not give to you, something in back of her eyes that said, 'If I really wanted to, I would be different to you from any woman you ever knew.'

"I know about that," said Jesus Maria, "for I ran after Gracie, too. And Petey ran after her. Only Petey was different." Jesus Maria looked sharply into his friends' eyes to emphasize his point.

"Petey wanted what Gracie had so much that he grew thin, and his eyes were as wide and pained as the eyes of one who smokes marihuana. Petey could not eat, and he was sick. Old Man Ravanno went over and talked to Gracie. He said, 'If you are not nice to Petey, he will die.' But she only laughed. She was not a very good one. And then her little sister 'Tonia came into the room. 'Tonia was fourteen years old. The old man looked at her and his breath stopped. 'Tonia was like Gracie, with that funny thing that she kept away from men. Old Man Ravanno could not help it. He said, 'Come to me, little girl.' But 'Tonia was not a little girl. She knew. So she laughed and ran out of the room.

"Old Man Ravanno went home then. Petey said, 'Something is the matter with thee, my father.'

" 'No, Petey,' the old man said, 'only I worry that you do not get this Gracie, so you can be well again.'

"Hot blooded, all those Ravannos were!

"And then what do you think?" Jesus Maria continued. "Petey went to cut squids for Chin Kee, and he made presents to Gracie, big bottles of Agua Florida and ribbons and garters. He paid to have her picture taken, with colors on the picture, too.

"Gracie took all the presents and she ran away from him, and laughed. You should have heard how she laughed. It made you want to choke her and pet her at the same time. It made you want to cut her open and get that thing that was inside of her. I know how it was. I ran after her, and Petey told me, too. But it made Petey crazy. He could not sleep any more. He said to me, 'If that Gracie will marry me in the church, then she will not dare to run away any more, because she will be married, and it will be a sin to run away.' So he asked her. She laughed that high laugh that made you want to choke her.

"Oh! Petey was crazy. He went home and put a rope over a rafter and he stood on a box and put the rope around his neck and then he kicked out the box. Well,

Petey's father came in then. He cut the rope and called the doctor. But it was two hours before Petey opened his eyes, and it was four days before he could talk."

Jesus Maria paused. He saw with pride that his friends were leaning in toward the story. "That was the way of it," he said.

"But Gracie Montez married that Petey Ravanno," Pilon cried excitedly. "I know her. She is a good woman. She never misses mass, and she goes once a month to confession."

"So it is now," Jesus Maria agreed. "Old man Ravanno was angry. He ran to Gracie's house, and he cried, 'See how you murder my boy with your foolishness. He tried to kill himself for you, dung-heap chicken.'

"Gracie was afraid, but she was pleased, too, because it is not many women who can make a man go so far. She went to see Petey where he was in bed with a crooked neck. After a little while they were married.

"It turned out the way Petey thought it would, too. When the church told her to be a good wife, she was a good wife. She didn't laugh to men any more. And she didn't run away so they chased her. Petey went on cutting squids, and pretty soon Chin Kee let him empty the squid boxes. And not long after that he was the mayordomo of the squid yard. You see," said Jesus Maria, "there is a good story. It would be a story for a priest to tell, if it stopped there."

"Oh, yes," said Pilon gravely. "There are things to be learned in this story."

The friends nodded appreciatively, for they liked a story with a meaning.

"I knew a girl in Texas like that," said Danny. "Only she didn't change. They called her the wife of the second platoon. 'Mrs. Second Platoon,' they said."

Pablo held up his hand. "There is more to this story," he said. "Let Jesus Maria tell the rest."

"Yes, there is more. And it is not such a good story, in the ending. There was the viejo, over sixty. And Petey and Gracie went to live in another house. The Viejo Ravanno was lonely, for he had always been with Petey. He didn't know how to take up his time. He just sat and looked sad, until one day he saw 'Tonia again. 'Tonia was fifteen, and she was prettier, even, than Gracie. Half the soldiers from the Presidio followed her around like little dogs.

"Now as it had been with Petey, so it was with the old man. His desire made him ache all over. He could not eat or sleep. His cheeks sunk in, and his eyes stared like the eyes of a marihuana smoker. He carried candy to 'Tonia, and she grabbed the candy out of his hands and laughed at him. He said, 'Come to me, little dear one, for I am thy friend.' She laughed again.

"Then the viejo told Petey about it. And Petey laughed too. 'You old fool,' Petey said. 'You've had enough women in your life. Don't run after babies.' But it did no good. Old Man Ravanno grew sick with longing. They are hot-blooded, those Ravannos. He hid in the grass and watched her pass by. His heart ached in his breast.

"He needed money to buy presents, so he got a job in the Standard Service Station. He raked the gravel and watered the flowers at that station. He put water in the radiators and cleaned the windshields. With every cent he bought presents for 'Tonia, candy and ribbons and dresses. He paid to have her picture taken with colors.

"She only laughed more, and the viejo was nearly crazy. So he thought, 'If marriage in the church made

Gracie a good woman, it will make 'Tonia a good woman, too.' He asked her to marry him. Then she laughed more than ever. She flung up her skirts at him to worry him. Oh, she was a devil, that 'Tonia."

"He was a fool," said Pilon smugly. "Old men should not run after babies. They should sit in the sun."

Jesus Maria went on irritably, "Those Ravannos are different," he said, "so hot-blooded."

"Well, it was not a decent thing," said Pilon. "It was a shame on Petey."

Pablo turned to him. "Let Jesus Maria go on. It is his story, Pilon, not thine. Sometime we will listen to thee."

Jesus Maria looked gratefully to Pablo. "I was telling.

"The viejo could not stand it any more. But he was not a man to invent anything. He was not like Pilon. He could not think of anything new. The Viejo Ravanno thought like this: 'Gracie married Petey because he hanged himself. I will hang myself, and maybe 'Tonia will marry me.' And then he thought, 'If no one finds me soon enough, I will be dead. Some one must find me.'

"You must know," said Jesus Maria, "at that service

station there is a tool house. Early in the morning, the viejo went down and unlocked the tool house and raked the gravel and watered the flowers before the station opened. The other men came to work at eight o'clock. So, one morning, the viejo went into the tool house and put up a rope. Then he waited until it was eight o'clock. He saw the men coming. He put the rope around his neck and stepped off a work bench. And just when he did that, the door of the tool shed blew shut."

Broad smiles broke out on the faces of the friends. Sometimes, they thought, life was very, very humorous.

"Those men did not miss him right away," Jesus Maria went on. "They said, 'He is probably drunk, that old one.' It was an hour later when they opened the door of that tool shed." He looked around.

The smiles were still on the faces of the friends, but they were changed smiles. "You see," Jesus Maria said, "it is funny. But it squeezes in you, too."

"What did 'Tonia say?" Pilon demanded. "Did she read a lesson and change her living?"

"No. She did not. Petey told her, and she laughed. Petey laughed too. But he was ashamed. 'Tonia said,

'What an old fool he was,' and 'Tonia looked at Petey that way she had.

"Then Petey said, 'It is good to have a little sister like thee. Some night I will walk in the woods with thee.' Then 'Tonia laughed again, and ran away a little. And she said, 'Do you think I am as pretty as Gracie?' So Petey followed her into the house."

Pilon complained, "It is not a good story. There are too many meanings and too many lessons in it. Some of those lessons are opposite. There is not a story to take into your head. It proves nothing."

"I like it," said Pablo. "I like it because it hasn't any meaning you can see, and still it does seem to mean something, I can't tell what."

The sun had turned across noon, and the air was hot.

"I wonder what the Pirate will bring to eat," said Danny.

"There is a mackerel run in the bay," Pablo observed.

Pilon's eyes brightened. "I have a plan that I thought out," he said. "When I was a little boy, we lived by the railroad. Every day when the train went by, my brothers and I threw rocks at the engine, and the fireman threw coal at us. Sometimes we picked up a big bucketful of coal, and took it in to our mother. Now I thought maybe we could take rocks down on the pier. When the boats come near, we will call names, we will throw rocks. How can those fishermen get back at us? Can they throw oars, or nets? No. They can only throw mackerel."

Danny stood up joyfully. "Now there is a plan!" he cried. "How this little Pilon of ours is our friend! What would we do without our Pilon? Come, I know where there is a great pile of rocks."

"I like mackerel better than any other fish," said Pablo.

# XV

*How Danny brooded and became mad. How the
devil in the shape of Torrelli assaulted Danny's
House.*

THERE is a changeless qual-
ity about Monterey. Nearly every day in the morning
the sun shines in the windows on the west sides of the
streets; and, in the afternoons, on the east sides of the
streets. Every day the red bus clangs back and forth
between Monterey and Pacific Grove. Every day the
canneries send a stink of reducing fish into the air.
Every afternoon the wind blows in from the bay and
sways the pines on the hills. The rock fishermen sit on
the rocks holding their poles, and their faces are graven
with patience and with cynicism.

On Tortilla Flat, above Monterey, the routine is
changeless, too; for there are only a given number of

adventures that Cornelia Ruiz can have with her slowly changing procession of sweethearts. She has been known to take again a man long since discarded.

In Danny's house there was even less change. The friends had sunk into a routine which might have been monotonous for any one but a paisano—up in the morning, to sit in the sun and wonder what the Pirate would bring. The Pirate still cut pitchwood and sold it in the streets of Monterey, but now he bought food with the quarter he earned every day. Occasionally the friends procured some wine, and then there was singing and fighting.

Time is more complex near the sea than in any other place, for in addition to the circling of the sun and the turning of the seasons, the waves beat out the passage of time on the rocks and the tides rise and fall as a great clepsydra.

Danny began to feel the beating of time. He looked at his friends, and saw how with them every day was the same. When he got out of his bed in the night and stepped over the sleeping paisanos, he was angry with them for being there. Gradually, sitting on the front porch, in the sun, Danny began to dream of the days of his freedom. He had slept in the woods in summer, and in the warm hay of barns when the winter cold was in. The weight of property was not upon him. He remembered that the name of Danny was a name of storm. Oh, the fights! The flights through the woods with an outraged chicken under his arm! The hiding places in the gulch when an outraged husband proclaimed feud! Storm and violence, sweet violence! When Danny thought of the old lost time, he could taste again how good the stolen food was, and he longed for that old time again. Since his inheritance had lifted him, he had not fought often. He had been drunk, but not adventurously so. Always the weight of the house was upon him; always the responsibility to his friends.

Danny began to mope on the front porch, so that his friends thought him ill.

"Tea made from yerba buena will be good," Pilon suggested. "If you will go to bed, Danny, we will put hot rocks to your feet."

It was not coddling Danny wanted, it was freedom. For a month he brooded, stared at the ground, looked with sullen eyes at his ubiquitous friends, kicked the friendly dogs out of his way.

In the end he gave up to his longing. One night he ran away. He went into the pine woods and disappeared.

When in the morning the friends awakened and found him missing, Pilon said, "It is some lady. He is in love."

They left it there, for every man has a right to love. The friends went on living as they had. But when a week passed with no sign of Danny, they began to worry. In a body they went to the woods to look for him.

"Love is nice," said Pilon. "We cannot blame any man for following a girl, but a week is a week. It must be a lively girl to keep Danny away for a week."

Pablo said, "A little love is like a little wine. Too much of either will make a man sick. Maybe Danny is already sick. Maybe this girl is too lively."

Jesus Maria was worried, too. "Is it not like the Danny we know to be gone so long. Some bad thing has happened."

The Pirate took his dogs into the woods. The friends advised the dogs, "Find Danny. He may be sick. Somewhere he may be dead, that good Danny who lets you sleep in his house."

The Pirate whispered to them, "Oh, evil, ungrateful dogs, find our friend." But the dogs waved their tails happily and sought out a rabbit and went kyoodling after it.

The paisanos ranged all day through the woods, calling Danny's name, looking in places they themselves might have chosen to sleep in, the good hollows between the roots of trees, the thick needle beds, encircled by bushes. They knew where a man would sleep, but they found no sign of Danny.

"Perhaps he is mad," Pilon suggested. "Some secret worry may have turned his wit."

In the evening they went back to Danny's house and opened the door and went in. Instantly they became intense. A thief had been busy. Danny's blankets were gone. All the food was stolen. Two pots were missing.

Pilon looked quickly at Big Joe Portagee, and then he shook his head. "No, you were with us. You didn't do it."

"Danny did it," Pablo said excitedly. "Truly he is mad. He is running through the woods like an animal."

Great care and worry settled on Danny's house. "We must find him," the friends assured one another. "Some harm will fall upon our friend in his craziness. We must search through the whole world until we find him."

They threw off their laziness. Every day they looked for him, and they began to hear curious rumors. "Yes, Danny was here last night. Oh, that drunk one! Oh, that thief! For see, Danny knocked down the viejo with a fence picket and he stole a bottle of grappa. What kind of friends are these who let their friend do such things?"

"Yes, we saw Danny. His eye was closed, and he was singing, 'Come into the woods and we will dance, little girls,' but we would not go. We were afraid. That Danny did not look very quiet."

At the wharf they found more evidence of their friend. "He was here," the fishermen said. "He wanted to fight everybody. Benito broke an oar on Danny's head. Then Danny broke some windows, and then a policeman took him to jail."

Hot on the path of their wayward friend, they continued. "McNear brought him in last night," the sergeant said. "Some way he got loose before morning. When we catch him, we'll give him six months."

The friends were tired of the chase. They went home, and to their horror, they found that the new sack of potatoes that Pilon had found only that morning was gone.

"Now it is too much," Pilon cried. "Danny is crazy, and he is in danger. Some terrible thing will happen to him if we do not save him."

"We will search," said Jesus Maria.

"We will look behind every tree and every shed," Pablo guaranteed.

"Under the boats on the beach," Big Joe suggested.

"The dogs will help," the Pirate said.

Pilon shook his head. "That is not the way. Every time we come to a place after Danny has gone. We must wait in some place where he will come. We must act as wise men, not as fools."

"But where will he come?"

The light struck all of them at once. "Torrelli's! Sooner or later, Danny will go to Torrelli's. We must go there to catch him, to restrain him in the madness that has fallen upon him."

"Yes," they agreed. "We must save Danny."

In a body they visited Torrelli, and Torrelli would not let them in. "Ask me," he cried through the door, "have I seen Danny? Danny brought three blankets and two cooking pots, and I gave him a gallon of wine. What did that devil do then? My wife he insulted and me he called bad names. My baby he spanked, my dog he kicked! He stole the hammock from my porch." Torrelli gasped with emotion. "I chased him to get my hammock back, and when I returned, he was with my wife! Seducer, thief, drunkard! That is your friend Danny! I myself will see that he goes to penitentiary."

The eyes of the friends glinted. "Oh, Corsican pig," Pilon said evenly. "You speak of our friend. Our friend is not well."

Torrelli locked the door. They could hear the bolt slide, but Pilon continued to speak through the door. "Oh, Jew," he said. "If thou wert a little more charitable with thy wine, these things would not happen. See that thou keepest that cold frog which is thy tongue from dirtying our friend. See thou treatest him gently, for his friends are many. We will tear thy stomach out if thou art not nice to him."

Torrelli made no sound inside the locked house, but he trembled with rage and fear at the ferocity of the tones. He was relieved when he heard the footsteps of the friends receding up the path.

That night, after the friends had gone to bed, they heard a stealthy step in the kitchen. They knew it was Danny, but he escaped before they could catch him. They wandered about in the dark, calling disconsolately, "Come, Danny, our little sugar friend, we need thee with us."

There was no reply, but a thrown rock struck Big Joe in the stomach and doubled him up on the ground. Oh, how the friends were dismayed, and how their hearts were heavy!

"Danny is running to his death," they said sadly. "Our little friend is in need, and we cannot help him."

It was difficult to keep house now, for Danny had stolen nearly everything in it. A chair turned up at a bootlegger's. All the food was taken, and once, when they were searching for Danny in the woods, he stole the air-tight stove; but it was heavy, he abandoned it in the gulch. Money there was none, for Danny stole the Pirate's wheelbarrow and traded it to Joe Ortiz for a bottle of whisky. Now all peace had gone from Danny's house, and there was only worry and sadness.

"Where is our happiness gone?" Pablo mourned. "Somewhere we have sinned. It is a judgment. We should go to confession."

No more did they discuss the marital parade of Cornelia Ruiz. Gone were the moralities, lost were the humanities. Truly the good life lay in ruins. And into the desolation came the rumors.

"Danny committed partial rape last night. '

"Danny has been milking Mrs. Palochico's goat."

"Danny was in a fight with some soldiers the night before last."

Sad as they were at his moral decay, the friends were not a little jealous of the good time Danny was having.

"If he is not crazy, he will be punished," said Pilon. "Be sure of that. Danny is sinning in a way which, sin for sin, beats any record I ever heard of. Oh, the penances when he wants to be decent again! In a few weeks Danny has piled up more sins than Old Ruiz did in a lifetime."

That night Danny, unhindered by the friendly dogs, crept into the house as silently as the moving shadow of a limb under a street light, and wantonly he stole Pilon's shoes. In the morning it did not take Pilon long to understand what had happened. He went firmly to the porch and sat down in the sun and regarded his feet.

"Now he has gone too far," Pilon said. "Pranks he has played, and we were patient. But now he turns to crime. This is not the Danny we know. This is another man, a bad man. We must capture this bad man."

Pablo looked complacently down at his shoes. "Maybe this is only a prank too," he suggested.

"No," Pilon said severely. "This is crime. They were not very good shoes, but it is a crime against friendship to take them. And that is the worst kind of crime. If Danny will steal the shoes of his friends, there is no crime he will stop at."

The friends nodded in agreement. "Yes, we must catch him," said Jesus Maria of the humanities. "We know he is sick. We will tie him to his bed and try to cure him of the sickness. We must try to wipe the darkness from his brain."

"But now," said Pablo, "before we catch him, we

must remember to put our shoes under our pillows when we sleep."

The house was in a state of siege. All about it raged Danny, and Danny was having a wonderful time.

Seldom did the face of Torrelli show any emotions but suspicion and anger. In his capacity as bootlegger, and in his dealings with the people of Tortilla Flat, those two emotions were often called into his heart, and their line was written on his face. Moreover, Torrelli had never visited any one. He had only to stay at home to have every one visit him. Consequently, when Torrelli walked up the road toward Danny's house in the morning, his face suffused with a ferocious smile of pleasure and anticipation, the children ran into their yards and peeked through the pickets at him; the dogs caressed their stomachs with their tails and fled with backward, fearful looks; men meeting him, stepped out of his path, and clenched their fists to repel a madman.

This morning the fog covered the sky. The sun, after a number of unsuccessful skirmishes, gave up and retired behind the gray folds. The pine trees dripped dusty dew on the ground; and in the faces of the few people who were about, the day was reflected with sombre looks and gray skins. There were no hearty greetings. There was none of that human idealism which blandly hopes this day will be better than all other days.

Old Roca, seeing Torrelli smiling, went home and told his wife, "That one has just killed and eaten his children. You will see!"

Torrelli was happy, for in his pocket there was a folded, precious paper. His fingers sought his coat again and again, and pressed until a little crackling sound assured Torrelli that the paper was still there. As he walked through the gray morning, he muttered to himself.

"Nest of snakes," he said. "I will wipe out this pestilence of Danny's friends. No more will I give wine for goods, and have the goods stolen again. Each man alone is not so bad, but the nest of them! Madonna, look down how I will cast them out into the street! The toads, the lice, the stinging flies! When they sleep in the woods again, they will not be so proud.

"I would have them know that Torrelli has triumphed. They thought to cheat me, to despoil my house of furniture and my wife of virtue! They will see that Torrelli, the great sufferer, can strike back. Oh, yes, they will see!"

Thus he muttered as he walked, and his fingers crackled the paper in his pocket. The trees dripped mournful drops into the dust. The seagulls circled in the air, screaming tragically. Torrelli moved like gray Fate on Danny's house.

In Danny's house there was gloom. The friends could not sit on the porch in the sunshine, for there was no sunshine. No one can produce a better reason for gloom. They had brought back the stolen stove from the gulch and set it up. They clustered to it now, and Johnny Pom-pom, who had come to call, told the news he had.

"Tito Ralph," he said, "is no longer the jailer down at the city jail. No, this morning the police judge sent him away."

"I liked Tito Ralph," said Pilon. "When a man was in jail, Tito Ralph would bring him a little wine. And he knew more stories than a hundred other men. Why did he lose his job, Johnny Pom-pom?"

'That is what I came to tell. Tito Ralph, you know, was often in jail, and he was a good prisoner. He knew how a jail should be run. After a while he knew more about the jail than any one. Then Daddy Marks, the old jailer, died, and Tito Ralph took his place. Never has there been such a good jailer as Tito Ralph. Everything he did just right. But he has one little fault. When he drinks wine, he forgets he is the jailer. He escapes, and they have to catch him."

The friends nodded. "I know," said Pablo. "I have heard he is hard to catch, too. He hides."

"Yes," continued Johnny Pom-pom, "except for that, he is the best jailer they ever had. Well, this is the thing that I came to tell. Last night Danny had enough wine for ten men, and he drank it. Then he drew pictures on windows. He was very rich; he bought eggs to throw at a Chinaman. And one of those eggs missed the Chinaman and hit a policeman. So, Danny was in jail.

"But he was rich. He sent Tito Ralph out to get some wine, and then some more wine. There were four men in the jail. They all drank wine. And at last that fault of Tito Ralph's came out. So he escaped, and all the others escaped with him. They caught Tito Ralph this morning and told him he could not be jailer any more. He was so sad that he broke a window, and now he is in jail again."

"But Danny," Pilon cried. "What about Danny?"

"Oh, Danny," said Johnny Pom-pom, "he escaped too. They did not catch him."

The friends sighed in dismay.

"Danny is getting bad," Pilon said seriously. "He will not come to a good end. I wonder where he got the money."

It was at this moment that the triumphant Torrelli opened the gate and strode up the path. The Pirate's dogs got up nervously from their corner and moved toward the door, snarling. The friends looked up and questioned one another with their eyes. Big Joe picked up the pick-handle that had so lately been used on him. The heavy confident step of Torrelli pounded on the porch. The door flew open, and there stood Torrelli, smiling. He did not bluster at them. No, he approached as delicately as a house cat. He patted them kindly, as a house cat pats a cockroach.

"Ah, my friends," he said gently, at their looks of alarm. "My dear good friends and customers. My heart is torn that I must be a carrier of bad news to those whom I love."

Pilon leaped up. "It is Danny. He is sick, he is hurt. Tell us."

Torrelli shook his head daintily. "No, my little ones, it is not Danny. My heart bleeds, but I must tell you that you cannot live here any more." His eyes gloated at the amazement his words wrought. Every mouth dropped open, every eye went blank with astonishment.

"That is foolish," Pablo cried. "Why can't we live here any more?"

Torrelli's hand went lovingly into his breast pocket, and his fingers brought out the precious paper and waved it in the air. "Imagine my suffering," Torrelli went on. "Danny does not own this house any more."

"What!" they cried. "What do you mean? How does not Danny own his house any more? Speak, oh, Corsican pig."

Torrelli giggled, a thing so terrible that the paisanos stepped back from him. "Because," he said, "the house belongs to me. Danny came to me and sold me his house for twenty-five dollars last night." Fiendishly he watched the thoughts crowd on their faces.

"It is a lie," their faces said. "Danny would not do such a thing." And then, "But Danny has been doing many bad things lately. He has been stealing from us. Maybe he has sold the house over our heads."

"It is a lie," Pilon cried aloud. "It is a dirty wop lie."

Torrelli smiled on and waved the paper. "Here I have proof," he said. "Here is the paper Danny signed. It is what we of business call a bill of sale."

Pablo came to him furiously. "You got him drunk. He did not know what he did."

Torrelli opened the paper a little bit. "The law will not be interested in that," he said. "And so, my dear little friends, it is my terrible duty to tell you that you must leave my house. I have plans for it." His face lost its smile, then, and all the cruelty came back into it. "If you are not out by noon, I will send a policeman."

Pilon moved gently toward him. Oh, beware, Torrelli, when Pilon moves smiling on you! Run, hide yourself in some iron room and weld up the door. "I do not understand these things," Pilon said gently. "Of course I am sad that Danny should do a thing like this."

Torrelli giggled again.

"I never had a house to sell," Pilon continued. "Danny signed this paper, is that it?"

"Yes," Torrelli mimicked him, "Danny signed this paper. That is it."

Pilon blundered on, stupidly. "That is the thing that proves you own this house?"

"Yes, oh, little fool. This is the paper that proves it."

Pilon looked puzzled. "I thought you must take it down and have some record made."

Torrelli laughed scornfully. Oh, beware, Torrelli! Do you not see how quietly these snakes are moving? There is Jesus Maria in front of the door. There is Pablo by the kitchen door. See Big Joe's knuckles white on the pick-handle.

Torrelli said, "You know nothing of business, little hoboes and tramps. When I leave here I shall take this paper down and——"

It happened so quickly that the last words belched out explosively. His feet flew up in the air. He landed with a great thump on the floor and clawed at the air with his fat hands. He heard the stove-lid clang.

"Thieves," he screamed. The blood pressed up his

neck and into his face. "Thieves, oh, rats and dogs, give me my paper."

Pilon, standing in front of him, looked amazed.

"Paper?" he asked politely. "What is this paper you speak of so passionately?"

"My bill of sale, my ownership. Oh, the police will hear of this!"

"I do not recall a paper," said Pilon. "Pablo, do you know what is this paper he talks about?"

"Paper?" said Pablo. "Does he mean a newspaper or a cigarette paper?"

Pilon continued with the roll. "Johnny Pom-pom?"

"He is dreaming, maybe, that one," said Johnny Pom-pom.

"Jesus Maria? Do you know of a paper?"

"I think he is drunk," Jesus Maria said in a scandalized voice. "It is too early in the morning to be drunk."

"Joe Portagee?"

"I wasn't here," Joe insisted. "I just came in now."

"Pirate?"

"He don't have no paper," the Pirate turned to his dogs, "do he?"

Pilon turned back to the apoplectic Torrelli. "You

are mistaken, my friend. It is possible that I might have been wrong about this paper, but you can see for yourself that no one but you saw this paper. Do you blame me when I think that maybe there was no paper? Maybe you should go to bed and rest a little."

Torrelli was too stunned to shout any more. They turned him about and helped him out of the door and sped him on his way, sunk in the awfulness of his defeat.

And then they looked at the sky, and were glad; for the sun had fought again, and this time won a pathway through the fog. The friends did not go back into the house. They sat happily down on the front porch.

"Twenty-five dollars," said Pilon. "I wonder what he did with the money."

The sun, once its first skirmish was won, drove the fog headlong from the sky. The porch boards warmed up, and the flies sang in the light. Exhaustion had settled on the friends.

"It was a close thing," Pablo said wearily. "Danny should not do such things."

"We will get all our wine from Torrelli to make it up to him," said Jesus Maria.

A bird hopped into the rose bush and flirted its tail.

Mrs. Morales' new chickens sang a casual hymn to the sun. The dogs, in the front yard, thoughtfully scratched all over and gnawed their tails.

At the sound of footsteps from the road, the friends looked up, and then stood up with welcoming smiles. Danny and Tito Ralph walked in the gate, and each of them carried two heavy bags. Jesus Maria darted into the house and brought out the fruit jars. The friends noticed that Danny looked a little tired when he set his jugs on the porch.

"It is hot climbing that hill," Danny said.

"Tito Ralph," cried Johnny Pom-pom, "I heard you were put in jail."

"I escaped again," Tito Ralph said wanly. "I still had the keys."

The fruit jars gurgled full. A great sigh escaped from the men, a sigh of relief that everything was over.

Pilon took a big drink. "Danny," he said, "that pig, Torrelli, came up here this morning with lies. He had a paper he said you signed."

Danny looked startled. "Where is that paper?" he demanded.

"Well," Pilon continued. "We knew it was a lie, so

we burned that paper. You didn't sign it, did you?"

"No," said Danny, and he drained his jar.

"It would be nice to have something to eat," observed Jesus Maria.

Danny smiled sweetly. "I forgot. In one of those bags are three chickens and some bread."

So great was Pilon's pleasure and relief that he stood up and made a little speech. "Where is there a friend like our friend?" he declaimed. "He takes us into his house out of the cold. He shares his good food with us, and his wine. Ohee, the good man, the dear friend."

Danny was embarrassed. He looked at the floor. "It is nothing," he murmured. "It has no merit."

But Pilon's joy was so great that it encompassed the world, and even the evil things of the world. "We must do something nice some time for Torrelli," he said.

# XVI

*Of the sadness of Danny. How through sacrifice
Danny's Friends gave a party. How Danny was
Translated.*

WHEN Danny came back to
his house and to his friends after his amok, he was not
conscience stricken, but he was very tired. The rough
fingers of violent experience had harped upon his soul.
He began to live listlessly, arising from bed only to sit
on the porch, under the rose of Castile; arising from the
porch only to eat; arising from the table only to go to
bed. The talk flowed about him and he listened, but he
did not care. Cornelia Ruiz had a quick and superb run
of husbands, and no emotion was aroused in Danny.
When Big Joe got in his bed one evening, so apathetic
was Danny that Pilon and Pablo had to beat Big Joe for
him. When Sammy Rasper, celebrating a belated New

Year with a shotgun and a gallon of whisky, killed a cow and went to jail, Danny could not even be drawn into a discussion of the ethics of the case, although the arguments raged about him and although his judgment was passionately appealed to.

After a while it came about that the friends began to worry about Danny. "He is changed," said Pilon. "He is old."

Jesus Maria suggested, "This Danny has crowded the good times of a life into a little three weeks. He is sick of fun."

In vain the friends tried to draw him from the cavern of his apathy. In the mornings, on the porch, they told their funniest stories. They reported details of the love life of Tortilla Flat so penetrating that they would have been of interest to a dissection class. Pilon winnowed the Flat for news, and brought home every seedling of interest to Danny; but there was age in Danny's eyes and weariness.

"Thou art not well," Jesus Maria insisted in vain. "There is some bitter secret in thine heart."

"No," said Danny.

It was noticed that he let flies crawl on his feet a

long time, and that when he did slap them off there was no art in his stroke. Gradually the high spirits, the ready laughter went out of Danny's house and tumbled into the dark pool of Danny's quietness.

Oh, it was a pity to see him, that Danny who had fought for lost causes, or any other kind; that Danny who could drink glass for glass with any man in the world; that Danny who responded to the look of love like an aroused tiger. Now he sat on his front porch in the sunlight, his blue-jeaned knees drawn up against his chest, his arms hanging over, his hands dangling from limp wrists, his head bent forward as though by a heavy black thought. His eyes had no light of desire nor displeasure nor joy nor pain.

Poor Danny, how has life left thee! Here thou sittest like the first man before the world grew up around him; and like the last man, after the world has eroded away. But see, Danny! Thou art not alone. Thy friends are caught in this state of thine. They look at thee from their eye-corners. They wait like expectant little dogs for the first waking movement of their master. One joyful word from thee, Danny, one joyful look, and they will bark and chase their tails. Thy life is not thine own to govern, Danny, for it controls other lives. See how thy friends suffer! Spring to life, Danny, that thy friends may live again!

This, in effect, although not in words so beautiful, was what Pilon said. Pilon held out a jar of wine to Danny. "Come on," he said. "Get up off your can."

Danny took the jar and drained it. And then he settled back and tried to find again his emotional Nirvana.

"Do you hurt any place?" Pilon asked.

"No," said Danny.

Pilon poured him another jar of wine and watched his face while the wine disappeared. The eyes lost their lack-lustre. Somewhere in the depths, the old Danny stirred to life for a moment. He killed a fly with a stroke that would have done justice to a master.

Slowly a smile spread over Pilon's face. And later he gathered all the friends, Pablo and Jesus Maria and Big Joe and the Pirate and Johnny Pom-pom and Tito Ralph.

Pilon led them all into the gulch behind the house. "I gave Danny the last of the wine, and it did him good.

What Danny needs is lots of wine, and maybe a party. Where can we get wine?"

Their minds combed the possibilities of Monterey like rat terriers in a barn, but there were no rats. These friends were urged on by altruism more pure than most men can conceive. They loved Danny.

Jesus Maria said, finally, "Chin Kee is packing squids."

Their minds bolted, turned with curiosity and looked at the thing, crept steathily back and sniffed it. It was several moments before their shocked imaginations could become used to the thing. "But after all, why not?" they argued silently. "One day would not be so bad—only one day."

Their faces showed the progress of the battle, and how they were defeating their fears in the interest of Danny's welfare.

"We will do it," Pilon said. "To-morrow we will all go down and cut squid, and to-morrow night we will give a party for Danny."

When Danny awakened the next morning, the house was deserted. He got up from his bed and looked through the silent rooms. But Danny was not a man to brood very long. He gave it up as a problem, and then as a thought. He went to the front porch and listlessly sat down.

Is it premonition, Danny? Do you fear the fate that is closing in on you? Are there no pleasures left? No. Danny is as sunk in himself as he had been for a week.

Not so Tortilla Flat. Early the rumor flew about, "Danny's friends are cutting squids for Chin Kee." It was a portent, like the overthrow of government, or even of the solar system. It was spoken of in the street, called over back fences to ladies who were just then hurrying to tell it. "All of Danny's friends are down cutting squids."

The morning was electric with the news. There must be some reason, some secret. Mothers instructed their children and sent them running toward Chin Kee's squid yard. Young matrons waited anxiously behind their curtains for later news. And news came.

"Pablo has cut his hand with a squid knife."

"Chin Kee has kicked the Pirate's dogs."

Riot.

"The dogs are back."

"Pilon looks grim."

A few small bets were laid. For months nothing so exciting had happened. During one whole morning not a single person spoke of Cornelia Ruiz. It was not until the noon hour that the real news leaked out, but then it came with a rush.

"They are going to give a big party for Danny."

"Every one is going."

Instructions began to emerge from the squid yard. Mrs. Morales dusted her phonograph and picked out her loudest records. Some spark flared, and Tortilla Flat was tinder. Seven friends, indeed, to give a party for Danny! It is as though to say Danny had only seven friends! Mrs. Soto descended upon her chicken yard with a cleaver. Mrs. Palochico poured a bag of sugar into her largest cooking pot to make dulces. A delegation of girls went into the Woolworth store in Monterey and bought the complete stock of colored crepe paper. Guitars and accordions cried experimentally through the Flat.

News! More news from the squid yard. They are going to make it. They are firm. They will have at least fourteen dollars. See that fourteen gallons of wine are ready.

Torrelli was overwhelmed with business. Every one wanted to buy a gallon to take to Danny's house. Torrelli himself, caught in the fury of the movement, said to his wife, "Maybe we will go to Danny's house. I will take a few gallons for my friends."

As the afternoon passed, waves of excitement poured over the flat. Dresses unworn in a lifetime were unpacked and hung to air. Shawls the moths had yearned for during two hundred years hung from porch railings and exuded the odor of moth balls.

And Danny? He sat like a half-melted man. He moved only when the sun moved. If he realized that every inhabitant of Tortilla Flat had passed his gate that afternoon, he gave no sign. Poor Danny! At least two dozen pairs of eyes watched his front gate. At about four o'clock he stood up, stretched and sauntered out of his yard, toward Monterey.

Why, they hardly waited until he was out of sight. Oh, the twisting and stringing of green and yellow and red crepe paper! Oh, the candles shaved, and the shavings thrown on the floor! Oh, the mad children who skated the wax in evenly.

Food appeared. Basins of rice, pots of steaming

chicken, dumplings to startle you! And the wine came, gallons and gallons of it. Martinez dug up a keg of potato whisky from his manure pile and carried it to Danny's house.

At five-thirty the friends marched up the hill, tired and bloody, but triumphant. So must the Old Guard have looked when they returned to Paris after Austerlitz. They saw the house, bristling with color. They laughed, and their weariness fell from them. They were so happy that tears came into their eyes.

Mama Chipo walked into the yard followed by her two sons who carried a washtub of salsa pura between them. Paulito, that rich scamp, rushed the fire under a big kettle of beans and chili. Shouts, songs broken off, shrieks of women, the general turmoil of excited children.

A carful of apprehensive policemen drove up from Monterey. "Oh, it is only a party. Sure, we'll have a glass of wine. Don't kill anybody."

Where is Danny? Lonely as smoke on a clear cold night, he drifts through Monterey in the evening. To the post-office he goes, to the station, to the pool rooms on Alvarado Street, to the wharf where the black water mourns among the piles. What is it, Danny? What makes you feel this way? Danny didn't know. There was an ache in his heart like the farewell to a dear woman; there was vague sorrow in him like the despair of autumn. He walked past the restaurants he used to smell with interest, and no appetite was aroused in him. He walked by Madam Zuca's great establishment, and exchanged no obscene jests with the girls in the windows. Back to the wharf he went. He leaned over the rail and looked into the deep, deep water. Do you know, Danny, how the wine of your life is pouring into the fruit jars of the gods? Do you see the procession of your days in the oily water among the piles? He remained motionless, staring down.

They were worried about him at Danny's house, when it began to get dark. The friends left the party and trotted down the hill into Monterey. They asked, "Have you seen Danny?"

"Yes, Danny walked by here an hour ago. He walked slow."

Pilon and Pablo hunted together. They traced their friend over the route he had followed, and at last they saw him, on the end of the dark pier. He was lighted by a dim electric wharf light. They hurried out to him.

Pablo did not mention it then, but ever afterwards it was his custom, when Danny was mentioned, to describe what he saw as he and Pilon walked out on the wharf toward Danny. "There he stood," Pablo always said. "I could just see him, leaning on the rail. I looked at him, and then I saw something else. At first it looked like a black cloud in the air over Danny's head. And then I saw it was a big black bird, as big as a man. It hung in the air like a hawk over a rabbit hole. I crossed myself and said two Hail Marys. The bird was gone when we came to Danny."

Pilon did not see it. Moreover, Pilon did not remember Pablo crossing himself and saying the Hail Marys. But he never interfered with the story, for it was Pablo's story.

They walked rapidly toward Danny; the wharf boards drummed hollowly under their feet. Danny did not turn. They took him by the arms and turned him about.

"Danny! What is wrong?"

"Nothing. I'm all right."

"Are you sick, Danny?"

"No."

"Then what is it that makes you so sad?"

"I don't know," said Danny. "I just feel this way. I don't want to do anything."

"Maybe a doctor could do something for you, Danny."

"I tell you I am not sick."

"Then look," Pilon cried. "We are having a party for you at your house. Everybody in Tortilla Flat is there, and music and wine and chicken! There are maybe twenty or thirty gallons of wine. And bright paper hanging up. Don't you want to come?"

Danny breathed deeply. For a moment he turned back to the deep black water. Perhaps he whispered to the gods a promise or a defiance.

He swung around again to his friends. His eyes were feverish. "You're goddam right I want to go. Hurry up. I am thirsty. Any girls there?"

"Lots of girls. All the girls."

"Come on, then. Hurry up."

He led them, running up the hill. Long before they arrived they could hear the sweetness of the music through the pines, and the shrill notes of excited happy voices. The three belated ones arrived at a dead run. Danny lifted his head and howled like a coyote. Jars of wine were held out to him. He took a gulp from each one.

That was a party for you! Always afterward when a man spoke of a party with enthusiasm, some one was sure to say with reverence, "Did you go to that party at Danny's house?" And, unless the first speaker were a newcomer, he had been there. That was a party for you! No one ever tried to give a better one. Such a thing was unthinkable; for within two days Danny's party was lifted out of possible comparison with all other parties that ever were. What man came out of that night without some glorious cuts and bruises? Never had there been so many fights; not fights between two men, but roaring battles that raged through whole clots of men, each one for himself.

Oh, the laughter of women! Thin and high and brittle as spun glass. Oh, the lady-like shrieks of protest from the gulch. Father Ramon was absolutely astounded and incredulous at the confessions the next week. The whole happy soul of Tortilla Flat tore itself from restraint and arose into the air, one ecstatic unit. They danced so hard that the floor gave way in one corner.

The accordions played so loudly that always afterwards they were windbroken, like foundered horses.

And Danny—just as this party knew no comparison, so Danny defied emulation as a celebrant. In the future

let some squirt say with excitement, "Did you see me? Did you see me ask that nigger wenches for a dance? Did you seen us go 'round and 'round like a tom-cats?" and some old, wise and baleful eye would be turned on him. Some voice, sated with having known the limit of possibilities, would ask quietly, "Did you see Danny the night of the party?"

Some time a historian may write a cold, dry, fungus-like history of The Party. He may refer to the moment when Danny defied and attacked the whole party, men, women and children, with a table-leg. He may conclude, "A dying organism is often observed to be capable of extraordinary endurance and strength." Referring to Danny's super-human amorous activity that night, this same historian may write with unshaking hand: "When any living organism is attacked, its whole function seems to aim toward reproduction."

But I say, and the people of Tortilla Flat would say, "To hell with it. That Danny was a man for you!" No one kept actual count, and afterwards, naturally, no lady would willingly admit that she had been ignored; so that the reputed prowess of Danny may be somewhat overstated. One tenth of it would be an overstatement for any one in the world.

Where Danny went, a magnificent madness followed. It is passionately averred in Tortilla Flat that Danny alone drank three gallons of wine. It must be remembered, however, that Danny is now a god. In a few years it may be thirty gallons. In twenty years it may be plainly remembered that the clouds flamed and spelled DANNY in tremendous letters; that the moon dripped blood; that the wolf of the world bayed prophetically from the mountains of the Milky Way.

Gradually a few of those whose stuff was less stern than Danny's began to wilt, to sag, to creep out from under foot. Those who were left, feeling the lack, shouted the louder, fought the more viciously, danced the harder. In Monterey the motors of the fire trucks were kept running and the firemen, in their red tin hats and raincoats silently sat in their places and waited.

The night passed quickly, and still Danny roared through the party.

What happened is attested by many witnesses, both men and women. And although their value as witnesses is sometimes attacked on the ground that they had drunk thirty gallons of wine and a keg of potato whisky, those people are sullenly sure of the major points. It took some weeks to get the story into line, some said one thing, some another. But gradually the account clarified into the reasonable form it now has and always will have.

Danny, say the people of Tortilla Flat, had been rapidly changing his form. He had grown huge and terrible. His eyes flared like the headlights of an automobile. There was something fearsome about him. There he stood, in the room of his own house. He held the pine table-leg in his right hand, and even it had grown. Danny challenged the world.

"Who will fight?" he cried. "Is there no one left in the world who is not afraid?" The people were afraid; that table-leg, so hideous and so alive, had become a terror to them all. Danny swung it back and forth. The accordions wheezed to silence. The dancing stopped. The room grew chill and a silence seemed to roar in the air like an ocean.

"No one?" Danny cried again. "Am I alone in the world? Will no one fight with me?" The men shuddered before his terrible eyes, and watched fascinated the slashing path of the table-leg through the air. And no one answered the challenge.

Danny drew himself up. It is said that his head just missed touching the ceiling. "Then I will go out to The One who can fight. I will find The Enemy who is worthy of Danny!" He stalked to the door, staggering a little as he went. The terrified people made a broad path for him. He bent to get out of the door. The people stood still and listened.

Outside the house they heard his roaring challenge. They heard the table-leg whistle like a meteor through the air. They heard his footsteps charging down the yard. And then, behind the house, in the gulch, they heard an answering challenge so fearful and so chill that their spines wilted like nasturtium stems under frost. Even now, when the people speak of Danny's Opponent, they lower their voices and look furtively about. They heard Danny charge to the fray. They heard his last shrill cry of defiance, and then a thump. And then silence.

For a long moment the people waited, holding their breaths lest the harsh rush of air from their lungs should obscure some sound. But they listened in vain. The night was hushed, and the gray dawn was coming.

Pilon broke the silence. "Something is wrong," he said. And Pilon it was who first rushed out of the door. Brave man, no terror could restrain him. The people followed him. Back of the house they went, where Danny's footsteps had sounded, and there was no Danny. They came to the edge of the gulch, where a sharp zig-zag path led down to the bottom of that ancient water-course wherein no stream had flowed for many genera-

tions. The following people saw Pilon dart down the path. They went after him, slowly. And they found Pilon at the bottom of the gulch, leaning over a broken and twisted Danny. He had fallen forty feet. Pilon lighted a match. "I think he is alive," he shrieked. "Run for a doctor. Run for Father Ramon."

The people scattered. Within fifteen minutes four doctors were awakened, dragged from their beds by frantic paisanos. They were not allowed that slow deliberateness by which doctors love to show that they are no slaves to emotion. No! They were hustled, rushed, pushed, their instrument cases were shoved into their hands by men hopelessly incapable of saying what they wanted. Father Ramon, dragged from his bed, came panting up the hill, uncertain whether it was a devil to drive out, a newborn baby to baptize before it died or a lynching to attend. Meanwhile Pilon and Pablo and Jesus Maria carried Danny up the hill and laid him on his bed. They stood candles all about him. Danny was breathing heavily.

First the doctors arrived. They glanced suspiciously at one another, considered precedence; but the moment of delay brought threatening looks into the eyes of the people. It did not take long to look Danny over. They were all through by the time Father Ramon arrived.

I shall not go into the bedroom with Father Ramon, for Pilon and Pablo and Jesus Maria and Big Joe and Johnny Pom-pom and Tito Ralph and the Pirate and the dogs were there; and they were Danny's family. The door was, and is, closed. For after all there is pride in men, and some things cannot decently be pried into.

But in the big room, crowded to suffocation with the people of Tortilla Flat, there was tenseness and a waiting silence. Priests and doctors have developed a subtle means of communication. When Father Ramon came out of the bedroom his face had not changed, but at sight of him the women broke into a high and terrible wail. The men shifted their feet like horses in a box-stall, and then went outside into the dawning. And the bedroom door remained closed.

# XVII

*How Danny's sorrowing Friends defied the conventions. How the Talismanic Bond was burned. How each Friend departed alone.*

DEATH is a personal matter, arousing sorrow, despair, fervor or dry-hearted philosophy. Funerals, on the other hand, are social functions. Imagine going to a funeral without first polishing the automobile. Imagine standing at a graveside not dressed in your best dark suit and your best black shoes, polished delightfully. Imagine sending flowers to a funeral with no attached card to prove you had done the correct thing. In no social institution is the codified ritual of behavior more rigid than in funerals. Imagine the indignation if the minister altered his sermon or experimented with facial expression. Consider the shock if, at the funeral parlors, any chairs were used but those little folding yellow torture chairs with the hard seats. No, dying, a man may be loved, hated, mourned, missed; but once dead he becomes the chief ornament of a complicated and formal social celebration.

Danny was dead, two days dead; and already he had ceased to be Danny. Although the faces of the people were decently and mournfully veiled with gloom, there was excitement in their hearts. The government has promised a military funeral to all of its ex-soldier sons who wish it. Danny was the first of Tortilla Flat to go, and Tortilla Flat was ready critically to test the government promises. Already news had been sent to the Presidio and Danny's body had been embalmed at government expense. Already a caisson was newly painted and waiting in the artillery shed with a neat new flag folded on top of it. Already orders of the day for Friday were made out:

"Ten to eleven A.M., funeral. Escort, Squadron A, 11th Cavalry, 11th Cavalry Band and Firing Squad."

Were these not things to set every woman in Tortilla Flat window shopping at the National Dollar Store in Monterey? During the day dark children walked the streets of Monterey begging flowers from the gardens for Danny's funeral. And at night the same children visited the same gardens to augment their bouquets.

At the party, the finest clothes had been worn. During the two-day interval, those clothes had to be cleaned, washed, starched, mended and ironed. The activity was frantic. The excitement was decently intense.

On the evening of the second day, Danny's friends were gathered in Danny's house. The shock and the wine had worn off; and now they were horror-stricken, for in all Tortilla Flat they, who had loved Danny most, who had received the most from his hands, they, the paisanos, were the only ones who could not attend Danny's funeral. Through the murk of the headaches they had been conscious of this appalling tragedy, but only on this evening had the situation become so concrete that it must be faced. Ordinarily, their clothes were unspeakable. The party had aged their jeans and blue shirts by years. Where was the trouser knee unburst? Where the shirt unripped? If any one else had died, they could have borrowed clothes; but there was no person in Tortilla Flat who was not going to wear his good clothes to the funeral. Only Cocky Riordan was not going, but Cocky was in quarantine for smallpox, and so were his clothes. Money might be begged or stolen to buy one good suit, but money for six suits was simply impossible to get.

You may say, did they not love Danny enough to go to his funeral in rags? Would you go in rags when your neighbors were dressed in finery? Would not the disrespect to Danny be more if they went in rags than if they did not go at all?

The despair that lay on their hearts was incalculable. They cursed their fate. Through the front door they could see Galvez parading by. Galvez had bought a new suit for the funeral, and he had it on twenty-four hours in advance. The friends sat, chin in hand, crushed by their ill fortune. Every possibility had been discussed.

Pilon, for once in his life, descended to absurdity. "We might go out to-night and each one steal a suit," he suggested. He knew that was silly, for every suit would be laid on a chair beside a bed that night. It would be death to steal a suit.

"The Salvation Army sometimes gives suits," said Jesus Maria.

"I have been there," Pablo said. "They have fourteen dresses this time, but no suits."

On every side Fate was against them. Tito Ralph came in with his new green handkerchief sticking out of his breast pocket, but the hostility he aroused made him back apologetically out of the room.

"If we had a week, we could cut squids," Pilon said heroically. "The funeral is tomorrow. We must look in the eye at this thing. Of course we can go to the funeral all right."

"How?" the friends demanded.

"We can go on the sidewalk, while the band and the people march in the street. It is all grass around the cemetery fence. We can lie there in the grass and see everything."

The friends looked at Pilon gratefully. They knew how his sharp wits had been digging over possibilities. But it was only half, less than half, to see the funeral. Being seen at the funeral was the more important half. This was the best that could be done.

"In this we learn a lesson," said Pilon. "We must take it to heart that we should always have a good suit of clothes laid by. We can never tell what may happen."

There they left it, but they felt that they had failed. All through the night they wandered in the town. What yard then was not plundered of its finest blooms? What flowering tree remained standing? In the morning the hole in the cemetery that was to receive Danny's body was almost hidden by a mound of the finest flowers from the best gardens in Monterey.

It is not always that Nature arranges her effects with good taste. Truly, it rained before Waterloo; forty feet of snow fell in the path of the Donner Party. But Friday turned out a nice day. The sun arose as though this were a day for a picnic. The gulls flew in across a smiling bay to the sardine canneries. The rock fishermen took their places on the rocks for the ebbing tide. The Palace Drug Company ran down its awnings to protect the red hot-water bottles in its windows from the chemical action of the sun. Mr. Machado, the tailor, put a sign in his window, Back In Ten Minutes, and went home to dress for the funeral. Three purse seiners came in, loaded with sardines. Louie Duarte painted his boat, and changed its name from Lolita to The Three Cousins. Jake Lake, the cop, arrested a roadster from Del Monte and turned it loose and bought a cigar.

It is a puzzle. How can life go on its stupid course on such a day? How can Mamie Jackson hose off her front sidewalk? How can George W. Merk write his fourth and angriest letter to the water company? How can Charlie Marsh be as dirtily drunk as usual? It is sacrilege. It is outrage.

Danny's friends awakened sadly, and got up off the floor. Danny's bed was empty. It was like the riderless charger of an officer which follows its master to his grave. Even Big Joe Portagee had cast no covetous glance at Danny's bed. The sun shone enthusiastically through the window and cast the delicate shadows of spider webs on the floor.

"Danny was glad on mornings like this," said Pilon.

After their trip to the gulch, the friends sat for a while on the front porch and celebrated the memory of their friend. Loyally they remembered and proclaimed Danny's virtues. Loyally they forgot his faults.

"And strong," said Pablo. "He was as strong as a mule! He could lift a bale of hay."

They told little stories of Danny, of his goodness, his courage, his piety.

All too soon it was time to go to the church, to stand

312

across the street in their ragged clothes. They blushed inwardly when luckier people went into the church, dressed so beautifully, smelling so prodigally of Agua Florida. The friends could hear the music and the shrill drone of the service. From their vantage point they saw the cavalry arrive, and the band with muffled drums, and the firing squad, and the caisson with its three pairs of horses, and a cavalryman on the near horse of each pair. The mournful clop-clop of shod horses on asphalt put despair in the hearts of the friends. Helplessly they watched the casket carried out and laid on the caisson, and the flag draped over it. The officer blew his whistle, raised his hand and threw it forward. The squadron moved, the firing squad dropped its rifles. The drums thundered their heart-breaking, slow rhythm. The band played its sodden march. The caisson moved. The people walked majestically behind, men straight and stern, women daintily holding their skirts up out of the indelible trail of the cavalry. Every one was there, Cornelia Ruiz, Mrs. Morales, Galvez, Torrelli and his plump wife, Mrs. Palochico, Tito Ralph the traitor, Sweets Ramirez, Mr. Machado, every one who amounted to anything on Tortilla Flat, and every one else, was there.

Is it any wonder that the friends could not stand the shame and misery of it? For a little while they slunk along the sidewalk, bolstered with heroism.

Jesus Maria broke down first. He sobbed with shame, for his father had been a rich and respected prize-fighter. Jesus Maria put down his head and bolted; and the five other friends followed, and the five dogs bounded behind them.

Before the procession was in sight, Danny's friends were lying in the tall grass that edged the cemetery. The service was short and military. The casket was lowered; the rifles cracked; the bugle sang taps, and at the sound Enrique and Fluff, Pajarito and Rudolph and Señor Alec Thompson laid back their heads and howled. The Pirate was proud of them then!

It was over too soon; the friends walked hurriedly away so that the people would not see them.

They had to pass Torrelli's deserted house anyway, on the way home. Pilon went in through a window and brought out two gallons of wine. And then they walked slowly back to the Danny's quiet house. Ceremoniously they filled the fruit jars and drank.

"Danny liked wine," they said. "Danny was happy when he had a little wine."

The afternoon passed, and the evening came. Each man, as he sipped his wine, roved through the past. At seven o'clock a shamed Tito Ralph came in with a box of cigars he had won on a punch board. The friends lighted the cigars and spat, and opened the second gallon. Pablo tried a few notes of the song "Tuli Pan," to see whether his voice was gone for good.

"Cornelia Ruiz was alone to-day," Pilon said speculatively.

"Maybe it would be all right to sing a few sad songs,' said Jesus Maria.

"But Danny did not like sad songs," Pablo insisted. "He liked the quick ones, about lively women."

They all nodded gravely. "Yes, Danny was a great one for women."

Pablo tried the second verse to "Tuli Pan," and Pilon helped a little, and the others joined in toward the end.

When the song was done, Pilon puffed at his cigar, but it had gone out. "Tito Ralph," he said, "Why don't you get your guitar so we can sing a little better?" He lighted his cigar and flipped the match.

The little burning stick landed on an old newspaper against the wall. Each man started up to stamp it out; and each man was struck with a celestial thought, and settled back. They found one another's eyes and smiled the wise smiles of the deathless and hopeless ones. In a reverie they watched the flame flicker and nearly die, and sprout to life again. They saw it bloom on the paper. Thus do the gods speak with tiny causes. And the men smiled on as the paper burned and the dry wooden wall caught.

Thus must it be, oh, wise friends of Danny. The cord that bound you together is cut. The magnet that drew you has lost its virtue. Some stranger will own the house, some joyless relative of Danny's. Better that this symbol of holy friendship, this good house of parties and fights, of love and comfort, should die as Danny died, in one last glorious hopeless assault on the gods.

They sat and smiled. And the flame climbed like a snake to the ceiling and broke through the roof and roared. Only then did the friends get up from their chairs and walk like dreaming men out of the door.

Pilon, who profited by every lesson, took what was left of the wine with him.

The sirens screamed from Monterey. The trucks roared up the hill in second gear. The searchlights played among the trees. When the Department arrived, the house was one great blunt spear of flame. The hoses wet the trees and brush to keep the flames from spreading.

Among the crowding people of Tortilla Flat Danny's friends stood entranced and watched until at last the house was a mound of black, steaming cinders. Then the fire trucks turned and coasted away down the hill.

The people of the Flat melted into the darkness. Danny's friends still stood looking at the smoking ruin. They looked at one another strangely, and then back to the burned house. And after a while they turned and walked slowly away, and no two walked together.

# OF MICE AND MEN

# I

A FEW MILES south of Soledad, the Salinas River drops in close to the hillside bank and runs deep and green. The water is warm too, for it has slipped twinkling over the yellow sands in the sunlight before reaching the narrow pool. On one side of the river the golden foothill slopes curve up to the strong and rocky Gabilan mountains, but on the valley side the water is lined with trees—willows fresh and green with every spring, carrying in their lower leaf junctures the debris of the winter's flooding; and sycamores with mottled, white, recumbent limbs and branches that arch over the pool. On the sandy bank under the trees the leaves lie deep and so crisp that a lizard makes a great skittering if he runs among them. Rabbits come out of the brush to sit on the sand in the evening, and the damp flats are covered with the night tracks of 'coons, and with the spread pads of dogs from the ranches, and with the split-wedge tracks of deer that come to drink in the dark.

There is a path through the willows and among the sycamores, a path beaten hard by boys coming down from the ranches to swim in the deep pool, and beaten hard by tramps who come wearily down from the highway in the evening to jungle-up near water. In front of the low horizontal limb of a giant sycamore there is an ash pile made by many fires; the limb is worn smooth by men who have sat on it.

Evening of a hot day started the little wind to moving among the leaves. The shade climbed up the hills toward the top. On the sand banks the rabbits sat as quietly as little gray, sculptured stones. And then from the direction of the state highway came the sound of footsteps on crisp sycamore leaves. The rabbits hurried noiselessly for cover. A stilted heron labored up into the air and pounded down river. For a moment the place was lifeless, and then two men emerged from the path and came into the opening by the green pool.

They had walked in single file down the path, and even in the open one stayed behind the other. Both were dressed in denim trousers and in denim coats with brass buttons. Both wore black, shapeless hats and both carried tight blanket rolls slung over their shoulders. The first man was small and quick, dark of face, with restless eyes and sharp, strong features. Every part of him was defined: small, strong hands, slender arms, a thin and bony nose. Behind him walked his opposite, a huge man, shapeless of face, with large, pale eyes, with wide, sloping shoulders; and he walked heavily, dragging his feet a little, the way a bear drags his paws. His arms did not swing at his sides, but hung loosely.

The first man stopped short in the clearing,

and the follower nearly ran over him. He took
off his hat and wiped the sweat-band with his
forefinger and snapped the moisture off. His
huge companion dropped his blankets and flung
himself down and drank from the surface of the
green pool; drank with long gulps, snorting into
the water like a horse. The small man stepped
nervously beside him.

"Lennie!" he said sharply. "Lennie, for God'
sakes don't drink so much." Lennie continued
to snort into the pool. The small man leaned
over and shook him by the shoulder. "Lennie.
You gonna be sick like you was last night."

Lennie dipped his whole head under, hat and
all, and then he sat up on the bank and his hat
dripped down on his blue coat and ran down his
back. "Tha's good," he said. "You drink some,
George. You take a good big drink." He smiled
happily.

George unslung his bindle and dropped it
gently on the bank. "I ain't sure it's good water,"
he said. "Looks kinda scummy."

Lennie dabbled his big paw in the water and wiggled his fingers so the water arose in little splashes; rings widened across the pool to the other side and came back again. Lennie watched them go. "Look, George. Look what I done."

George knelt beside the pool and drank from his hand with quick scoops. "Tastes all right," he admitted. "Don't really seem to be running, though. You never oughta drink water when it ain't running, Lennie," he said hopelessly. "You'd drink out of a gutter if you was thirsty." He threw a scoop of water into his face and rubbed it about with his hand, under his chin and around the back of his neck. Then he replaced his hat, pushed himself back from the river, drew up his knees and embraced them. Lennie, who had been watching, imitated George exactly. He pushed himself back, drew up his knees, embraced them, looked over to George to see whether he had it just right. He pulled his hat down a little more over his eyes, the way George's hat was.

George stared morosely at the water. The rims of his eyes were red with sun glare. He said angrily, "We could just as well of rode clear to the ranch if that bastard bus driver knew what he was talkin' about. 'Jes' a little stretch down the highway,' he says. 'Jes' a little stretch.' God damn near four miles, that's what it was! Didn't wanta stop at the ranch gate, that's what. Too God damn lazy to pull up. Wonder he isn't too damn good to stop in Soledad at all. Kicks us out and says, 'Jes' a little stretch down the road.' I bet it was *more* than four miles. Damn hot day."

Lennie looked timidly over to him. "George?"

"Yeah, what ya want?"

"Where we goin', George?"

The little man jerked down the brim of his hat and scowled over at Lennie. "So you forgot that awready, did you? I gotta tell you again, do I? Jesus Christ, you're a crazy bastard!"

"I forgot," Lennie said softly. "I tried not to forget. Honest to God I did, George."

"O.K.—O.K. I'll tell ya again. I ain't got nothing to do. Might jus' as well spen' all my time tellin' you things and then you forget 'em, and I tell you again."

"Tried and tried," said Lennie, "but it didn't do no good. I remember about the rabbits, George."

"The hell with the rabbits. That's all you ever can remember is them rabbits. O.K! Now you listen and this time you got to remember so we don't get in no trouble. You remember settin' in that gutter on Howard street and watchin' that blackboard?"

Lennie's face broke into a delighted smile. "Why sure, George. I remember that . . . . but . . . . what'd we do then? I remember some girls come by and you says . . . . you say . . . ."

"The hell with what I says. You remember about us goin' into Murray and Ready's, and they give us work cards and bus tickets?"

"Oh, sure, George. I remember that now." His hands went quickly into his side coat pockets. He said gently, "George . . . . I ain't got mine. I musta lost it." He looked down at the ground in despair.

"You never had none, you crazy bastard. I got both of 'em here. Think I'd let you carry your own work card?"

Lennie grinned with relief. "I . . . . I thought I put it in my side pocket." His hand went into the pocket again.

George looked sharply at him. "What'd you take outa that pocket?"

"Ain't a thing in my pocket," Lennie said cleverly.

"I know there ain't. You got it in your hand. What you got in your hand—hidin' it?"

"I ain't got nothin', George. Honest."

"Come on, give it here."

Lennie held his closed hand away from George's direction. "It's on'y a mouse, George."

"A mouse? A live mouse?"

"Uh-uh. Jus' a dead mouse, George. I didn' kill it. Honest! I found it. I found it dead."

"Give it here!" said George.

"Aw, leave me have it, George."

*"Give it here!"*

Lennie's closed hand slowly obeyed. George took the mouse and threw it across the pool to the other side, among the brush. "What you want of a dead mouse, anyways?"

"I could pet it with my thumb while we walked along," said Lennie.

"Well, you ain't petting no mice while you walk with me. You remember where we're goin' now?"

Lennie looked startled and then in embarrassment hid his face against his knees. "I forgot again."

"Jesus Christ," George said resignedly. "Well —look, we're gonna work on a ranch like the one we come from up north."

"Up north?"

"In Weed."

"Oh, sure. I remember. In Weed."

"That ranch we're goin' to is right down

there about a quarter mile. We're gonna go in an' see the boss. Now, look—I'll give him the work tickets, but you ain't gonna say a word. You jus' stand there and don't say nothing. If he finds out what a crazy bastard you are, we won't get no job, but if he sees ya work before he hears ya talk, we're set. Ya got that?"

"Sure, George. Sure I got it."

"O.K. Now when we go in to see the boss, what you gonna do?"

"I . . . . I," Lennie thought. His face grew tight with thought. "I . . . . ain't gonna say nothin'. Jus' gonna stan' there."

"Good boy. That's swell. You say that over two, three times so you sure won't forget it."

Lennie droned to himself softly, "I ain't gonna say nothin' . . . . I ain't gonna say nothin' . . . . I ain't gonna say nothin'."

"O.K.," said George. "An' you ain't gonna do no bad things like you done in Weed, neither."

Lennie looked puzzled. "Like I done in Weed?"

"Oh, so ya forgot that too, did ya? Well, I ain't gonna remind ya, fear ya do it again."

A light of understanding broke on Lennie's face. "They run us outa Weed," he exploded triumphantly.

"Run us out, hell," said George disgustedly. "We run. They was lookin' for us, but they didn't catch us."

Lennie giggled happily. "I didn't forget that, you bet."

George lay back on the sand and crossed his hands under his head, and Lennie imitated him, raising his head to see whether he were doing it right. "God, you're a lot of trouble," said George. "I could get along so easy and so nice if I didn't have you on my tail. I could live so easy and maybe have a girl."

For a moment Lennie lay quiet, and then he said hopefully, "We gonna work on a ranch, George."

"Awright. You got that. But we're gonna sleep here because I got a reason."

The day was going fast now. Only the tops of the Gabilan mountains flamed with the light of the sun that had gone from the valley. A water snake slipped along on the pool, its head held up like a little periscope. The reeds jerked slightly in the current. Far off toward the highway a man shouted something, and another man shouted back. The sycamore limbs rustled under a little wind that died immediately.

"George—why ain't we goin' on to the ranch and get some supper? They got supper at the ranch."

George rolled on his side. "No reason at all for you. I like it here. Tomorra we're gonna go to work. I seen thrashin' machines on the way down. That means we'll be bucking grain bags, bustin' a gut. Tonight I'm gonna lay right here and look up. I like it."

Lennie got up on his knees and looked down at George. "Ain't we gonna have no supper?"

"Sure we are, if you gather up some dead willow sticks. I got three cans of beans in my bindle. You get a fire ready. I'll give you a match when you get the sticks together. Then we'll heat the beans and have supper."

Lennie said, "I like beans with ketchup."

"Well, we ain't got no ketchup. You go get wood. An' don't you fool around. It'll be dark before long."

Lennie lumbered to his feet and disappeared in the brush. George lay where he was and whistled softly to himself. There were sounds of splashings down the river in the direction Lennie had taken. George stopped whistling and listened. "Poor bastard," he said softly, and then went on whistling again.

In a moment Lennie came crashing back through the brush. He carried one small willow stick in his hand. George sat up. "Awright," he said brusquely. "Gi'me that mouse!"

But Lennie made an elaborate pantomime of innocence. "What mouse, George? I ain't got no mouse."

George held out his hand. "Come on. Give it to me. You ain't puttin' nothing over."

Lennie hesitated, backed away, looked wildly at the brush line as though he contemplated running for his freedom. George said coldly, "You gonna give me that mouse or do I have to sock you?"

"Give you what, George?"

"You know God damn well what. I want that mouse."

Lennie reluctantly reached into his pocket. His voice broke a little. "I don't know why I can't keep it. It ain't nobody's mouse. I didn't steal it. I found it lyin' right beside the road."

George's hand remained outstretched imperiously. Slowly, like a terrier who doesn't want to bring a ball to its master, Lennie approached, drew back, approached again. George snapped his fingers sharply, and at the sound Lennie laid the mouse in his hand.

"I wasn't doin' nothing bad with it, George. Jus' strokin' it."

George stood up and threw the mouse as far as he could into the darkening brush, and then he stepped to the pool and washed his hands. "You crazy fool. Don't you think I could see your feet was wet where you went acrost the river to get it?" He heard Lennie's whimpering cry and wheeled about. "Blubberin' like a baby! Jesus Christ! A big guy like you." Lennie's lip quivered and tears started in his eyes. "Aw, Lennie!" George put his hand on Lennie's shoulder. "I ain't takin' it away jus' for meanness. That mouse ain't fresh, Lennie; and besides, you've broke it pettin' it. You get another mouse that's fresh and I'll let you keep it a little while."

Lennie sat down on the ground and hung his head dejectedly. "I don't know where there is no other mouse. I remember a lady used to give 'em to me—ever' one she got. But that lady ain't here."

George scoffed. "Lady, huh? Don't even remember who that lady was. That was your own Aunt Clara. An' she stopped givin' 'em to ya. You always killed 'em."

Lennie looked sadly up at him. "They was so

little," he said, apologetically. "I'd pet 'em, and pretty soon they bit my fingers and I pinched their heads a little and then they was dead—because they was so little."

"I wish't we'd get the rabbits pretty soon, George. They ain't so little."

"The hell with the rabbits. An' you ain't to be trusted with no live mice. Your Aunt Clara give you a rubber mouse and you wouldn't have nothing to do with it."

"It wasn't no good to pet," said Lennie.

The flame of the sunset lifted from the mountaintops and dusk came into the valley, and a half darkness came in among the willows and the sycamores. A big carp rose to the surface of the pool, gulped air and then sank mysteriously into the dark water again, leaving widening rings on the water. Overhead the leaves whisked again and little puffs of willow cotton blew down and landed on the pool's surface.

"You gonna get that wood?" George demanded. "There's plenty right up against the back of that sycamore. Floodwater wood. Now you get it."

Lennie went behind the tree and brought out a litter of dried leaves and twigs. He threw them in a heap on the old ash pile and went back for more and more. It was almost night now. A dove's wings whistled over the water. George walked to the fire pile and lighted the dry leaves. The flame cracked up among the twigs and fell to work. George undid his bindle and brought out three cans of beans. He stood them about the fire, close in against the blaze, but not quite touching the flame.

"There's enough beans for four men," George said.

Lennie watched him from over the fire. He said patiently, "I like 'em with ketchup."

"Well, we ain't got any," George exploded. "Whatever we ain't got, that's what you want. God a'mighty, if I was alone I could live so easy. I could go get a job an' work, an' no trouble. No mess at all, and when the end of the month come I could take my fifty bucks and go into town and get whatever I want. Why, I could stay in a cat house all night. I could eat any place I want, hotel or any place, and order any damn thing I could think of. An' I could do all that every damn month. Get a gallon of whisky, or set in a pool room and play cards or shoot pool." Lennie knelt and looked over the fire at the angry George. And Lennie's face was drawn with terror. "An' whatta I got," George went on furiously. "I got you! You can't keep a job and you lose me ever' job I get. Jus' keep me shovin' all over the country all the time. An' that ain't the worst. You get in trouble. You do bad things and I got to get you out." His voice rose nearly to a shout. "You crazy son-of-a-bitch. You keep me in hot water all the time." He took on the elaborate manner of little girls when they are mimicking one another. "Jus' wanted to feel that girl's dress—jus' wanted to pet it like it was a mouse—— Well, how the hell did she know you jus' wanted to feel her dress?

She jerks back and you hold on like it was a mouse. She yells and we got to hide in a irrigation ditch all day with guys lookin' for us, and we got to sneak out in the dark and get outta the country. All the time somethin' like that—all the time. I wisht I could put you in a cage with about a million mice an' let you have fun." His anger left him suddenly. He looked across the fire at Lennie's anguished face, and then he looked ashamedly at the flames.

It was quite dark now, but the fire lighted the trunks of the trees and the curving branches overhead. Lennie crawled slowly and cautiously around the fire until he was close to George. He sat back on his heels. George turned the bean cans so that another side faced the fire. He pretended to be unaware of Lennie so close beside him.

"George," very softly. No answer. "George!"

"Whatta you want?"

"I was only foolin', George. I don't want no ketchup. I wouldn't eat no ketchup if it was right here beside me."

"If it was here, you could have some."

"But I wouldn't eat none, George. I'd leave it all for you. You could cover your beans with it and I wouldn't touch none of it."

George still stared morosely at the fire. "When I think of the swell time I could have without you, I go nuts. I never get no peace."

Lennie still knelt. He looked off into the darkness across the river. "George, you want I should go away and leave you alone?"

"Where the hell could you go?"

"Well, I could. I could go off in the hills there. Some place I'd find a cave."

"Yeah? How'd you eat. You ain't got sense enough to find nothing to eat."

"I'd find things, George. I don't need no nice food with ketchup. I'd lay out in the sun and nobody'd hurt me. An' if I foun' a mouse, I could keep it. Nobody'd take it away from me."

George looked quickly and searchingly at him. "I been mean, ain't I?"

"If you don' want me I can go off in the hills

an' find a cave. I can go away any time."

"No—look! I was jus' foolin', Lennie. 'Cause I want you to stay with me. Trouble with mice is you always kill 'em." He paused. "Tell you what I'll do, Lennie. First chance I get I'll give you a pup. Maybe you wouldn't kill *it*. That'd be better than mice. And you could pet it harder."

Lennie avoided the bait. He had sensed his advantage. "If you don't want me, you only jus' got to say so, and I'll go off in those hills right there—right up in those hills and live by myself. An' I won't get no mice stole from me."

George said, "I want you to stay with me, Lennie. Jesus Christ, somebody'd shoot you for a coyote if you was by yourself. No, you stay with me. Your Aunt Clara wouldn't like you running off by yourself, even if she is dead."

Lennie spoke craftily, "Tell me—like you done before."

"Tell you what?"

"About the rabbits."

George snapped, "You ain't gonna put nothing over on me."

Lennie pleaded, "Come on, George. Tell me. Please, George. Like you done before."

"You get a kick outta that, don't you? Awright, I'll tell you, and then we'll eat our supper. . . ."

George's voice became deeper. He repeated his words rhythmically as though he had said them many times before. "Guys like us, that work on ranches, are the loneliest guys in the world. They got no family. They don't belong no place. They come to a ranch an' work up a stake and then they go inta town and blow their stake, and the first thing you know they're poundin' their tail on some other ranch. They ain't got nothing to look ahead to."

Lennie was delighted. 'That's it—that's it. Now tell how it is with us."

George went on. "With us it ain't like that. We got a future. We got somebody to talk to that gives a damn about us. We don't have to sit in no bar room blowin' in our jack jus' because we got no place else to go. If them other guys gets in jail they can rot for all anybody gives a damn. But not us."

Lennie broke in. *"But not us! An' why? Because . . . . because I got you to look after me, and you got me to look after you, and that's why."* He laughed delightedly. "Go on now, George!"

"You got it by heart. You can do it yourself."

"No, you. I forget some a' the things. Tell about how it's gonna be."

"O.K. Someday—we're gonna get the jack together and we're gonna have a little house and a couple of acres an' a cow and some pigs and——"

*"An' live off the fatta the lan',"* Lennie shouted. "An' have *rabbits*. Go on, George! Tell about what we're gonna have in the garden and about the rabbits in the cages and about the rain in the winter and the stove, and how thick the

cream is on the milk like you can hardly cut it. Tell about that, George."

"Why'n't you do it yourself? You know all of it."

"No . . . . you tell it. It ain't the same if I tell it. Go on . . . . George. How I get to tend the rabbits."

"Well," said George, "we'll have a big vegetable patch and a rabbit hutch and chickens. And when it rains in the winter, we'll just say the hell with goin' to work, and we'll build up a fire in the stove and set around it an' listen to the rain comin' down on the roof—Nuts!" He took out his pocket knife. "I ain't got time for no more." He drove his knife through the top of one of the bean cans, sawed out the top and passed the can to Lennie. Then he opened a second can. From his side pocket he brought out two spoons and passed one of them to Lennie.

They sat by the fire and filled their mouths with beans and chewed mightily. A few beans slipped out of the side of Lennie's mouth.

George gestured with his spoon. "What you gonna say tomorrow when the boss asks you questions?"

Lennie stopped chewing and swallowed. His face was concentrated. "I . . . . I ain't gonna . . . . say a word."

"Good boy! That's fine, Lennie! Maybe you're gettin' better. When we get the coupla acres I can let you tend the rabbits all right. 'Specially if you remember as good as that."

Lennie choked with pride. "I can remember," he said.

George motioned with his spoon again. "Look, Lennie. I want you to look around here. You can remember this place, can't you? The ranch is about a quarter mile up that way. Just follow the river?"

"Sure," said Lennie. "I can remember this. Di'n't I remember about not gonna say a word?"

" 'Course you did. Well, look. Lennie—if you jus' happen to get in trouble like you always

done before, I want you to come right here an'
hide in the brush."

"Hide in the brush," said Lennie slowly.

"Hide in the brush till I come for you. Can
you remember that?"

"Sure I can, George. Hide in the brush till
you come."

"But you ain't gonna get in no trouble, because if you do, I won't let you tend the rabbits." He threw his empty bean can off into
the brush.

"I won't get in no trouble, George. I ain't
gonna say a word."

"O.K. Bring your bindle over here by the
fire. It's gonna be nice sleepin' here. Lookin' up,
and the leaves. Don't build up no more fire.
We'll let her die down."

They made their beds on the sand, and as the
blaze dropped from the fire the sphere of light
grew smaller; the curling branches disappeared
and only a faint glimmer showed where the tree
trunks were. From the darkness Lennie called,
"George—you asleep?"

"No. Whatta you want?"

"Let's have different color rabbits, George."

"Sure we will," George said sleepily. "Red and blue and green rabbits, Lennie. Millions of 'em."

"Furry ones, George, like I seen in the fair in Sacramento."

"Sure, furry ones."

" 'Cause I can jus' as well go away, George, an' live in a cave."

"You can jus' as well go to hell," said George. "Shut up now."

The red light dimmed on the coals. Up the hill from the river a coyote yammered, and a dog answered from the other side of the stream. The sycamore leaves whispered in a little night breeze.

# 2

THE bunk house was a long, rectangular building. Inside, the walls were whitewashed and the floor unpainted. In three walls there were small, square windows, and in the fourth, a solid door with a wooden latch. Against the walls were eight bunks, five of them made up with blankets and the other three showing their burlap ticking. Over each bunk there was nailed an apple box with the opening forward so that it made two shelves for the personal belongings of the occupant of the bunk. And these shelves were loaded with little articles, soap and talcum powder, razors and those Western magazines ranch men love to read and scoff at and secretly believe. And there were medicines on the shelves, and little vials, combs; and from nails on the box sides, a few neckties. Near one wall there was a black cast-iron stove, its stovepipe going straight up through the ceiling. In the middle of the room stood a big square table littered with playing cards, and around it were grouped boxes for the players to sit on.

At about ten o'clock in the morning the sun threw a bright dust-laden bar through one of the side windows, and in and out of the beam flies shot like rushing stars.

The wooden latch raised. The door opened and a tall, stoop-shouldered old man came in. He was dressed in blue jeans and he carried a big push-broom in his left hand. Behind him came George, and behind George, Lennie.

"The boss was expectin' you last night," the old man said. "He was sore as hell when you wasn't here to go out this morning." He pointed with his right arm, and out of the sleeve came a round stick-like wrist, but no hand. "You can have them two beds there," he said, indicating two bunks near the stove.

George stepped over and threw his blankets down on the burlap sack of straw that was a mattress. He looked into his box shelf and then picked a small yellow can from it. "Say. What the hell's this?"

"I don't know," said the old man.

"Says 'positively kills lice, roaches and other scourges.' What the hell kind of bed you giving us, anyways. We don't want no pants rabbits."

The old swamper shifted his broom and held it between his elbow and his side while he held out his hand for the can. He studied the label carefully. "Tell you what—" he said finally, "last guy that had this bed was a blacksmith—hell of a nice fella and as clean a guy as you want to meet. Used to wash his hands even *after* he ate."

"Then how come he got graybacks?" George was working up a slow anger. Lennie put his bindle on the neighboring bunk and sat down. He watched George with open mouth.

"Tell you what," said the old swamper. "This

here blacksmith—name of Whitey—was the kind of guy that would put that stuff around even if there wasn't no bugs—just to make sure, see? Tell you what he used to do— At meals he'd peel his boil' potatoes, an' he'd take out ever' little spot, no matter what kind, before he'd eat it. And if there was a red splotch on an egg, he'd scrape it off. Finally quit about the food. That's the kinda guy he was—clean. Used ta dress up Sundays even when he wasn't going no place, put on a necktie even, and then set in the bunkhouse."

"I ain't so sure," said George skeptically. "What did you say he quit for?"

The old man put the yellow can in his pocket, and he rubbed his bristly white whiskers with his knuckles. "Why . . . . he . . . . just quit, the way a guy will. Says it was the food. Just wanted to move. Didn't give no other reason but the food. Just says 'gimme my time' one night, the way any guy would."

George lifted his tick and looked underneath

it. He leaned over and inspected the sacking closely. Immediately Lennie got up and did the same with his bed. Finally George seemed satisfied. He unrolled his bindle and put things on the shelf, his razor and bar of soap, his comb and bottle of pills, his liniment and leather wristband. Then he made his bed up neatly with blankets. The old man said, "I guess the boss'll be out here in a minute. He was sure burned when you wasn't here this morning. Come right in when we was eatin' breakfast and says, 'Where the hell's them new men?' An' he give the stable buck hell, too."

George patted a wrinkle out of his bed, and sat down. "Give the stable buck hell?" he asked.

"Sure. Ya see the stable buck's a nigger."

"Nigger, huh?"

"Yeah. Nice fella too. Got a crooked back where a horse kicked him. The boss gives him hell when he's mad. But the stable buck don't give a damn about that. He reads a lot. Got books in his room."

"What kind of a guy is the boss?" George asked.

"Well, he's a pretty nice fella. Gets pretty mad sometimes, but he's pretty nice. Tell ya what—know what he done Christmas? Brang a gallon of whisky right in here and says, 'Drink hearty boys. Christmas comes but once a year.'"

"The hell he did! Whole gallon?"

"Yes sir. Jesus, we had fun. They let the nigger come in that night. Little skinner name of Smitty took after the nigger. Done pretty good, too. The guys wouldn't let him use his feet, so the nigger got him. If he coulda used his feet, Smitty says he woulda killed the nigger. The guys said on account of the nigger's got a crooked back, Smitty can't use his feet." He paused in relish of the memory. "After that the guys went into Soledad and raised hell. I didn't go in there. I ain't got the poop no more."

Lennie was just finishing making his bed. The wooden latch raised again and the door opened. A little stocky man stood in the open doorway.

He wore blue jean trousers, a flannel shirt, a black, unbuttoned vest and a black coat. His thumbs were stuck in his belt, on each side of a square steel buckle. On his head was a soiled brown Stetson hat, and he wore high-heeled boots and spurs to prove he was not a laboring man.

The old swamper looked quickly at him, and then shuffled to the door rubbing his whiskers with his knuckles as he went. "Them guys just come," he said, and shuffled past the boss and out the door.

The boss stepped into the room with the short, quick steps of a fat-legged man. "I wrote Murray and Ready I wanted two men this morning. You got your work slips?" George reached into his pocket and produced the slips and handed them to the boss. "It wasn't Murray and Ready's fault. Says right here on the slip that you was to be here for work this morning."

George looked down at his feet. "Bus driver

give us a bum steer," he said. "We hadda walk ten miles. Says we was here when we wasn't. We couldn't get no rides in the morning."

The boss squinted his eyes. "Well, I had to send out the grain teams short two buckers. Won't do any good to go out now till after dinner." He pulled his time book out of his pocket and opened it where a pencil was stuck between the leaves. George scowled meaningfully at Lennie, and Lennie nodded to show that he understood. The boss licked his pencil. "What's your name?"

"George Milton."

"And what's yours?"

George said, "His name's Lennie Small."

The names were entered in the book. "Le's see, this is the twentieth, noon the twentieth." He closed the book. "Where you boys been working?"

"Up around Weed," said George.

"You, too?" to Lennie.

"Yeah, him too," said George.

The boss pointed a playful finger at Lennie. "He ain't much of a talker, is he?"

"No, he ain't, but he's sure a hell of a good worker. Strong as a bull."

Lennie smiled to himself. "Strong as a bull," he repeated.

George scowled at him, and Lennie dropped his head in shame at having forgotten.

The boss said suddenly, "Listen, Small!" Lennie raised his head. "What can you do?"

In a panic, Lennie looked at George for help. "He can do anything you tell him," said George. "He's a good skinner. He can rassel grain bags, drive a cultivator. He can do anything. Just give him a try."

The boss turned on George. "Then why don't you let him answer? What you trying to put over?"

George broke in loudly, "Oh! I ain't saying he's bright. He ain't. But I say he's a God damn good worker. He can put up a four hundred pound bale."

The boss deliberately put the little book in his pocket. He hooked his thumbs in his belt and squinted one eye nearly closed. "Say—what you sellin'?"

"Huh?"

"I said what stake you got in this guy? You takin' his pay away from him?"

"No, 'course I ain't. Why ya think I'm sellin' him out?"

"Well, I never seen one guy take so much trouble for another guy. I just like to know what your interest is."

George said, "He's my . . . . cousin. I told his old lady I'd take care of him. He got kicked in the head by a horse when he was a kid. He's awright. Just ain't bright. But he can do anything you tell him."

The boss turned half away. "Well, God knows he don't need any brains to buck barley bags. But don't you try to put nothing over, Milton. I got my eye on you. Why'd you quit in Weed?"

"Job was done," said George promptly.

"What kinda job?"

"We . . . . we was diggin' a cesspool."

"All right. But don't try to put nothing over, 'cause you can't get away with nothing. I seen wise guys before. Go on out with the grain teams after dinner. They're pickin' up barley at the threshing machine. Go out with Slim's team."

"Slim?"

"Yeah. Big tall skinner. You'll see him at dinner." He turned abruptly and went to the door, but before he went out he turned and looked for a long moment at the two men.

When the sound of his footsteps had died away, George turned on Lennie. "So you wasn't gonna say a word. You was gonna leave your big flapper shut and leave me do the talkin'. Damn near lost us the job."

Lennie stared hopelessly at his hands. "I forgot, George."

"Yeah, you forgot. You always forget, an' I

got to talk you out of it." He sat down heavily on the bunk. "Now he's got his eye on us. Now we got to be careful and not make no slips. You keep your big flapper shut after this." He fell morosely silent.

"George."

"What you want now?"

"I wasn't kicked in the head with no horse, was I, George?"

"Be a damn good thing if you was," George said viciously. "Save ever'body a hell of a lot of trouble."

"You said I was your cousin, George."

"Well, that was a lie. An' I'm damn glad it was. If I was a relative of yours I'd shoot myself." He stopped suddenly, stepped to the open front door and peered out. "Say, what the hell you doin' listenin'?"

The old man came slowly into the room. He had his broom in his hand. And at his heels there walked a dragfooted sheepdog, gray of muzzle, and with pale, blind old eyes. The dog struggled lamely to the side of the room and lay down, grunting softly to himself and licking his grizzled, moth-eaten coat. The swamper watched him until he was settled. "I wasn't listenin'. I was jus' standin' in the shade a minute scratchin' my dog. I jus' now finished swampin' out the wash house."

"You was pokin' your big ears into our business," George said. "I don't like nobody to get nosey."

The old man looked uneasily from George to Lennie, and then back. "I jus' come there," he said. "I didn't hear nothing you guys was sayin'. I ain't interested in nothing you was sayin'. A guy on a ranch don't never listen nor he don't ast no questions."

"Damn right he don't," said George, slightly mollified, "not if he wants to stay workin' long." But he was reassured by the swamper's defense. "Come on in and set down a minute," he said. "That's a hell of an old dog."

"Yeah. I had 'im ever since he was a pup. God,

he was a good sheep dog when he was younger." He stood his broom against the wall and he rubbed his white bristled cheek with his knuckles. "How'd you like the boss?" he asked.

"Pretty good. Seemed awright."

"He's a nice fella," the swamper agreed. "You got to take him right."

At that moment a young man came into the bunk house; a thin young man with a brown face, with brown eyes and a head of tightly curled hair. He wore a work glove on his left hand, and, like the boss, he wore high-heeled boots. "Seen my old man?" he asked.

The swamper said, "He was here jus' a minute ago, Curley. Went over to the cook house, I think."

"I'll try to catch him," said Curley. His eyes passed over the new men and he stopped. He glanced coldly at George and then at Lennie. His arms gradually bent at the elbows and his hands closed into fists. He stiffened and went into a slight crouch. His glance was at once calculating and pugnacious. Lennie squirmed under the look and shifted his feet nervously. Curley stepped gingerly close to him. "You the new guys the old man was waitin' for?"

"We just come in," said George.

"Let the big guy talk."

Lennie twisted with embarrassment.

George said, "S'pose he don't want to talk?"

Curley lashed his body around. "By Christ, he's gotta talk when he's spoke to. What the hell are you gettin' into it for?"

"We travel together," said George coldly.

"Oh, so it's that way."

George was tense, and motionless. "Yeah, it's that way."

Lennie was looking helplessly to George for instruction.

"An' you won't let the big guy talk, is that it?"

"He can talk if he wants to tell you anything." He nodded slightly to Lennie.

"We jus' come in," said Lennie softly.

Curley stared levelly at him. "Well, nex' time you answer when you're spoke to." He turned toward the door and walked out, and his elbows were still bent out a little.

George watched him out, and then he turned back to the swamper. "Say, what the hell's he got on his shoulder? Lennie didn't do nothing to him."

The old man looked cautiously at the door to make sure no one was listening. "That's the boss's son," he said quietly. "Curley's pretty handy. He done quite a bit in the ring. He's a lightweight, and he's handy."

"Well, let him be handy," said George. "He don't have to take after Lennie. Lennie didn't do nothing to him. What's he got against Lennie?"

The swamper considered. . . . . "Well . . . . tell you what. Curley's like a lot of little guys. He hates big guys. He's alla time picking scraps with big guys. Kind of like he's mad at 'em because he ain't a big guy. You seen little guys like that, ain't you? Always scrappy?"

"Sure," said George. "I seen plenty tough little guys. But this Curley better not make no mistakes about Lennie. Lennie ain't handy, but this Curley punk is gonna get hurt if he messes around with Lennie."

"Well, Curley's pretty handy," the swamper said skeptically. "Never did seem right to me. S'pose Curley jumps a big guy an' licks him. Ever'body says what a game guy Curley is. And s'pose he does the same thing and gets licked. Then ever'body says the big guy oughtta pick somebody his own size, and maybe they gang up on the big guy. Never did seem right to me. Seems like Curley ain't givin' nobody a chance."

George was watching the door. He said ominously, "Well, he better watch out for Lennie. Lennie ain't no fighter, but Lennie's strong and quick and Lennie don't know no rules." He walked to the square table and sat down on one of the boxes. He gathered some of the cards together and shuffled them.

The old man sat down on another box.

"Don't tell Curley I said none of this. He'd slough me. He just don't give a damn. Won't ever get canned 'cause his old man's the boss."

George cut the cards and began turning them over, looking at each one and throwing it down on a pile. He said, "This guy Curley sounds like a son-of-a-bitch to me. I don't like mean little guys."

"Seems to me like he's worse lately," said the swamper. "He got married a couple of weeks ago. Wife lives over in the boss's house. Seems like Curley is cockier'n ever since he got married."

George grunted, "Maybe he's showin' off for his wife."

The swamper warmed to his gossip. "You seen that glove on his left hand?"

"Yeah. I seen it."

"Well, that glove's fulla vaseline."

"Vaseline? What the hell for?"

"Well, I tell ya what—Curley says he's keepin' that hand soft for his wife."

George studied the cards absorbedly. "That's a dirty thing to tell around," he said.

The old man was reassured. He had drawn a derogatory statement from George. He felt safe now, and he spoke more confidently. "Wait'll you see Curley's wife."

George cut the cards again and put out a solitaire lay, slowly and deliberately. "Purty?" he asked casually.

"Yeah. Purty . . . . but——"

George studied his cards. "But what?"

"Well—she got the eye."

"Yeah? Married two weeks and got the eye? Maybe that's why Curley's pants is full of ants."

"I seen her give Slim the eye. Slim's a jerk-line skinner. Hell of a nice fella. Slim don't need to wear no high-heeled boots on a grain team. I seen her give Slim the eye. Curley never seen it. An' I seen her give Carlson the eye."

George pretended a lack of interest. "Looks like we was gonna have fun."

The swamper stood up from his box. "Know

what I think?" George did not answer. "Well, I think Curley's married . . . . a tart."

"He ain't the first," said George. "There's plenty done that."

The old man moved toward the door, and his ancient dog lifted his head and peered about, and then got painfully to his feet to follow. "I gotta be settin' out the wash basins for the guys. The teams'll be in before long You guys gonna buck barley?"

"Yeah."

"You won't tell Curley nothing I said?"

"Hell no."

"Well, you look her over, mister. You see if she ain't a tart." He stepped out the door into the brilliant sunshine.

George laid down his cards thoughtfully, turned his piles of three. He built four clubs on his ace pile. The sun square was on the floor now, and the flies whipped through it like sparks. A sound of jingling harness and the croak of heavy-laden axles sounded from outside. From the distance came a clear call. "Stable Buck—ooh, sta-able Buck! And then, "Where the hell is that God damn nigger?"

George stared at his solitaire lay, and then he flounced the cards together and turned around to Lennie. Lennie was lying down on the bunk watching him.

"Look, Lennie! This here ain't no set up. I'm scared. You gonna have trouble with that Curley guy. I seen that kind before. He was kinda feelin' you out. He figures he's got you scared and he's gonna take a sock at you the first chance he gets."

Lennie's eyes were frightened. "I don't want no trouble," he said plaintively. "Don't let him sock me, George."

George got up and went over to Lennie's bunk and sat down on it. "I hate that kinda bastard," he said. "I seen plenty of 'em. Like the old guy says, Curley don't take no chances. He always wins." He thought for a moment. "If he tangles with you, Lennie, we're gonna get the can. Don't make no mistake about that. He's the boss's son. Look, Lennie. You try to keep away from him, will you? Don't never speak to him. If he comes in here you move clear to the other side of the room. Will you do that, Lennie?"

"I don't want no trouble," Lennie mourned. "I never done nothing to him."

"Well, that won't do you no good if Curley wants to plug himself up for a fighter. Just don't have nothing to do with him. Will you remember?"

"Sure, George. I ain't gonna say a word."

The sound of the approaching grain teams was louder, thud of big hooves on hard ground, drag of brakes and the jingle of trace chains. Men were calling back and forth from the teams. George, sitting on the bunk beside Lennie, frowned as he thought. Lennie asked timidly, "You ain't mad, George?"

"I ain't mad at you. I'm mad at this here Curley bastard. I hoped we was gonna get a little stake together—maybe a hundred dollars." His tone grew decisive. "You keep away from Curley, Lennie."

"Sure I will, George. I won't say a word."

"Don't let him pull you in—but—if the son-of-a-bitch socks you—let 'im have it."

"Let 'im have what, George?"

"Never mind, never mind. I'll tell you when. I hate that kind of a guy. Look, Lennie, if you get in any kind of trouble, you remember what I told you to do?"

Lennie raised up on his elbow. His face contorted with thought. Then his eyes moved sadly to George's face. "If I get in any trouble, you ain't gonna let me tend the rabbits."

"That's not what I meant. You remember where we slep' last night? Down by the river?"

"Yeah. I remember. Oh, sure I remember! I go there an' hide in the brush."

"Hide till I come for you. Don't let nobody see you. Hide in the brush by the river. Say that over."

"Hide in the brush by the river, down in the brush by the river."

"If you get in trouble."

"If I get in trouble."

A brake screeched outside. A call came, "Stable—Buck. Oh! Sta-able Buck."

George said, "Say it over to yourself, Lennie, so you won't forget it."

Both men glanced up, for the rectangle of sunshine in the doorway was cut off. A girl was standing there looking in. She had full, rouged lips and wide-spaced eyes, heavily made up. Her fingernails were red. Her hair hung in little rolled clusters, like sausages. She wore a cotton house dress and red mules, on the insteps of which were little bouquets of red ostrich feathers. "I'm lookin' for Curley," she said. Her voice had a nasal, brittle quality.

George looked away from her and then back. "He was in here a minute ago, but he went."

"Oh!" She put her hands behind her back and leaned against the door frame so that her body was thrown forward. "You're the new fellas that just come, ain't ya?"

"Yeah."

Lennie's eyes moved down over her body, and though she did not seem to be looking at Lennie she bridled a little. She looked at her fingernails. "Sometimes Curley's in here," she explained.

George said brusquely, "Well he ain't now."

"If he ain't, I guess I better look some place else," she said playfully.

Lennie watched her, fascinated. George said, "If I see him, I'll pass the word you was looking for him."

She smiled archly and twitched her body. "Nobody can't blame a person for lookin'," she said. There were footsteps behind her, going by. She turned her head. "Hi, Slim," she said.

Slim's voice came through the door. "Hi, Good-lookin'."

"I'm tryin' to find Curley, Slim."

"Well, you ain't tryin' very hard. I seen him goin' in your house."

She was suddenly apprehensive. " 'Bye, boys," she called into the bunk house, and she hurried away.

George looked around at Lennie. "Jesus, what a tramp," he said. "So that's what Curley picks for a wife."

"She's purty," said Lennie defensively.

"Yeah, and she's sure hidin' it. Curley got his work ahead of him. Bet she'd clear out for twenty bucks."

Lennie still stared at the doorway where she had been. "Gosh, she was purty." He smiled admiringly. George looked quickly down at him and then he took him by an ear and shook him.

"Listen to me, you crazy bastard," he said fiercely. "Don't you even take a look at that bitch. I don't care what she says and what she does. I seen 'em poison before, but I never seen no piece of jail bait worse than her. You leave her be."

Lennie tried to disengage his ear. "I never done nothing, George."

"No, you never. But when she was standin'
in the doorway showin' her legs, you wasn't
lookin' the other way, neither."

"I never meant no harm, George. Honest I
never."

"Well, you keep away from her, 'cause she's
a rat-trap if I ever seen one. You let Curley take
the rap. He let himself in for it. Glove fulla
vaseline," George said disgustedly. "An' I bet
he's eatin' raw eggs and writin' to the patent
medicine houses."

Lennie cried out suddenly—"I don' like this
place, George. This ain't no good place. I wanna
get outa here."

"We gotta keep it till we get a stake. We
can't help it, Lennie. We'll get out jus' as soon
as we can. I don't like it no better than you do."
He went back to the table and set out a new
solitaire hand. "No, I don't like it," he said.
"For two bits I'd shove out of here. If we can
get jus' a few dollars in the poke we'll shove off
and go up the American River and pan gold.

We can make maybe a couple of dollars a day there, and we might hit a pocket."

Lennie leaned eagerly toward him. "Le's go, George. Le's get outta here. It's mean here."

"We gotta stay," George said shortly. "Shut up now. The guys'll be comin' in."

From the washroom nearby came the sound of running water and rattling basins. George studied the cards. "Maybe we oughtta wash up," he said. "But we ain't done nothing to get dirty."

A tall man stood in the doorway. He held a crushed Stetson hat under his arm while he combed his long, black, damp hair straight back. Like the others he wore blue jeans and a short denim jacket. When he had finished combing his hair he moved into the room, and he moved with a majesty only achieved by royalty and master craftsmen. He was a jerkline skinner, the prince of the ranch, capable of driving ten, sixteen, even twenty mules with a single line to the leaders. He was capable of killing a fly on the wheeler's butt with a bull whip without touching the mule. There was a gravity in his manner and a quiet so profound that all talk stopped when he spoke. His authority was so great that his word was taken on any subject, be it politics or love. This was Slim, the jerkline skinner. His hatchet face was ageless. He might have been thirty-five or fifty. His ear heard more than was said to him, and his slow speech had overtones not of thought, but of understanding beyond thought. His hands, large and lean, were as delicate in their action as those of a temple dancer.

He smoothed out his crushed hat, creased it in the middle and put it on. He looked kindly at the two in the bunk house. "It's brighter'n a bitch outside," he said gently. "Can't hardly see nothing in here. You the new guys?"

"Just come," said George.

"Gonna buck barley?"

"That's what the boss says."

Slim sat down on a box across the table from George. He studied the solitaire hand that was upside down to him. "Hope you get on my team," he said. His voice was very gentle. "I gotta pair of punks on my team that don't know a barley bag from a blue ball. You guys ever bucked any barley?"

"Hell, yes," said George. "I ain't nothing to scream about, but that big bastard there can put up more grain alone than most pairs can."

Lennie, who had been following the conversation back and forth with his eyes, smiled complacently at the compliment. Slim looked approvingly at George for having given the compliment. He leaned over the table and snapped the corner of a loose card. "You guys travel around together?" His tone was friendly. It invited confidence without demanding it.

"Sure," said George. "We kinda look after each other." He indicated Lennie with his thumb. "He ain't bright. Hell of a good worker, though. Hell of a nice fella, but he ain't bright. I've knew him for a long time."

Slim looked through George and beyond him.

"Ain't many guys travel around together," he mused. "I don't know why. Maybe ever'body in the whole damn world is scared of each other."

"It's a lot nicer to go around with a guy you know," said George.

A powerful, big-stomached man came into the bunk house. His head still dripped water from the scrubbing and dousing. "Hi, Slim," he said, and then stopped and stared at George and Lennie.

"These guys jus' come," said Slim by way of introduction.

"Glad ta meet ya," the big man said. "My name's Carlson."

"I'm George Milton. This here's Lennie Small."

"Glad ta meet ya," Carlson said again. "He ain't very small." He chuckled softly at his joke. "Ain't small at all," he repeated. "Meant to ask you, Slim—how's your bitch? I seen she wasn't under your wagon this morning."

"She slang her pups last night," said Slim. "Nine of 'em. I drowned four of 'em right off. She couldn't feed that many."

"Got five left, huh?"

"Yeah, five. I kept the biggest."

"What kinda dogs you think they're gonna be?"

"I dunno," said Slim. "Some kinda shepherds, I guess. That's the most kind I seen around here when she was in heat."

Carlson went on, "Got five pups, huh. Gonna keep all of 'em?"

"I dunno. Have to keep 'em a while so they can drink Lulu's milk."

Carlson said thoughtfully, "Well, looka here, Slim. I been thinkin'. That dog of Candy's is so God damn old he can't hardly walk. Stinks like hell, too. Ever' time he comes into the bunk house I can smell him for two, three days. Why'n't you get Candy to shoot his old dog and give him one of the pups to raise up? I can smell that dog a mile away. Got no teeth, damn near blind, can't eat. Candy feeds him milk. He can't chew nothing else."

George had been staring intently at Slim. Suddenly a triangle began to ring outside, slowly at first, and then faster and faster until the beat of it disappeared into one ringing sound. It stopped as suddenly as it had started.

"There she goes," said Carlson.

Outside, there was a burst of voices as a group of men went by.

Slim stood up slowly and with dignity. "You guys better come on while they's still something to eat. Won't be nothing left in a couple of minutes."

Carlson stepped back to let Slim precede him, and then the two of them went out the door.

Lennie was watching George excitedly. George rumpled his cards into a messy pile. "Yeah!" George said, "I heard him, Lennie. I'll ask him."

"A brown and white one," Lennie cried excitedly.

"Come on. Le's get dinner. I don't know whether he got a brown and white one."

Lennie didn't move from his bunk. "You ask him right away, George, so he won't kill no more of 'em."

"Sure. Come on now, get up on your feet."

Lennie rolled off his bunk and stood up, and the two of them started for the door. Just as they reached it, Curley bounced in.

"You seen a girl around here?" he demanded angrily.

George said coldly. " 'Bout half an hour ago maybe."

"Well what the hell was she doin'?"

George stood still, watching the angry little man. He said insultingly, "She said—she was lookin' for you."

Curley seemed really to see George for the first time. His eyes flashed over George, took in his height, measured his reach, looked at his trim middle. "Well, which way'd she go?" he demanded at last.

"I dunno," said George. "I didn' watch her go."

Curley scowled at him, and turning, hurried out the door.

George said, "Ya know, Lennie, I'm scared I'm gonna tangle with that bastard myself. I hate his guts. Jesus Christ! Come on. They won't be a damn thing left to eat."

They went out the door. The sunshine lay in a thin line under the window. From a distance there could be heard a rattle of dishes.

After a moment the ancient dog walked lamely in through the open door. He gazed about with mild, half-blind eyes. He sniffed, and then lay down and put his head between his paws. Curley popped into the doorway again and stood looking into the room. The dog raised his head, but when Curley jerked out, the grizzled head sank to the floor again.

# 3

ALTHOUGH there was evening brightness showing through the windows of the bunk house, inside it was dusk. Through the open door came the thuds and occasional clangs of a horseshoe game, and now and then the sound of voices raised in approval or derision.

Slim and George came into the darkening bunkhouse together. Slim reached up over the card table and turned on the tin-shaded electric light. Instantly the table was brilliant with light, and the cone of the shade threw its brightness straight downward, leaving the corners of the bunk house still in dusk. Slim sat down on a box and George took his place opposite.

"It wasn't nothing," said Slim. "I would of had to drowned most of 'em anyways. No need to thank me about that."

George said, "It wasn't much to you, maybe, but it was a hell of a lot to him. Jesus Christ, I don't know how we're gonna get him to sleep in here. He'll want to sleep right out in the barn with 'em. We'll have trouble keepin' him from getting right in the box with them pups."

"It wasn't nothing," Slim repeated. "Say, you sure was right about him. Maybe he ain't bright, but I never seen such a worker. He damn near killed his partner buckin' barley. There ain't nobody can keep up with him. God awmighty I never seen such a strong guy."

George spoke proudly. "Jus' tell Lennie what to do an' he'll do it if it don't take no figuring. He can't think of nothing to do himself, but he sure can take orders."

There was a clang of horseshoe on iron stake outside and a little cheer of voices.

Slim moved back slightly so the light was not on his face. "Funny how you an' him string along together." It was Slim's calm invitation to confidence.

"What's funny about it?" George demanded defensively.

"Oh, I dunno. Hardly none of the guys ever travel together. I hardly never seen two guys travel together. You know how the hands are, they just come in and get their bunk and work a month, and then they quit and go out alone. Never seem to give a damn about nobody. It jus' seems kinda funny a cuckoo like him and a smart little guy like you travelin' together."

"He ain't no cuckoo," said George. "He's dumb as hell, but he ain't crazy. An' I ain't so bright neither, or I wouldn't be buckin' barley for my fifty and found. If I was bright, if I was even a little bit smart, I'd have my own little place, an' I'd be bringin' in my own crops, 'stead of doin' all the work and not getting what comes up outa the ground." George fell silent. He wanted to talk. Slim neither encouraged nor discouraged him. He just sat back quiet and receptive.

"It ain't so funny, him an' me goin' aroun' together," George said at last. "Him and me was both born in Auburn. I knowed his Aunt Clara. She took him when he was a baby and raised him up. When his Aunt Clara died, Lennie just come along with me out workin'. Got kinda used to each other after a little while."

"Umm," said Slim.

George looked over at Slim and saw the calm, God-like eyes fastened on him. "Funny," said George. "I used to have a hell of a lot of fun with 'im. Used to play jokes on 'im 'cause he was too dumb to take care of 'imself. But he was too dumb even to know he had a joke played on him. I had fun. Made me seem God damn smart alongside of him. Why he'd do any damn thing I tol' him. If I tol' him to walk over a cliff, over he'd go. That wasn't so damn much fun after a while. He never got mad about it, neither. I've beat the hell outa him, and he coulda bust every bone in my body jus' with his han's, but he never lifted a finger against me." George's voice was taking on the tone of confession. "Tell you what made me stop that. One day a bunch of guys was standin' around up on the Sacramento River. I was feelin' pretty smart. I turns to Lennie and says, 'Jump in.' An' he jumps. Couldn't swim a stroke. He damn near drowned before we could get him. An' he was so damn nice to me for pullin' him out. Clean forgot I told him to jump in. Well, I ain't done nothing like that no more."

"He's a nice fella," said Slim. "Guy don't need no sense to be a nice fella. Seems to me sometimes it jus' works the other way around. Take a real smart guy and he ain't hardly ever a nice fella."

George stacked the scattered cards and began to lay out his solitaire hand. The shoes thudded on the ground outside. At the windows the light of the evening still made the window squares bright.

"I ain't got no people," George said. "I seen the guys that go around on the ranches alone. That ain't no good. They don't have no fun.

After a long time they get mean. They get wantin' to fight all the time."

"Yeah, they get mean," Slim agreed. "They get so they don't want to talk to nobody."

" 'Course Lennie's a God damn nuisance most of the time," said George. "But you get used to goin' around with a guy an' you can't get rid of him."

"He ain't mean," said Slim. "I can see Lennie ain't a bit mean."

" 'Course he ain't mean. But he gets in trouble alla time because he's so God damn dumb. Like what happened in Weed——" He stopped, stopped in the middle of turning over a card. He looked alarmed and peered over at Slim. "You wouldn't tell nobody?"

"What'd he do in Weed?" Slim asked calmly.

"You wouldn' tell? . . . . No, 'course you wouldn'."

"What'd he do in Weed?" Slim asked again.

"Well, he seen this girl in a red dress. Dumb bastard like he is, he wants to touch ever'thing he likes. Just wants to feel it. So he reaches out to feel this red dress an' the girl lets out a squawk, and that gets Lennie all mixed up, and he holds on 'cause that's the only thing he can think to do. Well, this girl squawks and squawks. I was jus' a little bit off, and I heard all the yellin', so I comes running, an' by that time Lennie's so scared all he can think to do is jus' hold on. I socked him over the head with a fence picket to make him let go. He was so scairt he couldn't let go of that dress. And he's so God damn strong, you know."

Slim's eyes were level and unwinking. He nodded very slowly. "So what happens?"

George carefully built his line of solitaire cards. "Well, that girl rabbits in an' tells the law she been raped. The guys in Weed start a party out to lynch Lennie. So we sit in a irrigation ditch under water all the rest of that day. Got on'y our heads sticking outa water, an' up under the grass that sticks out from the side of the ditch. An' that night we scrammed outa there."

Slim sat in silence for a moment. "Didn't hurt the girl none, huh?" he asked finally.

"Hell, no. He just scared her. I'd be scared too if he grabbed me. But he never hurt her. He jus' wanted to touch that red dress, like he wants to pet them pups all the time."

"He ain't mean," said Slim. "I can tell a mean guy a mile off."

" 'Course he ain't, and he'll do any damn thing I——"

Lennie came in through the door. He wore his blue denim coat over his shoulders like a cape, and he walked hunched way over.

"Hi, Lennie," said George. "How you like the pup now?"

Lennie said breathlessly, "He's brown an' white jus' like I wanted." He went directly to his bunk and lay down and turned his face to the wall and drew up his knees.

George put down his cards very deliberately. "Lennie," he said sharply.

Lennie twisted his neck and looked over his shoulder. "Huh? What you want, George?"

"I tol' you you couldn't bring that pup in here."

"What pup, George? I ain't got no pup."

George went quickly to him, grabbed him by the shoulder and rolled him over. He reached down and picked the tiny puppy from where Lennie had been concealing it against his stomach.

Lennie sat up quickly. "Give 'um to me, George."

George said, "You get right up an' take this pup back to the nest. He's gotta sleep with his mother. You want to kill him? Just born last night an' you take him out of the nest. You take him back or I'll tell Slim not to let you have him."

Lennie held out his hands pleadingly. "Give 'um to me, George. I'll take 'um back. I didn't mean no harm, George. Honest I didn't. I jus' wanted to pet 'um a little."

George handed the pup to him. "Awright. You get him back there quick, and don't you take him out no more. You'll kill him, the first thing you know." Lennie fairly scuttled out of the room.

Slim had not moved. His calm eyes followed Lennie out the door. "Jesus," he said. "He's jes' like a kid, ain't he."

"Sure he's jes' like a kid. There ain't no more harm in him than a kid neither, except he's so strong. I bet he won't come in here to sleep tonight. He'd sleep right alongside that box in the barn. Well—let 'im. He ain't doin' no harm out there."

It was almost dark outside now. Old Candy, the swamper, came in and went to his bunk, and behind him struggled his old dog. "Hello, Slim. Hello, George. Didn't neither of you play horseshoes?"

"I don't like to play ever' night," said Slim.

Candy went on, "Either you guys got a slug of whisky? I gotta gut ache."

"I ain't," said Slim. "I'd drink it myself if I had, an' I ain't got a gut ache neither."

"Gotta bad gut ache," said Candy. "Them God damn turnips give it to me. I knowed they was going to before I ever eat 'em."

The thick-bodied Carlson came in out of the darkening yard. He walked to the other end of the bunk house and turned on the second shaded light. "Darker'n hell in here," he said. "Jesus, how that nigger can pitch shoes."

"He's plenty good," said Slim.

"Damn right he is," said Carlson. "He don't give nobody else a chance to win——" He stopped and sniffed the air, and still sniffing, looked down at the old dog. "God awmighty, that dog stinks. Get him outa here, Candy! I don't know nothing that stinks as bad as an old dog. You gotta get him out."

Candy rolled to the edge of his bunk. He reached over and patted the ancient dog, and he apologized, "I been around him so much I never notice how he stinks."

"Well, I can't stand him in here," said Carlson. "That stink hangs around even after he's gone. He walked over with his heavy-legged stride and looked down at the dog. "Got no teeth," he said. "He's all stiff with rheumatism. He ain't no good to you, Candy. An' he ain't no good to himself. Why'n't you shoot him, Candy?"

The old man squirmed uncomfortably. "Well —hell! I had him so long. Had him since he was a pup. I herded sheep with him." He said proudly, "You wouldn't think it to look at him now, but he was the best damn sheep dog I ever seen."

George said, "I seen a guy in Weed that had an Airedale could herd sheep. Learned it from the other dogs."

Carlson was not to be put off. "Look, Candy. This ol' dog jus' suffers hisself all the time. If you was to take him out and shoot him right in the back of the head—" he leaned over and pointed, "—right there, why he'd never know what hit him."

Candy looked about unhappily. "No," he said

softly. "No, I couldn' do that. I had 'im too long."

"He don't have no fun," Carlson insisted. "And he stinks to beat hell. Tell you what. I'll shoot him for you. Then it won't be you that does it."

Candy threw his legs off his bunk. He scratched the white stubble whiskers on his cheek nervously. "I'm so used to him," he said softly. "I had him from a pup."

"Well, you ain't bein' kind to him keepin' him alive," said Carlson. "Look, Slim's bitch got a litter right now. I bet Slim would give you one of them pups to raise up, wouldn't you, Slim?"

The skinner had been studying the old dog with his calm eyes. "Yeah," he said. "You can have a pup if you want to." He seemed to shake himself free for speech. "Carl's right, Candy. That dog ain't no good to himself. I wisht some-body'd shoot me if I get old an' a cripple."

Candy looked helplessly at him, for Slim's opinions were law. "Maybe it'd hurt him," he suggested. "I don't mind takin' care of him."

Carlson said, "The way I'd shoot him, he wouldn't feel nothing. I'd put the gun right there." He pointed with his toe. "Right back of the head. He wouldn't even quiver."

Candy looked for help from face to face. It was quite dark outside by now. A young laboring man came in. His sloping shoulders were bent forward and he walked heavily on his heels, as though he carried the invisible grain bag. He went to his bunk and put his hat on his shelf. Then he picked a pulp magazine from his shelf and brought it to the light over the table. "Did I show you this, Slim?" he asked.

"Show me what?"

The young man turned to the back of the magazine, put it down on the table and pointed with his finger. "Right there, read that." Slim bent over it. "Go on," said the young man. "Read it out loud."

" 'Dear Editor' ": Slim read slowly. " 'I read your mag for six years and I think it is the best on the market. I like stories by Peter Rand. I think he is a whing-ding. Give us more like the Dark Rider. I don't write many letters. Just thought I would tell you I think your mag is the best dime's worth I ever spent.' "

Slim looked up questioningly. "What you want me to read that for?"

Whit said, "Go on. Read the name at the bottom."

Slim read, " 'Yours for success, William Tenner.' " He glanced up at Whit again. "What you want me to read that for?"

Whit closed the magazine impressively. "Don't you remember Bill Tenner? Worked here about three months ago?"

Slim thought. . . . "Little guy?" he asked. "Drove a cultivator?"

"That's him," Whit cried. "That's the guy!"

"You think he's the guy wrote this letter?"

"I know it. Bill and me was in here one day. Bill had one of them books that just come. He was lookin' in it and he says, 'I wrote a letter.

Wonder if they put it in the book!' But it wasn't there. Bill says, 'Maybe they're savin' it for later.' An' that's just what they done. There it is."

"Guess you're right," said Slim. "Got it right in the book."

George held out his hand for the magazine. "Let's look at it?"

Whit found the place again, but he did not surrender his hold on it. He pointed out the letter with his forefinger. And then he went to his box shelf and laid the magazine carefully in. "I wonder if Bill seen it," he said. "Bill and me worked in that patch of field peas. Run cultivators, both of us. Bill was a hell of a nice fella."

During the conversation Carlson had refused to be drawn in. He continued to look down at the old dog. Candy watched him uneasily. At last Carlson said, "If you want me to, I'll put the old devil out of his misery right now and get it over with. Ain't nothing left for him. Can't eat, can't see, can't even walk without hurtin'."

Candy said hopefully, "You ain't got no gun."

"The hell I ain't. Got a Luger. It won't hurt him none at all."

Candy said, "Maybe tomorra. Le's wait till tomorra."

"I don't see no reason for it," said Carlson. He went to his bunk, pulled his bag from underneath it and took out a Luger pistol. "Le's get it over with," he said. "We can't sleep with him stinkin' around in here." He put the pistol in his hip pocket.

Candy looked a long time at Slim to try to find some reversal. And Slim gave him none. At last Candy said softly and hopelessly, "Awright —take 'im." He did not look down at the dog at all. He lay back on his bunk and crossed his arms behind his head and stared at the ceiling.

From his pocket Carlson took a little leather thong. He stooped over and tied it around the old dog's neck. All the men except Candy watched him. "Come boy. Come on, boy," he said gently. And he said apologetically to Candy, "He won't even feel it." Candy did not move nor answer him. He twitched the thong. "Come on, boy." The old dog got slowly and stiffly to his feet and followed the gently pulling leash.

Slim said, "Carlson."

"Yeah?"

"You know what to do."

"What ya mean, Slim?"

"Take a shovel," said Slim shortly.

"Oh, sure! I get you." He led the dog out into the darkness.

George followed to the door and shut the door and set the latch gently in its place. Candy lay rigidly on his bed staring at the ceiling.

Slim said loudly, "One of my lead mules got a bad hoof. Got to get some tar on it." His voice trailed off. It was silent outside. Carlson's footsteps died away. The silence come into the room. And the silence lasted.

George chuckled, "I bet Lennie's right out there in the barn with his pup. He won't want to come in here no more now he's got a pup."

Slim said, "Candy, you can have any one of them pups you want."

Candy did not answer. The silence fell on the room again. It came out of the night and invaded the room. George said, "Anybody like to play a little euchre?"

"I'll play out a few with you," said Whit.

They took places opposite each other at the table under the light, but George did not shuffle the cards. He rippled the edge of the deck nervously, and the little snapping noise drew the eyes of all the men in the room, so that he stopped doing it. The silence fell on the room again. A minute passed, and another minute. Candy lay still, staring at the ceiling. Slim gazed at him for a moment and then looked down at his hands; he subdued one hand with the other, and held it down. There came a little gnawing sound from under the floor and all the men looked down toward it gratefully. Only Candy continued to stare at the ceiling.

"Sounds like there was a rat under there," said George. "We ought to get a trap down there."

Whit broke out, "What the hell's takin' him so long? Lay out some cards, why don't you? We ain't going to get no euchre played this way."

George brought the cards together tightly and studied the backs of them. The silence was in the room again.

A shot sounded in the distance. The men looked quickly at the old man. Every head turned toward him.

For a moment he continued to stare at the ceiling. Then he rolled slowly over and faced the wall and lay silent.

George shuffled the cards noisily and dealt them. Whit drew a scoring board to him and set the pegs to start. Whit said, "I guess you guys really come here to work."

"How do ya mean?" George asked.

Whit laughed. "Well, ya come on a Friday. You got two days to work till Sunday."

"I don't see how you figure," said George.

Whit laughed again. "You do if you been

around these big ranches much. Guy that wants to look over a ranch comes in Sat'day afternoon. He gets Sat'day night supper an' three meals on Sunday, and he can quit Monday mornin' after breakfast without turning his hand. But you come to work Friday noon. You got to put in a day an' a half no matter how you figure."

George looked at him levelly. "We're gonna stick aroun' a while," he said. "Me an' Lennie's gonna roll up a stake."

The door opened quietly and the stable buck put in his head; a lean negro head, lined with pain, the eyes patient. "Mr. Slim."

Slim took his eyes from old Candy. "Huh? Oh! Hello, Crooks. What's'a matter?"

"You told me to warm up tar for that mule's foot. I got it warm."

"Oh! Sure, Crooks. I'll come right out an' put it on."

"I can do it if you want, Mr. Slim."

"No. I'll come do it myself." He stood up. Crooks said, "Mr. Slim."

"Yeah."

"That big new guy's messin' around your pups out in the barn."

"Well, he ain't doin' no harm. I give him one of them pups."

"Just thought I'd tell ya," said Crooks. "He's takin' 'em outa the nest and handlin' them. That won't do them no good."

"He won't hurt 'em," said Slim. "I'll come along with you now."

George looked up. "If that crazy bastard's foolin' around too much, jus' kick him out, Slim."

Slim followed the stable buck out of the room.

George dealt and Whit picked up his cards and examined them. "Seen the new kid yet?" he asked.

"What kid?" George asked.

"Why, Curley's new wife."

"Yeah, I seen her."

"Well, ain't she a looloo?"

"I ain't seen that much of her," said George.

Whit laid down his cards impressively. "Well, stick around an' keep your eyes open. You'll see plenty. She ain't concealin' nothing. I never seen nobody like her. She got the eye goin' all the time on everybody. I bet she even gives the stable buck the eye. I don't know what the hell she wants."

George asked casually, "Been any trouble since she got here?"

It was obvious that Whit was not interested in his cards. He laid his hand down and George scooped it in. George laid out his deliberate solitaire hand—seven cards, and six on top, and five on top of those.

Whit said, "I see what you mean. No, they ain't been nothing yet. Curley's got yella-jackets in his drawers, but that's all so far. Ever' time the guys is around she shows up. She's lookin' for Curley, or she thought she lef' somethin' layin' around and she's lookin' for it. Seems like she can't keep away from guys. An' Curley's

pants is just crawlin' with ants, but they ain't
nothing come of it yet."

George said, "She's gonna make a mess.
They's gonna be a bad mess about her. She's a
jail bait all set on the trigger. That Curley got
his work cut out for him. Ranch with a bunch
of guys on it ain't no place for a girl, specially
like her."

Whit said, "If you got idears, you ought ta
come in town with us guys tomorra night."

"Why? What's doin'?"

"Jus' the usual thing. We go in to old Susy's
place. Hell of a nice place. Old Susy's a laugh—
always crackin' jokes. Like she says when we
come up on the front porch las' Sat'day night.
Susy opens the door and then she yells over her
shoulder, 'Get yor coats on, girls, here comes
the sheriff.' She never talks dirty, neither. Got
five girls there."

"What's it set you back?" George asked.

"Two an' a half. You can get a shot for two
bits. Susy got nice chairs to set in, too. If a guy

don't want a flop, why he can just set in the chairs and have a couple or three shots and pass the time of day and Susy don't give a damn. She ain't rushin' guys through and kickin' 'em out if they don't want a flop."

"Might go in and look the joint over," said George.

"Sure. Come along. It's a hell of a lot of fun—her crackin' jokes all the time. Like she says one time, she says, 'I've knew people that if they got a rag rug on the floor an' a kewpie doll lamp on the phonograph they think they're running a parlor house.' That's Clara's house she's talkin' about. An' Susy says, 'I know what you boys want,' she says. 'My girls is clean,' she says, 'an' there ain't no water in my whisky,' she says. 'If any you guys wanta look at a kewpie doll lamp an' take your own chance gettin' burned, why you know where to go.' An' she says, 'There's guys around here walkin' bow-legged 'cause they like to look at a kewpie doll lamp.'"

George asked, "Clara runs the other house, huh?"

"Yeah," said Whit. "We don't never go there. Clara gets three bucks a crack and thirty-five cents a shot, and she don't crack no jokes. But Susy's place is clean and she got nice chairs. Don't let no goo-goos in, neither."

"Me an' Lennie's rollin' up a stake," said George. "I might go in an' set and have a shot, but I ain't puttin' out no two and a half."

"Well, a guy got to have some fun sometime," said Whit.

The door opened and Lennie and Carlson came in together. Lennie crept to his bunk and sat down, trying not to attract attention. Carlson reached under his bunk and brought out his bag. He didn't look at old Candy, who still faced the wall. Carlson found a little cleaning rod in the bag and a can of oil. He laid them on his bed and then brought out the pistol, took out the magazine and snapped the loaded shell from the chamber. Then he fell to cleaning the barrel with the little rod. When the ejector snapped, Candy turned over and looked for a moment at the gun before he turned back to the wall again.

Carlson said casually, "Curley been in yet?"

"No," said Whit. "What's eatin' on Curley?"

Carlson squinted down the barrel of his gun. "Lookin' for his old lady. I seen him going round and round outside."

Whit said sarcastically, "He spends half his time lookin' for her, and the rest of the time she's lookin' for him."

Curley burst into the room excitedly. "Any you guys seen my wife?" he demanded.

"She ain't been here," said Whit.

Curley looked threateningly about the room. "Where the hell's Slim?"

"Went out in the barn," said George. "He was gonna put some tar on a split hoof."

Curley's shoulders dropped and squared. "How long ago'd he go?"

"Five—ten minutes."

Curley jumped out the door and banged it after him.

Whit stood up. "I guess maybe I'd like to see this," he said. "Curley's just spoilin' or he wouldn't start for Slim. An' Curley's handy, God damn handy. Got in the finals for the Golden Gloves. He got newspaper clippings about it." He considered. "But jus' the same, he better leave Slim alone. Nobody don't know what Slim can do."

"Thinks Slim's with his wife, don't he?" said George.

"Looks like it," Whit said. " 'Course Slim ain't. Least I don't think Slim is. But I like to see the fuss if it comes off. Come on, le's go."

George said, "I'm stayin' right here. I don't want to get mixed up in nothing. Lennie and me got to make a stake."

Carlson finished the cleaning of the gun and put it in the bag and pushed the bag under his bunk. "I guess I'll go out and look her over," he said. Old Candy lay still, and Lennie, from his bunk, watched George cautiously.

When Whit and Carlson were gone and the

door closed after them, George turned to Lennie. "What you got on your mind?"

"I ain't done nothing, George. Slim says I better not pet them pups so much for a while. Slim says it ain't good for them; so I come right in. I been good, George."

"I coulda told you that," said George.

"Well, I wasn't hurtin' 'em none. I jus' had mine in my lap pettin' it."

George asked, "Did you see Slim out in the barn?"

"Sure I did. He tol' me I better not pet that pup no more."

"Did you see that girl?"

"You mean Curley's girl?"

"Yeah. Did she come in the barn?"

"No. Anyways I never seen her."

"You never seen Slim talkin' to her?"

"Uh-uh. She ain't been in the barn."

"O.K.," said George. "I guess them guys ain't gonna see no fight. If there's any fightin', Lennie, you keep out of it."

"I don't want no fights," said Lennie. He got up from his bunk and sat down at the table, across from George. Almost automatically George shuffled the cards and laid out his solitaire hand. He used a deliberate, thoughtful, slowness.

Lennie reached for a face card and studied it, then turned it upside down and studied it. "Both ends the same," he said. "George, why is it both end's the same?"

"I don't know," said George. "That's jus' the way they make 'em. What was Slim doin' in the barn when you seen him?"

"Slim?"

"Sure. You seen him in the barn, an' he tol' you not to pet the pups so much."

"Oh, yeah. He had a can a' tar an' a paint brush. I don't know what for."

"You sure that girl didn't come in like she come in here today?"

"No. She never come."

George sighed. "You give me a good whore

house every time," he said. "A guy can go in an' get drunk and get ever'thing outa his system all at once, an' no messes. And he knows how much it's gonna set him back. These here jail baits is just set on the trigger of the hoosegow."

Lennie followed his words admiringly, and moved his lips a little to keep up. George continued, "You remember Andy Cushman, Lennie? Went to grammar school?"

"The one that his old lady used to make hot cakes for the kids?" Lennie asked.

"Yeah. That's the one. You can remember anything if there's anything to eat in it." George looked carefully at the solitaire hand. He put an ace up on his scoring rack and piled a two, three and four of diamonds on it. "Andy's in San Quentin right now on account of a tart," said George.

Lennie drummed on the table with his fingers. "George?"

"Huh?"

"George, how long's it gonna be till we get

that little place an' live on the fatta the lan—an' rabbits?"

"I don' know," said George. "We gotta get a big stake together. I know a little place we can get cheap, but they ain't givin' it away."

Old Candy turned slowly over. His eyes were wide open. He watched George carefully.

Lennie said, "Tell about that place, George."

"I jus' tol' you, jus' las' night."

"Go on—tell again, George."

"Well, it's ten acres," said George. "Got a little win'mill. Got a little shack on it, an' a chicken run. Got a kitchen, orchard, cherries, apples, peaches, 'cots, nuts, got a few berries. They's a place for alfalfa and plenty water to flood it. They's a pig pen——"

"An' rabbits, George."

"No place for rabbits now, but I could easy build a few hutches and you could feed alfalfa to the rabbits."

"Damn right, I could," said Lennie. "You God damn right I could."

George's hands stopped working with the cards. His voice was growing warmer. "An' we could have a few pigs. I could build a smoke house like the one gran'pa had, an' when we kill a pig we can smoke the bacon and the hams, and make sausage an' all like that. An' when the salmon run up river we could catch a hundred of 'em an' salt 'em down or smoke 'em. We could have them for breakfast. They ain't nothing so nice as smoked salmon. When the fruit come in we could can it—and tomatoes, they're easy to can. Ever' Sunday we'd kill a chicken or a rabbit. Maybe we'd have a cow or a goat, and the cream is so God damn thick you got to cut it with a knife and take it out with a spoon."

Lennie watched him with wide eyes, and old Candy watched him too. Lennie said softly, "We could live offa the fatta the lan'."

"Sure," said George. "All kin's a vegetables in the garden, and if we want a little whisky we can sell a few eggs or something, or some milk. We'd jus' live there. We'd belong there.

There wouldn't be no more runnin' round the country and gettin' fed by a Jap cook. No, sir, we'd have our own place where we belonged and not sleep in no bunk house."

"Tell about the house, George," Lennie begged.

"Sure, we'd have a little house an' a room to ourself. Little fat iron stove, an' in the winter we'd keep a fire goin' in it. It ain't enough land so we'd have to work too hard. Maybe six, seven hours a day. We wouldn't have to buck no barley eleven hours a day. An' when we put in a crop, why, we'd be there to take the crop up. We'd know what come of our planting."

"An' rabbits," Lennie said eagerly. "An' I'd take care of 'em. Tell how I'd do that, George."

"Sure, you'd go out in the alfalfa patch an' you'd have a sack. You'd fill up the sack and bring it in an' put it in the rabbit cages."

"They'd nibble an' they'd nibble," said Lennie, "the way they do. I seen 'em."

"Ever' six weeks or so," George continued,

"them does would throw a litter so we'd have plenty rabbits to eat an' to sell. An' we'd keep a few pigeons to go flyin' around the win'mill like they done when I was a kid." He looked raptly at the wall over Lennie's head. "An' it'd be our own, an' nobody could can us. If we don't like a guy we can say, 'Get the hell out,' and by God he's got to do it. An' if a fren' come along, why we'd have an extra bunk, an' we'd say, 'Why don't you spen' the night?' an' by God he would. We'd have a setter dog and a couple stripe cats, but you gotta watch out them cats don't get the little rabbits."

Lennie breathed hard. "You jus' let 'em try to get the rabbits. I'll break their God damn necks. I'll . . . . I'll smash 'em with a stick." He subsided, grumbling to himself, threatening the future cats which might dare to disturb the future rabbits.

George sat entranced with his own picture.

When Candy spoke they both jumped as

though they had been caught doing something reprehensible. Candy said, "You know where's a place like that?"

George was on guard immediately. "S'pose I do," he said. "What's that to you?"

"You don't need to tell me where it's at. Might be any place."

"Sure," said George. "That's right. You couldn't find it in a hundred years."

Candy went on excitedly, "How much they want for a place like that?"

George watched him suspiciously. "Well—I could get it for six hundred bucks. The ol' people that owns it is flat bust an' the ol' lady needs an operation. Say—what's it to you? You got nothing to do with us."

Candy said, "I ain't much good with on'y one hand. I lost my hand right here on this ranch. That's why they give me a job swampin'. An' they give me two hunderd an' fifty dollars 'cause I los' my hand. An' I got fifty more saved up right in the bank, right now. Tha's three hunderd, and I got fifty more comin' the end a the month. Tell you what——" He leaned forward eagerly. "S'pose I went in with you guys. Tha's three hunderd an' fifty bucks I'd put in. I ain't much good, but I could cook and tend the chickens and hoe the garden some. How'd that be?"

George half-closed his eyes. "I gotta think about that. We was always gonna do it by ourselves."

Candy interrupted him, "I'd make a will an' leave my share to you guys in case I kick off, 'cause I ain't got no relatives nor nothing. You guys got any money? Maybe we could do her right now?"

George spat on the floor disgustedly. "We got ten bucks between us." Then he said thoughtfully, "Look, if me an' Lennie work a month an' don't spen' nothing, we'll have a hunderd bucks. That'd be four fifty. I bet we could swing her for that. Then you an' Lennie could go get her started an' I'd get a job an' make up the res', an' you could sell eggs an' stuff like that."

They fell into a silence. They looked at one another, amazed. This thing they had never really believed in was coming true. George said reverently, "Jesus Christ! I bet we could swing her." His eyes were full of wonder. "I bet we could swing her," he repeated softly.

Candy sat on the edge of his bunk. He scratched the stump of his wrist nervously. "I got hurt four year ago," he said. "They'll can me purty soon. Jus' as soon as I can't swamp out no bunk houses they'll put me on the county. Maybe if I give you guys my money, you'll let me hoe in the garden even after I ain't no good at it. An' I'll wash dishes an' little chicken stuff like that. But I'll be on our own place, an' I'll be let to work on our own place." He said miserably, "You seen what they done to my dog tonight? They says he wasn't no good to himself nor nobody else. When they can me here I wisht somebody'd shoot me. But they won't do nothing like that. I won't have no place to go, an' I can't get no more jobs. I'll have thirty dollars more comin', time you guys is ready to quit."

George stood up. "We'll do her," he said. "We'll fix up that little old place an' we'll go live there." He sat down again. They all sat still, all bemused by the beauty of the thing, each mind was popped into the future when this lovely thing should come about.

George said wonderingly, "S'pose they was a carnival or a circus come to town, or a ball game, or any damn thing." Old Candy nodded in appreciation of the idea. "We'd just go to her," George said. "We wouldn't ask nobody if we could. Jus' say, 'We'll go to her,' an' we would. Jus' milk the cow and sling some grain to the chickens an' go to her."

"An' put some grass to the rabbits," Lennie broke in. "I wouldn't never forget to feed them. When we gon'ta do it, George?"

"In one month. Right squack in one month. Know what I'm gon'ta do? I'm gon'ta write to them old people that owns the place that we'll take it. An' Candy'll send a hunderd dollars to bind her."

"Sure will," said Candy. "They got a good stove there?"

"Sure, got a nice stove, burns coal or wood."

"I'm gonna take my pup," said Lennie. "I bet by Christ he likes it there, by Jesus."

Voices were approaching from outside. George said quickly, "Don't tell nobody about it. Jus' us three an' nobody else. They li'ble to can us so we can't make no stake. Jus' go on like we was gonna buck barley the rest of our lives, then all of a sudden some day we'll go get our pay an' scram outa here."

Lennie and Candy nodded, and they were grinning with delight. "Don't tell nobody," Lennie said to himself.

Candy said, "George."

"Huh?"

"I ought to of shot that dog myself, George. I shouldn't ought to of let no stranger shoot my dog."

The door opened. Slim came in, followed by Curley and Carlson and Whit. Slim's hands were black with tar and he was scowling. Curley hung close to his elbow.

Curley said, "Well, I didn't mean nothing, Slim. I just ast you."

Slim said, "Well, you been askin' me too often. I'm gettin' God damn sick of it. If you can't look after your own God damn wife, what you expect me to do about it? You lay offa me."

"I'm jus' tryin' to tell you I didn't mean nothing," said Curley. "I jus' thought you might of saw her."

"Why'n't you tell her to stay the hell home where she belongs?" said Carlson. "You let her hang around bunk houses and pretty soon you're gonna have som'pin on your hands and you won't be able to do nothing about it."

Curley whirled on Carlson. "You keep outta this les' you wanta step outside."

Carlson laughed. "You God damn punk," he

said. "You tried to throw a scare into Slim, an' you couldn't make it stick. Slim throwed a scare inta you. You're yella as a frog belly. I don't care if you're the best welter in the country. You come for me, an' I'll kick your God damn head off."

Candy joined the attack with joy. "Glove fulla vaseline," he said disgustedly. Curley glared at him. His eyes slipped on past and lighted on Lennie; and Lennie was still smiling with delight at the memory of the ranch.

Curley stepped over to Lennie like a terrier. "What the hell you laughin' at?"

Lennie looked blankly at him. "Huh?"

Then Curley's rage exploded. "Come on, ya big bastard. Get up on your feet. No big son-of-a-bitch is gonna laugh at me. I'll show ya who's yella."

Lennie looked helplessly at George, and then he got up and tried to retreat. Curley was balanced and poised. He slashed at Lennie with his left, and then smashed down his nose with a right. Lennie gave a cry of terror. Blood welled from his nose. "George," he cried. "Make 'um let me alone, George." He backed until he was against the wall, and Curley followed, slugging him in the face. Lennie's hands remained at his sides; he was too frightened to defend himself.

George was on his feet yelling, "Get him, Lennie. Don't let him do it."

Lennie covered his face with his huge paws and bleated with terror. He cried, "Make 'um stop, George." Then Curley attacked his stomach and cut off his wind.

Slim jumped up. "The dirty little rat," he cried, "I'll get 'um myself."

George put out his hand and grabbed Slim. "Wait a minute," he shouted. He cupped his hands around his mouth and yelled, "Get 'im, Lennie!"

Lennie took his hands away from his face and looked about for George, and Curley slashed at his eyes. The big face was covered with blood. George yelled again, "I said get him."

Curley's fist was swinging when Lennie reached for it. The next minute Curley was flopping like a fish on a line, and his closed fist was lost in Lennie's big hand. George ran down the room. "Leggo of him, Lennie. Let go."

But Lennie watched in terror the flopping little man whom he held. Blood ran down Lennie's face, one of his eyes was cut and closed. George slapped him in the face again and again, and still Lennie held on to the closed fist. Curley was white and shrunken by now, and his struggling had become weak. He stood crying, his fist lost in Lennie's paw.

George shouted over and over, "Leggo his hand, Lennie. Leggo. Slim, come help me while the guy got any hand left."

Suddenly Lennie let go his hold. He crouched cowering against the wall. "You tol' me to, George," he said miserably.

Curley sat down on the floor, looking in wonder at his crushed hand. Slim and Carlson bent over him. Then Slim straightened up and regarded Lennie with horror. "We got to get him in to a doctor," he said. "Looks to me like ever' bone in his han' is bust."

"I didn't wanta," Lennie cried. "I didn't wanta hurt him."

Slim said, "Carlson, you get the candy wagon hitched up. We'll take 'um into Soledad an' get 'um fixed up." Carlson hurried out. Slim turned to the whimpering Lennie. "It ain't your fault," he said. "This punk sure had it comin' to him. But—Jesus! He ain't hardly got no han' left." Slim hurried out, and in a moment returned with a tin cup of water. He held it to Curley's lips.

George said, "Slim, will we get canned now? We need the stake. Will Curley's old man can us now?"

Slim smiled wryly. He knelt down beside Curley. "You got your senses in hand enough to listen?" he asked. Curley nodded. "Well, then listen," Slim went on. "I think you got your han' caught in a machine. If you don't tell nobody what happened, we ain't going to. But you jus' tell an' try to get this guy canned and we'll tell ever'body, an' then will you get the laugh."

"I won't tell," said Curley. He avoided looking at Lennie.

Buggy wheels sounded outside. Slim helped Curley up. "Come on now. Carlson's gonna take you to a doctor." He helped Curley out the door. The sound of wheels drew away. In a moment Slim came back into the bunk house. He looked at Lennie, still crouched fearfully against the wall. "Le's see your hands," he asked.

Lennie stuck out his hands.

"Christ awmighty, I hate to have you mad at me," Slim said.

George broke in, "Lennie was jus' scairt," he explained. "He didn't know what to do. I told you nobody ought never to fight him. No, I guess it was Candy I told."

Candy nodded solemnly. "That's jus' what you done," he said. "Right this morning when

Curley first lit intil your fren', you says, 'He better not fool with Lennie if he knows what's good for 'um.' That's jus' what you says to me."

George turned to Lennie. "It ain't your fault," he said. "You don't need to be scairt no more. You done jus' what I tol' you to. Maybe you better go in the wash room an' clean up your face. You look like hell."

Lennie smiled with his bruised mouth. "I didn't want no trouble," he said. He walked toward the door, but just before he came to it, he turned back. "George?"

"What you want?"

"I can still tend the rabbits, George?"

"Sure. You ain't done nothing wrong."

"I di'n't mean no harm, George."

"Well, get the hell out and wash your face."

# 4

CROOKS, the negro stable buck, had his bunk
in the harness room; a little shed that leaned off
the wall of the barn. On one side of the little
room there was a square four-paned window,
and on the other, a narrow plank door leading
into the barn. Crooks' bunk was a long box
filled with straw, on which his blankets were
flung. On the wall by the window there were
pegs on which hung broken harness in process
of being mended; strips of new leather; and
under the window itself a little bench for
leather-working tools, curved knives and needles
and balls of linen thread, and a small hand riv-
eter. On pegs were also pieces of harness, a split
collar with the horsehair stuffing sticking out, a
broken hame, and a trace chain with its leather

covering split. Crooks had his apple box over his bunk, and in it a range of medicine bottles, both for himself and for the horses. There were cans of saddle soap and a drippy can of tar with its paint brush sticking over the edge. And scattered about the floor were a number of personal possessions; for, being alone, Crooks could leave his things about, and being a stable buck and a cripple, he was more permanent than the other men, and he had accumulated more possessions than he could carry on his back.

Crooks possessed several pairs of shoes, a pair of rubber boots, a big alarm clock and a single-barreled shotgun. And he had books, too; a tattered dictionary and a mauled copy of the California civil code for 1905. There were battered magazines and a few dirty books on a special shelf over his bunk. A pair of large gold-rimmed spectacles hung from a nail on the wall above his bed.

This room was swept and fairly neat, for Crooks was a proud, aloof man. He kept his distance and demanded that other people keep theirs. His body was bent over to the left by his crooked spine, and his eyes lay deep in his head, and because of their depth seemed to glitter with intensity. His lean face was lined with deep black wrinkles, and he had thin, pain-tightened lips which were lighter than his face.

It was Saturday night. Through the open door that led into the barn came the sound of moving horses, of feet stirring, of teeth champing on hay, of the rattle of halter chains. In the stable buck's room a small electric globe threw a meager yellow light.

Crooks sat on his bunk. His shirt was out of his jeans in back. In one hand he held a bottle of liniment, and with the other he rubbed his spine. Now and then he poured a few drops of the liniment into his pink-palmed hand and reached up under his shirt to rub again. He flexed his muscles against his back and shivered.

Noiselessly Lennie appeared in the open doorway and stood there looking in, his big shoulders nearly filling the opening. For a moment Crooks did not see him, but on raising his eyes he stiffened and a scowl came on his face. His hand came out from under his shirt.

Lennie smiled helplessly in an attempt to make friends.

Crooks said sharply, "You got no right to come in my room. This here's my room. Nobody got any right in here but me."

Lennie gulped and his smile grew more fawning. "I ain't doing nothing," he said. "Just come to look at my puppy. And I seen your light," he explained.

"Well, I got a right to have a light. You go on get outta my room. I ain't wanted in the bunk house, and you ain't wanted in my room."

"Why ain't you wanted?" Lennie asked.

" 'Cause I'm black. They play cards in there, but I can't play because I'm black. They say I stink. Well, I tell you, you all of you stink to me."

Lennie flapped his big hands helplessly.

"Ever'body went into town," he said. "Slim an' George an' ever'body. George says I gotta stay here an' not get in no trouble. I seen your light."

"Well, what do you want?"

"Nothing—I seen your light. I thought I could jus' come in an' set."

Crooks stared at Lennie, and he reached behind him and took down the spectacles and adjusted them over his pink ears and stared again. "I don't know what you're doin' in the barn anyway," he complained. "You ain't no skinner. They's no call for a bucker to come into the barn at all. You ain't no skinner. You ain't got nothing to do with the horses."

"The pup," Lennie repeated. "I come to see my pup."

"Well, go see your pup, then. Don't come in a place where you're not wanted."

Lennie lost his smile. He advanced a step into the room, then remembered and backed to the door again. "I looked at 'em a little. Slim says I ain't to pet 'em very much."

Crooks said, "Well, you been takin' 'em out of the nest all the time. I wonder the old lady don't move 'em someplace else."

"Oh, she don't care. She lets me." Lennie had moved into the room again.

Crooks scowled, but Lennie's disarming smile defeated him. "Come on in and set a while," Crooks said. " 'Long as you won't get out and leave me alone, you might as well set down." His tone was a little more friendly. "All the boys gone into town, huh?"

"All but old Candy. He just sets in the bunk house sharpening his pencil and sharpening and figuring."

Crooks adjusted his glasses. "Figuring? What's Candy figuring about?"

Lennie almost shouted, " 'Bout the rabbits."

"You're nuts," said Crooks. "You're crazy as a wedge. What rabbits you talkin' about?"

"The rabbits we're gonna get, and I get to

435

tend 'em, cut grass an' give 'em water, an' like that."

"Jus' nuts," said Crooks. "I don't blame the guy you travel with for keepin' you outa sight."

Lennie said quietly, "It ain't no lie. We're gonna do it. Gonna get a little place an' live on the fatta the lan'."

Crooks settled himself more comfortably on his bunk. "Set down," he invited. "Set down on the nail keg."

Lennie hunched down on the little barrel. "You think it's a lie," Lennie said, "But it ain't no lie. Ever' word's the truth, an' you can ast George."

Crooks put his dark chin into his pink palm. "You travel aroun' with George, don't ya?"

"Sure. Me an' him goes ever' place together."

Crooks continued. "Sometimes he talks, and you don't know what the hell he's talkin' about. Ain't that so?" He leaned forward, boring Lennie with his deep eyes. "Ain't that so?"

"Yeah . . . . sometimes."

"Jus' talks on, an' you don't know what the hell it's all about?"

"Yeah . . . . sometimes. But . . . . not always."

Crooks leaned forward over the edge of the bunk. "I ain't a southern negro," he said. "I was born right here in California. My old man had a chicken ranch, 'bout ten acres. The white kids come to play at our place, an' sometimes I went to play with them, and some of them was pretty nice. My ol' man didn't like that. I never knew till long later why he didn't like that. But I know now." He hesitated, and when he spoke again his voice was softer. "There wasn't another colored family for miles around. And now there ain't a colored man on this ranch an' there's jus' one family in Soledad." He laughed. "If I say something, why it's just a nigger sayin' it."

Lennie asked, "How long you think it'll be before them pups will be old enough to pet?"

Crooks laughed again. "A guy can talk to you

437

an' be sure you won't go blabbin'. Couple of weeks an' them pups'll be all right. George knows what he's about. Jus' talks, an' you don't understand nothing." He leaned forward excitedly. "This is just a nigger talkin', an' a busted-back nigger. So it don't mean nothing, see? You couldn't remember it anyways. I seen it over an' over—a guy talkin' to another guy and it don't make no difference if he don't hear or understand. The thing is, they're talkin', or they're settin' still not talkin'. It don't make no difference, no difference." His excitement had increased until he pounded his knee with this hand. "George can tell you screwy things, and it don't matter. It's just the talking. It's just bein' with another guy. That's all." He paused.

His voice grew soft and persuasive. "S'pose George don't come back no more. S'pose he took a powder and just ain't coming back. What'll you do then?"

Lennie's attention came gradually to what had been said. "What?" he demanded.

"I said s'pose George went into town tonight and you never heard of him no more." Crooks pressed forward some kind of private victory. "Just s'pose that," he repeated.

"He won't do it," Lennie cried. "George wouldn't do nothing like that. I been with George a long time. He'll come back to-night——" But the doubt was too much for him. "Don't you think he will?"

Crooks' face lighted with pleasure in his torture. "Nobody can't tell what a guy'll do," he observed calmly. "Le's say he wants to come back and can't. S'pose he gets killed or hurt so he can't come back."

Lennie struggled to understand. "George won't do nothing like that," he repeated. "George is careful. He won't get hurt. He ain't never been hurt, 'cause he's careful."

"Well, s'pose, jus' s'pose he don't come back. What'll you do then?"

Lennie's face wrinkled with apprehension. "I don' know. Say, what you doin' anyways?" he cried. "This ain't true. George ain't got hurt."

Crooks bored in on him. "Want me ta tell ya what'll happen? They'll take ya to the booby hatch. They'll tie ya up with a collar, like a dog."

Suddenly Lennie's eyes centered and grew quiet, and mad. He stood up and walked dangerously toward Crooks. "Who hurt George?" he demanded.

Crooks saw the danger as it approached him. He edged back on his bunk to get out of the way. "I was just supposin'," he said. "George ain't hurt. He's all right. He'll be back all right."

Lennie stood over him. "What you supposin' for? Ain't nobody goin' to suppose no hurt to George."

Crooks removed his glasses and wiped his eyes with his fingers. "Jus' set down," he said. "George ain't hurt."

Lennie growled back to his seat on the nail

keg. "Ain't nobody goin' to talk no hurt to George," he grumbled.

Crooks said gently, "Maybe you can see now. You got George. You *know* he's goin' to come back. S'pose you didn't have nobody. S'pose you couldn't go into the bunk house and play rummy 'cause you was black. How'd you like that? S'pose you had to sit out here an' read books. Sure you could play horseshoes till it got dark, but then you got to read books. Books ain't no good. A guy needs somebody—to be near him." He whined, "A guy goes nuts if he ain't got nobody. Don't make no difference who the guy is, long's he's with you. I tell ya," he cried, "I tell ya a guy gets too lonely an' he gets sick."

"George gonna come back," Lennie reassured himself in a frightened voice. "Maybe George come back already. Maybe I better go see."

Crooks said, "I didn't mean to scare you. He'll come back. I was talkin' about myself. A

guy sets alone out here at night, maybe readin'
books or thinkin' or stuff like that. Sometimes
he gets thinkin', an' he got nothing to tell him
what's so an' what ain't so. Maybe if he sees
somethin', he don't know whether it's right or
not. He can't turn to some other guy and ast
him if he sees it too. He can't tell. He got nothing to measure by. I seen things out here. I
wasn't drunk. I don't know if I was asleep. If
some guy was with me, he could tell me I was
asleep, an' then it would be all right. But I jus'
don't know." Crooks was looking across the
room now, looking toward the window.

Lennie said miserably, "George wun't go
away and leave me. I know George wun't do
that."

The stable buck went on dreamily, "I remember when I was a little kid on my old man's
chicken ranch. Had two brothers. They was always near me, always there. Used to sleep right
in the same room, right in the same bed—all
three. Had a strawberry patch. Had an alfalfa

patch. Used to turn the chickens out in the alfalfa on a sunny morning. My brothers'd set on a fence rail an' watch 'em—white chickens they was."

Gradually Lennie's interest came around to what was being said. "George says we're gonna have alfalfa for the rabbits."

"What rabbits?"

"We're gonna have rabbits an' a berry patch."

"You're nuts."

"We are too. You ast George."

"You're nuts." Crooks was scornful. "I seen hunderds of men come by on the road an' on the ranches, with their bindles on their back an' that same damn thing in their heads. Hunderds of them. They come, an' they quit an' go on; an' every damn one of 'em's got a little piece of land in his head. An' never a God damn one of 'em ever gets it. Just like heaven. Ever'body wants a little piece of lan'. I read plenty of books out here. Nobody never gets to heaven, and nobody gets no land. It's just in their head. They're all the time talkin' about it, but it's jus' in their head." He paused and looked toward the open door, for the horses were moving restlessly and the halter chains clinked. A horse whinnied. "I guess somebody's out there," Crooks said. "Maybe Slim. Slim comes in sometimes two, three times a night. Slim's a real skinner. He looks out for his team." He pulled himself painfully upright and moved toward the door. "That you, Slim?" he called.

Candy's voice answered. "Slim went in town. Say, you seen Lennie?"

"Ya mean the big guy?"

"Yeah. Seen him around any place?"

"He's in here," Crooks said shortly. He went back to his bunk and lay down.

Candy stood in the doorway scratching his bald wrist and looking blindly into the lighted room. He made no attempt to enter. "Tell ya what, Lennie. I been figuring out about them rabbits."

Crooks said irritably, "You can come in if you want."

Candy seemed embarrassed. "I do' know. 'Course, if ya want me to."

"Come on in. If ever'body's comin' in, you might just as well." It was difficult for Crooks to conceal his pleasure with anger.

Candy came in, but he was still embarrassed. "You got a nice cozy little place in here," he said to Crooks. "Must be nice to have a room all to yourself this way."

"Sure," said Crooks. "And a manure pile under the window. Sure, it's swell."

Lennie broke in, "You said about them rabbits."

Candy leaned against the wall beside the broken collar while he scratched the wrist stump. "I been here a long time," he said. "An' Crooks been here a long time. This's the first time I ever been in his room."

Crooks said darkly, "Guys don't come into a colored man's room very much. Nobody been here but Slim. Slim an' the boss."

Candy quickly changed the subject. "Slim's as good a skinner as I ever seen."

Lennie leaned toward the old swamper. "About them rabbits," he insisted.

Candy smiled. "I got it figured out. We can make some money on them rabbits if we go about it right."

"But I get to tend 'em," Lennie broke in. "George says I get to tend 'em. He promised."

Crooks interrupted brutally. "You guys is just kiddin' yourself. You'll talk about it a hell of a lot, but you won't get no land. You'll be a swamper here till they take you out in a box. Hell, I seen too many guys. Lennie here'll quit an' be on the road in two, three weeks. Seems like ever' guy got land in his head."

Candy rubbed his cheek angrily. "You God damn right we're gonna do it. George says we are. We got the money right now."

"Yeah?" said Crooks. "An' where's George now? In town in a whore house. That's where your money's goin'. Jesus, I seen it happen too many times. I seen too many guys with land in their head. They never get none under their hand."

Candy cried, "Sure they all want it. Everybody wants a little bit of land, not much. Jus' som'thin' that was his. Som'thin' he could live on and there couldn't nobody throw him off of it. I never had none. I planted crops for damn near ever'body in this state, but they wasn't my crops, and when I harvested 'em, it wasn't none of my harvest. But we gonna do it now, and don't you make no mistake about that. George ain't got the money in town. That money's in the bank. Me an' Lennie an' George. We gonna have a room to ourself. We're gonna have a dog an' rabbits an' chickens. We're gonna have green corn an' maybe a cow or a goat." He stopped, overwhelmed with his picture.

Crooks asked, "You say you got the money?"

"Damn right. We got most of it. Just a little bit more to get. Have it all in one month. George got the land all picked out, too."

Crooks reached around and explored his spine with his hand. "I never seen a guy really do it," he said. "I seen guys nearly crazy with loneliness for land, but ever' time a whore house or a blackjack game took what it takes." He hesitated. " . . . . If you . . . . guys would want a hand to work for nothing—just his keep, why I'd come an' lend a hand. I ain't so crippled I can't work like a son-of-a-bitch if I want to."

"Any you boys seen Curley?"

They swung their heads toward the door. Looking in was Curley's wife. Her face was heavily made up. Her lips were slightly parted. She breathed strongly, as though she had been running.

"Curley ain't been here," Candy said sourly.

She stood still in the doorway, smiling a little at them, rubbing the nails of one hand with the thumb and forefinger of the other. And her eyes traveled from one face to another. "They left all the weak ones here," she said finally. "Think